hunter. . . . Fans of Anita Blake and Charlaine Harris' Sookie Stackhouse vampire series will be rewarded."
—*Publishers Weekly*

"Unbridled lust and kick-ass action are the hallmarks of this first novel in a brand-new paranormal series. . . . 'Sizzling' is the only word to describe this heated, action-filled, suspenseful romantic drama."
—*Curled Up with a Good Book*

"Desert island keeper . . . Grade: A . . . I wanted to read this book in one sitting, and was terribly offended that the real world intruded on my reading time! . . . Inevitable comparisons can be made to Anita Blake, Kim Harrison, and Kelley Armstrong's books, but I think Ms. Arthur has a clear voice of her own and her characters speak for themselves. . . . I am hooked!"
—*All About Romance*

Praise for *Kissing Sin*

"The second book in this paranormal guardian series is just as phenomenal as the first. . . . I am addicted!!"
—*Fresh Fiction*

"Arthur's world building skills are absolutely superb and I recommend this story to any reader who enjoys tales of the paranormal."
—*Coffee Time Romance and More*

"Fast paced and filled with deliciously sexy characters, readers will find *Kissing Sin* a fantastic urban fantasy with a hot serving of romance that continues to sizzle long after the last page is read."
—*Darque Reviews*

"Keri Arthur's unique characters and the imaginative world she's created will make this series one that readers won't want to miss."

—*A Romance Review*

Praise for *Tempting Evil*

"Riley Jenson is kick-ass . . . genuinely tough and strong, but still vulnerable enough to make her interesting. . . . Arthur is not derivative of early [Laurell K.] Hamilton—far from it—but the intensity of her writing and the complexity of her heroine and her stories is reminiscent."

—*All About Romance*

"This paranormal romance series gets better and better with each new book. . . . An exciting adventure that delivers all you need for a fabulous read—sexy shapeshifters, hot vampires, wild uncontrollable sex and the slightest hint of a love that's meant to be forever."

—*Fresh Fiction*

"Pure sexy action adventure . . . I found the world vividly realized and fascinating. . . . So, if you like your erotic scenes hot, fast, and frequent, your heroine sassy, sexy, and tough, and your stories packed with hard-hitting action in a vividly realized fantasy world, then *Tempting Evil* and its companion novels could be just what you're looking for."

—*SFRevu*

"Keri Arthur's Riley Jenson series just keeps getting better and better and is sure to call to fans of other authors with kick-ass heroines such as Christine Feehan and Laurell K. Hamilton. I have become a steadfast fan of this marvelous series and I am greatly looking for-

ward to finding out what is next in store for this fascinating and strong character."
—*A Romance Review*

Praise for *Dangerous Games*

"One of the best books I have ever read. . . . The storyline is so exciting I did not realize I was literally sitting on the edge of my chair. . . . Arthur has a real winner on her hands. Five cups."
—*Coffee Time Romance and More*

"The depths of emotion, the tense plot, and the conflict of powerful driving forces inside the heroine made for [an] absorbing read."
—*SFRevu*

"This series is phenomenal! *Dangerous Games* is an incredibly original and devastatingly sexy story. It keeps you spellbound and mesmerized on every page. Absolutely perfect!!"
—*Fresh Fiction*

Praise for *Embraced by Darkness*

"Arthur is positively one of the best urban fantasy authors in print today. The characters have been well-drawn from the start and the mysteries just keep getting better. A creative, sexy and adventure filled world that readers will just love escaping to."
—*Darque Reviews*

"Arthur's storytelling is getting better and better with each book. *Embraced by Darkness* has suspense, interesting concepts, terrific main and secondary characters, well developed story arcs, and the world-building is

highly entertaining. . . . I think this series is worth the time and emotional investment to read."
—Reuters.com

"Once again, Keri Arthur has created a perfect, exciting and thrilling read with intensity that kept me vigilantly turning each page, hoping it would never end."
—*Fresh Fiction*

"Reminiscent of Laurell K. Hamilton back when her books had mysteries to solve, Arthur's characters inhabit a dark sexy world of the paranormal."
—*The Parkersburg News and Sentinel*

"I love this series."
—*All About Romance*

Praise for *The Darkest Kiss*

"The paranormal Australia that Arthur concocts works perfectly, and the plot speeds along at a breakneck pace. Riley fans won't be disappointed."
—*Publishers Weekly*

Praise for *Bound to Shadows*

"The Riley Jenson Guardian series ROCKS! Riley is one bad-ass heroine with a heart of gold. Keri Arthur never disappoints and always leaves me eagerly anticipating the next book. A classic, fabulous read!"
—*Fresh Fiction*

Praise for *Moon Sworn*

"Huge kudos to Arthur for giving readers an impressive series they won't soon forget! 4½ stars, Top pick!"
—*RT Book Reviews*

"The superb final Guardian urban fantasy saga ends with quite a bang that will please the fans of the series. Riley is terrific as she goes through a myriad of emotions with no time to mourn her losses. . . . Readers will enjoy Riley's rousing last stand."
—*Midwest Book Review*

Praise for *Darkness Unbound*

"A thrilling ride."
—*Publishers Weekly*

Praise for *Darkness Rising*

"Arthur ratchets up the intrigue . . . in this powerful sequel."
—*Publishers Weekly*

By Keri Arthur

THE DAMASK CIRCLE SERIES
Circle of Fire
Circle of Death

THE NIKKI AND MICHAEL SERIES
Dancing with the Devil
Hearts in Darkness
Chasing the Shadows
Kiss the Night Goodbye

THE RIPPLE CREEK WEREWOLF SERIES
Beneath a Rising Moon
Beneath a Darkening Moon

THE DARK ANGELS SERIES
Darkness Unbound
Darkness Rising
Darkness Devours
Darkness Hunts
Darkness Unmasked
Darkness Splintered

THE MYTH AND MAGIC SERIES
Destiny Kills
Mercy Burns

THE RILEY JENSON GUARDIAN SERIES
Full Moon Rising
Kissing Sin
Tempting Evil
Dangerous Games
Embraced by Darkness
The Darkest Kiss
Deadly Desire
Bound to Shadows
Moon Sworn

CIRCLE OF DEATH

KERI ARTHUR

DELL

NEW YORK

Circle of Death is a work of fiction. Names, characters, places, and incidents either are the product of the author's imagination or are used fictitiously. Any resemblance to actual persons, living or dead, events, or locales is entirely coincidental.

2014 Dell Mass Market Edition

Published in the United States by Dell, an imprint of The Random House Publishing Group, a division of Random House LLC, a Penguin Random House Company, New York.

DELL and the HOUSE colophon are registered trademarks of Random House LLC.

Originally published in trade paperback in the United States by Ima-Jinn Books, Hickory Corners, MI, in 2002.

This book contains an excerpt from the forthcoming book *Circle of Desire* by Keri Arthur. This excerpt has been set for this edition only and may not reflect the final content of the forthcoming edition.

ISBN 978-0-440-24656-5
eBook ISBN 978-0-345-53907-6

Cover design: Lynn Andreozzi
Cover illustration: Juliana Kolesova

Printed in the United States of America

www.bantamdell.com

9 8 7 6 5 4 3 2 1

Dell mass market edition: February 2014

CIRCLE OF DEATH

ONE

AUSTRALIA, PRESENT DAY

DEATH HAD COME CALLING ON A WINDBLOWN, WIN-
try evening. It smashed past the dead bolts lining the
front door and grabbed the living with unparalleled
glee, sucking the life from them until there was nothing left but husks. Then it tore the remains apart, as
if determined to erase any evidence of humanity.

Kirby hadn't been home at the time—but her best
friend had been.

Kirby stood on the edge of the porch, in the wind
and the rain, and felt nothing. No pain. No anger.
Not even the chill from the wild storm that had shattered the warm Australian summer.

It was as if part of her sat in a vacuum, waiting . . .
but for what, she wasn't sure.

"Miss Brown? Did you hear my question?"

The voice held an edge of impatience. She turned,
vaguely recognizing the red-haired police officer who
stood before her. "Sorry. My mind was elsewhere."

On walking into the kitchen and seeing the blood
spattered like paint across the walls. Or the dismem-

bered parts of Helen and Ross, strewn like forgotten toys throughout the house.

She swallowed heavily, then crossed her arms and licked the rain from her lips. It tasted salty, like tears.

"I asked why you were late coming home tonight." His blue eyes studied her closely. Not with suspicion, not exactly. He was just a cop being a cop, asking questions.

"There was an accident on the West Gate Bridge. It held up traffic for hours. I was supposed to have been home by six."

If she'd been on time, death would have caught her, too. But fate had stepped in and saved her life. She wondered why.

"What time *did* you get home, then?"

"Eight thirty. I stopped at the KFC down the road and got something to eat." It had been her turn to cook, but because of the late hour, she'd decided to wimp out and just grab takeout for everyone. The chicken still sat in its box, just inside the door where she'd dropped it. She wondered if she'd ever be able to eat KFC again. "I called in the murder not long after that."

But the constable knew all that. He'd been there earlier, taking notes, when the other detectives had questioned her. She wondered what it was he didn't believe.

He checked his notes. "And you saw nothing, heard nothing, as you walked up to the house?"

She shook her head. "Everything was dark. I didn't even notice the door was open until I got close."

He raised an eyebrow. "And you didn't find that unusual?"

In all honesty, she hadn't. She'd merely grinned, thinking that perhaps Helen and Ross had been too involved with each other to worry about mundane things like locking the front door. "Helen had only known Ross for a week. They were still at the 'fucking like rabbits' stage, I'm afraid."

She wasn't entirely sure why she'd said that. She wasn't usually the swearing type. Maybe it was simply the need to shock the half-smug smile from the young officer's lips.

A faint hint of red crept across his cheeks and he cleared his throat softly. "Yes, well, that would no doubt explain why the victims had no clothes on."

"No doubt," she mimicked, voice remote.

She stared past the emergency vehicles' swirling red and blue lights, a cold sense of dread enveloping her. She rubbed her arms and wished she had a whisky or a scotch. Even a beer would do. Something—anything— to drown the knowledge that death stood out there, watching and waiting.

"Do you have anyplace to go, Miss Brown?"

Her gaze jumped back to the police officer. "Go?"

He nodded. "You can't stay here. It's a crime scene."

"Oh." She hadn't thought of that. Hadn't thought of anything, really, once she'd stepped through that door.

"Have you got parents nearby?"

She shook her head. No use explaining that she didn't have parents at all. None that she remembered, anyway, and certainly none she wanted to find. As near as she knew, she'd been a ward of the state since birth, and she'd spent her formative years being bounced from one foster home to another. Helen had been the one permanent fixture in her life. They shared everything, even down to a birthday. They'd met in a government facility at the age of eleven, and had run away after it burned down and they'd been faced with separation again. Now Helen was gone, and Kirby was alone. Again.

She raised her face and let the rain wash the heat from her eyes. *Don't cry for me,* Helen would have said. *Just find the answers.*

"No friends you can bunk with for the night?" the officer continued.

Again she shook her head. They'd moved into the Essendon area only a few weeks ago. She'd barely had time to unpack, let alone make new friends. And she'd always been slower than Helen in that department anyway.

"Perhaps we can book you a hotel room for the next couple of nights."

She nodded, though she didn't really care one way or another. The young officer studied her for a moment longer, then walked away. Her gaze fell on the door. A symbol had been carved deep into the wood—a star point sitting at the top of a circle. If there were meant to be other star points, then they were missing. She wondered if this were deliberate, or if perhaps the intruder had been interrupted before he'd finished his design. Instinct said it was the former, though she had no idea why she was so certain of this.

The police had asked her several times about it. She had a feeling they were as perplexed by its presence as she was.

She crossed her arms again and turned her back on the house. The chill night wind picked up the wet strands of her hair, flinging them across her face. Absently, she tucked them back behind her ear and listened to the wind sigh through the old birches lining the front yard. It was a mournful sound, as if the wind cried for the dead.

Helen would have called it the wind of change. Normally, she would have sat under the old trees, letting the cold fingers of air wrap around her, communing with forces Kirby could feel but never see. She would have read their futures in the nuances of the breeze and planned a path around them.

If she had talked to the wind tonight, she might still be alive.

Tears tracked heat down Kirby's cheeks. She raised her face to the sky again, letting the rain chill her skin. *Don't cry for Helen,* she thought. *Find the answers. Make sense of her death.*

But where to start?

Footsteps sounded behind her. She turned slightly, watching the young police officer approach. Just for an instant, her vision blurred, and instead of the policeman, it was a gnarled, twisted being with red hair and malevolent yellow eyes. It reached out to grasp her soul—to kill, as it had killed Helen and Ross. Fear squeezed her throat tight, making it suddenly difficult to breathe. She stepped back, half turning, ready to run, but then the being became the young officer again. He dropped his hand, a surprised look on his face.

"I didn't mean to startle you, Miss Brown."

"You didn't. I just . . ." She hesitated, then shrugged.

He nodded, as if understanding. "Arrangements have been made for you to spend the night at the motel down the road—if that's okay with you."

"Yeah, sure." Where she was didn't really matter right now. It wasn't as if she'd be able to sleep.

He frowned slightly, as though her attitude bothered him in some way. "Would you like to collect some clothes or toiletries before you go?"

"I'm allowed inside?" she asked, surprised.

He nodded. "Only upstairs. The kitchen and living rooms are still out of bounds, I'm afraid."

And would be for some time—for her, at least. It was doubtful whether she'd ever be able to enter the house without remembering. She rubbed her arms again, suddenly chilled. Though she was soaked through to the skin, she knew that wasn't the cause. It was more the sense that death was out there—and that it wasn't finished yet.

"Ready when you are, Miss Brown," the young officer prompted when she didn't move.

Her hand brushed his as she headed for the door. His skin was cold—colder even than hers. As cold as the dead. She shivered and shoved her imagination back in its box. It was natural for his hands to be cold. The night was bitter, and he'd spent a good amount of time out on the veranda, watching her.

She kept her eyes averted from the living room as she ran up the stairs. Her bedroom was the first on the left, Helen's on the right. Helen's door was open and the bed still made. She and Ross had obviously been making out on the sofa again.

Swallowing heavily, Kirby headed for her wardrobe

and grabbed a backpack. She shoved whatever came to hand into it—sweaters, jeans and a couple of T-shirts—then headed over to the dressing table to collect underwear. And saw, on top of the dresser, a small, gift-wrapped package.

She stared at it for several seconds without moving. Helen had known, she thought. Or at least had sensed that she might not be around for their mutual birthday, in two days. Tears blurred her vision, and a sob caught at her throat. She grabbed the present, shoving it into the pack, then opened the drawer, grabbed a handful of underwear and stuffed that in as well.

She turned and found the young officer standing in the doorway, watching her closely. Though his stance was casual, there was a coldness in his eyes that sent another chill down her spine.

"Ready to go?" he asked, pushing away from the door frame.

She hesitated, then felt stupid for doing so. He was here to help her, not hurt her. She bit her lip and walked toward him. He didn't move, forcing her to brush past him again. Once more her vision seemed to blur, and it was leathery, scaly skin she was brushing past, not the uniformed presence of the young police officer.

"Want me to carry that backpack for you?" he asked, reaching for it.

She stepped away quickly. "No. I'm okay."

He frowned again, then shrugged. "This way, then, Miss Brown."

He led the way down the stairs. Another officer, a blond-haired man in his mid-forties, joined him at the base. "Constable John Ryan," he said to her, his voice as kind as his brown eyes. "Constable Dicks and I have been assigned to keep an eye on you for the night."

Her fear stirred anew. "You think the murderer might be after me as well?" She knew he was, but it was not something she wanted to say out loud—as if by voicing her fears she would invite the presence to step further into her life.

"Just precautionary measures, that's all."

His smile never touched his eyes, and she knew he was lying. He motioned her to follow the young officer. They stepped into the wind and rain and sloshed their way across to the nearest squad car. Constable Ryan held open the back door and ushered her inside.

"It won't be long," he said. "Then you can finally relax."

Relax? Knowing death was out there, waiting for her? But she forced a smile, knowing he meant well.

Constable Dicks climbed into the driver's side and started the car. It took only five minutes to reach the motel. Dicks pulled up near the front office, and Constable Ryan climbed out and returned with the key.

The motel was L-shaped and single-story. Her room was number thirteen. Some thought it unlucky, she knew, though up until now she had never considered it so. Dicks parked the car in the room's allotted space and Ryan got out, quickly opening the door and inspecting the room. He came back moments later and opened the squad car's back door. Kirby grabbed her pack and climbed out.

The room was basically a small suite—there were two sofas and a couple of armchairs in the main room, along with a kitchenette, a table, and a TV. A bedroom lay to her right, with the bathroom next to it.

She headed for the bathroom. She needed a shower, needed to wash the smell of death from her skin. She wished she could do the same with her memories.

"Need anything to eat, Miss Brown?" Constable Ryan asked, picking up the phone. "I'm going to order some pizza."

The thought made her stomach turn. She shook her head, then closed the bathroom door. Leaning her forehead against the wood for a moment, she took a deep, long breath. She wanted—*needed*—to be alone.

But she wasn't, so she couldn't let go just yet. Couldn't allow herself to feel the pain. She had a bad habit of doing that—of repressing emotion, and *not* just hurt, Helen had once told her.

She dumped her backpack against the bathtub and reached into the shower, turning on the tap. The water was icy, so she let it run while she hunted around for the little packets of soap and shampoo. She found several of both in the cupboard under the sink and shoved a couple in the shower. Out of habit, she put the rest into her pack. Never waste anything had been her and Helen's motto for as long as she could remember.

From the living room came an odd sound—a gurgling sort of cry that was quickly cut short. Goose bumps chased their way up her arm. There had been fear in that cry, and the recognition of death.

Swallowing heavily, she opened the bathroom door and peered out. Constable Ryan sat in one of the two armchairs, but he didn't react in any way to her reappearance, and there was something decidedly odd about his posture. Something that sent a chill through her soul—a sensation that only increased when her gaze met Dicks's.

"Something wrong, Miss Brown?"

The coldness she'd noticed earlier in his eyes was deeper, almost inhuman. She clenched a fist, resisting the impulse to slam the door shut. "Did you call out? I thought I heard someone call my name."

The lie tasted lame on her tongue, and amusement gleamed briefly in Dicks's blue eyes.

"Maybe you heard the TV."

And maybe it was all in her imagination. Maybe she was finally going mad, as one of her many foster parents had insisted she would. But that parent had been a devout Catholic and had believed magic to be the devil's work. And while she couldn't actually raise magic—not in the same manner Helen had been able to—she *could* bend the energy of the air and the earth to her will. Which sounded more dangerous than it was, because in reality she could to do little more than create a net that had the power to bind one thing to another. Still, it was quite amazing that she'd lasted in that particular home for three months.

But as she stared at Dicks, she knew it wasn't imagination or madness. Something odd was happening in the room. The feel of magic was in the air.

"I'll just go have my shower, then," she said, closing the door.

There was no lock on the door. She bit her bottom lip and looked quickly around. There was a towel rack on the wall next to the door. Better than nothing, she supposed. She grabbed a sweater out of her pack and roped it between the handle and the towel rack, knotting the arms as tightly as she could. It wouldn't hold for more than the time it took to scream, but for some reason, she felt a little safer.

She stripped off her jacket and thrust a hand through her wet hair. What she needed was a drink. If nothing else, it would calm her nerves and perhaps help her forget, if only for a few hours—another bad habit of hers, according to Helen.

But to get a drink, she'd have to leave the bathroom, and instinct warned her that might not be a good move right now. Over the years, she'd learned to trust that inner voice—and in doing so, she had saved both her own and Helen's lives more than once.

She wished it had spoken up earlier tonight and saved Helen for her.

Tears stung her eyes. She wiped them away with the heel of her hand and noticed the steam was beginning to fog the room. She frowned and flicked the fan switch up and down a couple of times. It didn't seem to help.

In the other room, the doorbell rang. Constable Ryan's pizzas had obviously arrived. Her stomach turned, and she wondered how he could eat after what he'd seen at her house. Maybe a lead-lined gut was a prerequisite for a cop. She walked across to open the window.

Kirby, get out. Leave, while you still can.

The voice sounded so close, the warmth of the speaker's breath seemed to brush past her ear. Her heart leapt to the vicinity of her throat, and she spun, fists clenched against the sudden rush of electricity across her fingertips. But there was no one in the room with her.

Now she was hearing things, on top of imagining them. *Great. Just great.* She took a deep breath, then reached up and opened the window.

As she did, the screaming began.

TWO

THE DOOR OPENED WITH A CRASH THAT RATTLED THE empty soda cans and coffee mugs lining the bookcase to his right. Doyle Fitzgerald glanced up to watch his best friend and sometimes partner drip in.

"You're wet," he said, leaning back in his chair with a grin. Russell was more than just wet. He looked like the proverbial drowned rat—brown hair plastered to his face and accentuating his sharp features, nose and cheeks mottled red, clothes sodden and shoes squelching.

"No kidding." Russ stripped off his coat and threw it roughly into the corner. "It *is* supposed to be summer here, isn't it?"

They'd come to Australia from the U.S. a week ago and had yet to see any real sunshine. Not that it really mattered, Doyle thought grimly. Most of their work was done at night. "The lady in the coffee shop down the road said you could get all four seasons in one day here."

Russell snorted. "The only season we're getting at the moment is winter. Is the boss in?"

He glanced toward the interview room. It was dark except for the occasional flicker of warmth from the candle Camille had lit earlier. "Yeah. She's trying to do another reading."

"She'll want to see this." Russell undid the top few buttons of his shirt and dug out a manila folder.

Doyle groaned. "Don't tell me our murderer has finally found one of his marks."

Russ's brown eyes were grim. "Yep. One point down, three to go."

"Damn." They'd been sent here to stop these murders, but so far they'd had little success in tracking down the victims, let alone the killer. "Who did he get?"

"One Helen Smith and her boyfriend, Ross Gibson."

Camille had done a reading the moment they'd arrived here and confirmed the list of possible victims they'd been given. Smith had been on it, but not Gibson. Doyle scrubbed a hand across his eyes. Was it simply a matter of Gibson being in the wrong place at the wrong time, or was the list inaccurate? And if it *was*, where the hell did that leave them? "Where did it happen?"

"Essendon. They rented the place two weeks ago, but hadn't got around to notifying anyone about their change of address." Russ's voice was grim. "Let's go see the boss. I'll be damned if I'm going to repeat everything."

He headed for the interview room. Doyle grabbed three mugs from the top of the bookcase and followed. Russ knocked softly on the door.

"Stop making all that damn noise and just come in," a raspy voice ordered.

Russ cocked an eyebrow. "The old witch sounds in fine form tonight."

"The old witch has fine hearing, too, Russell, so mind your tongue and get in here."

Russ rolled his eyes and opened the door. Restraining his grin, Doyle walked through the candlelit darkness to the coffeepot.

"That the police file?" Camille asked.

"It's as much information as I could get—which isn't much, given the murder only happened a few hours ago."

"First impressions are better than nothing." Camille snatched the folder from Russell's hands and, after pushing her blue-rimmed glasses back up to the bridge of her nose, opened it and peered at the contents with a frown.

Doyle filled the mugs, handing them out before sitting down at the table next to Russell. He sipped his coffee and watched Camille, an odd sort of trepidation filling his gut. The surprises hadn't ended with these two murders, of that he was certain.

"Damn it, this is the one thing we *didn't* need." Camille threw the file on the table, her voice filled with frustration. "Now that the killings have begun, they'll proceed quickly. We've got forty-eight hours, if that, to save the remaining three women."

Forty-eight hours to do what they hadn't been able to in a week, Doyle thought grimly. He picked up one of the crime scene photos and studied it. Even though he'd seen a hell of a lot worse in his time with the Circle, anger still burned through him. These people hadn't just been killed; they'd been desecrated. There was nothing ritualistic about the destruction, either, despite the fact that Camille had foreseen that *that* was the method by which these women would die. This death was fury, pure and simple. But why? What had Helen Smith done that had angered their killer so greatly?

"If we want to save some time," Doyle said, "it might be worth trying to capture the *manarei* so we can pull whatever information we can from its mind."

"It's doubtful a *manarei* would be given anything more than the necessary information to get the job done," Russ said. "Although the point has to be made—if the person behind these murders is powerful enough to control one of the most dangerous shapeshifters around, why would that person risk using it in the first place?"

Camille shook her head, her silver hair gleaming in the flickering candlelight. "It's hard to understand motives when we have no idea who our killer is. Russell, did you get a chance to look at the house?"

"Yeah, I got invited in with the forensic team. Brains consumed, bodies dismembered, although there was no obvious pattern to the destruction and certainly no sign of a ritual circle, despite the marking on the door. If I had to guess, I'd say it was done in anger."

She frowned and tapped a gnarled finger on the photo. "Nothing else? Nothing out of the ordinary?"

Russell frowned. "Yeah. The living room looked as if the storm had raged inside for a moment. The whole place was sodden."

Camille's gray eyebrows shot up. "What did the cops make of that?"

"Both the door and the window had been left

open." Russ shrugged. "They figured it was probably that."

"But you don't?" Doyle asked.

Russ shook his head. "I'm not magic-sensitive like you, but the air felt . . . electric." He shrugged. "Whatever happened, it still wasn't enough to protect them."

Doyle grimaced. The only thing that really stopped a *manarei* was a silver bullet to the brain. But the *manarei* weren't just powerful killers. They were hunters beyond compare, and they could assume the shape of anyone they killed. Which made them damn hard to track down.

"Storm witch," Camille muttered. "Damn it, I wish I knew *why* these women are being hunted."

"There has to be *some* sort of connection between all four," Russell said.

"Obviously," Camille snapped. "But *what* is the question."

Doyle reached for the folder. "We're obviously missing something."

"Yeah, a motive." Russell's voice was dry. "And the name of the person pulling the *manarei*'s strings."

Doyle grinned. "I meant specifically with this murder, moron. What do we know about this Helen Smith?"

"Not a lot. She was placed into the foster care system at the age of six when her adoptive parents were killed in a crash. She was eleven when she was sent to a government-run facility for troubled teenagers."

"No relatives?" Doyle asked.

Russell shook his head. "None listed, though I dare say she has some somewhere."

"Anything else?"

"Not much. She moved around a lot, from what I can gather. She'd just taken a job as a chef at a local vegetarian restaurant. Shared the house with a girl-friend, one Kirby Brown. It was Kirby who found her, apparently."

"You get a chance to talk to this woman?" Camille asked, voice sharp.

"No. The cops have her under protection at a local motel."

Camille made a sound of disgust. Her dislike for the police stemmed from her brief stint on the force. She never talked about it much, but Doyle had gathered over the years that it wasn't so much the rules she disliked as the unwillingness of those in charge to see beyond the material aspects of a case in order to solve it.

But the police force's loss was the Damask Circle's gain. Camille had been quickly pulled from the ranks of general investigators and now helped Seline White-shore run the huge organization. That Seline had sent her here with them spoke of the seriousness with which she viewed this situation.

"They do their best, given the limited resources and expertise they have." Though Russell's voice was mild, there was a flash of annoyance in his brown eyes. He'd been a cop himself before he'd crossed the line between the living and the dead, and even now, he readily defended them.

"What do we know about this Kirby Brown?" Doyle asked, before Russ and Camille could get into yet another argument on the merits of the police.

"Very little. She paints houses for a living and portraits for fun, and she has apparently known Helen most of her life."

"Photo?"

"Yeah, in the back of the folder. I took it from one of the bedrooms."

He shuffled through to find it. The two women could have passed for sisters. They had the same build and the same dusky-brown hair, only Kirby's was highlighted with streaks of pale gold. Their eyes differed, too. Helen Smith had the eyes of a storm witch— a smoldering, ethereal gray. Kirby's were a vibrant green. Even though it was only a photo, those eyes seemed to cut right through him and touch something deep in his soul.

Frowning, he slid the picture across to Camille. "What if it was a mistake? What if the *manarei* went after the wrong woman?"

"Aside from the fact she's not on the list?"

"We don't know how accurate your list actually is," he replied.

"Oh, that's a brave comment," Russell murmured.

Camille cast them both a withering look. "That list is all we've got, so you'd better hope it's at least partially accurate. And Helen Smith *was* on it."

Kirby Brown wasn't. And yet, looking at that picture, at those eyes, he couldn't escape the notion that *she* was the key they were searching for. "But what if the cops were right? What if the only reason Kirby Brown isn't also dead is the fact that she'd arrived home late?"

Camille picked up the photo and studied it for several seconds. "Well, it's possible. There's certainly power in her gaze, and our killer might be after something as simple as that."

Doyle frowned. "Meaning what?"

Camille looked at him, her expression surprised. "You mean to say you've been around magic more than half your life, and you didn't know it's possible to siphon powers?"

"I certainly didn't." He frowned. "How is something like that even possible? How can you siphon someone's psychic abilities like they're nothing more than blood?"

Camille snorted. "Boy, there are things in this world that can suck the energy from a person until they're nothing more than a husk. There are even creatures that feed on souls. Why wouldn't it be possible to siphon psychic energy or abilities?"

He shrugged. Put like that, it almost seemed reasonable. "So the real question is, why these particular girls?"

"Until we uncover what the link is between the women on the list—and there is one, have no doubt of that—then we won't know." She glanced back at Russell. "Did you get anything personal from the house?"

Russ reached into his shirt and pulled out a plastic bag. Inside were two hairbrushes.

Camille smiled. "Such a clever boy."

"Such a damn thief," Doyle muttered dryly.

Russ raised an eyebrow, his expression amused. "Now, *there's* a case of the pot calling the kettle black."

Doyle grinned and didn't deny it.

Camille drew one of the brushes out of the bag. She

unwound several strands of hair from the bristles, then closed her eyes and ran the lengths through her fingers. A shudder shook her slender frame. "This was Helen's," she said softly. "She could call to the storms, was a friend to the wind, and one with the air. But she was the weaker of the two."

He shared a glance with Russell. Storm witches were pretty damn powerful. If she was the weaker, then what kind of power did Kirby have?

"They've been on the run for years." Camille hesitated, frowning. "Running not from the past but the future."

"She obviously didn't see *this* future," Russ commented.

Camille's frown deepened. "I feel she did . . . but chose to accept her fate."

Another shudder rocked the old woman's frame. Sweat began to bead her forehead. The hair slipped from her fingers, falling softly to the desk. Camille leaned back in her chair and took a deep breath. "I can't read much farther. There's some sort of force blocking me."

Doyle reached across to touch the spiderweb of hair. Energy tingled across his fingertips, a muted echo of the power Helen Smith had controlled. The *manarei* should not have been able to kill her. At the very least, she should have been able to keep it at bay until help arrived.

But she'd chosen to die. He wondered why.

Camille took another deep breath, then leaned forward and took the second brush from the bag. "Kirby's," she said. "She is a part of this, even if her name is missing from our list. She is the key to all of them, the one that binds. She is . . ."

Her eyes flew open. "The *manarei* is after her. Doyle, go. Go now! Or she'll die."

He rose so swiftly his chair toppled backward. "Where?"

"Grice Street, Essendon. Hurry."

He was gone before she'd even finished speaking.

THREE

THE SCREAM CUT THROUGH THE NIGHT, A HIGH-pitched wail of distress. The hair along the nape of Kirby's neck stood on end, and for a minute she froze. The screamer was male, but the voice was too high, too young, to be Constable Ryan's. More than likely the screamer was the delivery boy. The sound cut off as suddenly as it had begun, and in the silence she could hear movement—gentle thumps, as if something soft were being thrown around in the next room.

Move, instinct said. *Move, before it comes for you.*

She thrust her coat into her pack and threw it out the window. It dropped with a splat into a puddle, and brown water splashed upward.

The sounds from the living room ceased. She froze again, listening, as she knew the thing in that room was listening. Her heart was beating so hard it was all she could hear.

Sweat trickled down her face. She clenched her fists and fought the urge to move. If she ran, it would come after her. She had to wait until it was distracted, otherwise she'd die. As the others in that room had died.

Time seemed to stretch, sawing against her nerves. Sweat dripped off her chin and splashed to the floor near her feet. For an instant, her vision blurred, and she saw blood instead of sweat pooling at her right foot.

A shiver stole across her. She blinked, but otherwise remained still. In the other room, the noise began again, this time accompanied by a soft, slurping sound.

Drinking the life of its victim, she thought, and knew that didn't mean blood.

Swallowing heavily, she stepped onto the rim of the tub. The window was on the small side and, even though she was small herself, it was a tight fit. She went out sideways, twisting as she fell so that she landed on her back rather than her head. There she lay for several seconds, gasping for breath and seeing stars.

Something thumped against the bathroom door. The creature she'd known as Dicks was coming after her. She scrambled to her feet, grabbed her backpack, and ran like hell.

In the bathroom, wood splintered and something metallic hit the tiles—the towel rack, giving way. Fear thrust energy through her limbs, and she raced toward the end of the motel.

Glass shattered behind her. She risked a look over her shoulder and saw a reptilian head snake through the window, eyes gleaming like yellow fire in the night. It hissed—an angry, alien sound that sent chills shuddering down her spine. She stumbled over something in the grass and threw out a hand to stop herself from falling. But she didn't see the glass hidden by the weeds, and she sliced her palm open. The smell of blood seemed to permeate the storm-clad night, and the creature screamed a second time.

A fence loomed in front of her. She threw her pack over it and grabbed the railing, climbing up. Splinters tore into her palms and sawed at the cut on her left hand, but she ignored the pain and scrambled to the top of the fence.

The wind hit her full force, the rain like bullets against her flesh. Suddenly unbalanced, she grabbed the fence, clinging precariously and wasting valuable seconds.

The creature's roar filled the night with anger. She felt it launch with a sudden gust of wind, and before she could react, it grabbed her leg. Claws ripped into her flesh and pain flamed. She screamed—a sound swept away by the wind.

The energy of the night and the storm surged through her, and she grabbed at it desperately, binding it within to create a power that crackled like lightning between her fingertips. But the creature didn't seem to notice, grabbing her leg more securely and pulling back, hard. He was strong—too strong. She had nothing but the top of the fence to hold on to, and against the creature it wasn't enough.

She fell, landing in a heap at its feet. Her breath left in a whoosh of air, and stars danced in front of her eyes. She battled to breathe but didn't move. In Dicks's malevolent yellow eyes she saw the elation of victory. A smug smile twisted his thin lips—the same sort of smile that had irritated her earlier.

"Now you too must die." His voice was guttural, almost scratchy, as if he wasn't used to talking in this form.

"It's not my time just yet," she muttered, and rolled *under* his blow rather than away from it.

This close, he smelled of blood and death and unclean flesh. Gagging, she gripped one thick leg and imagined a web of power encasing his body. Energy surged through her fingers and leapt up his scaly flesh, forming a spiderweb of blue-white tendrils that not only encased him in heat but locked him to the ground.

He roared in fury, slashing with thick claws at the net encasing him. It rippled and moved but for the moment, contained him. It wouldn't for long. She'd bought herself time, not freedom.

She scrambled to her feet. For an instant, the world spun, and she had to grab the fence to keep from falling. Lethargy made her muscles shake, and her heart felt as if it were planning to leap out of her chest. She hadn't used her abilities much in the past, but the few times she had, the same thing had happened.

All magic costs, Helen had once told her. In her case, the cost was physical—and in a situation like this, that could be deadly.

She took several deep breaths, then grabbed the top of the fence and climbed over. Her right leg buckled as she landed on the far side and crashed to one knee. Tears stung her eyes, and she swore vehemently. Red-colored water pooled at her feet, only to be swept away by the lashing rain.

Just what she'd seen in her vision in the bathroom, she thought absently, and she grabbed her coat from her pack. After throwing it on, she pushed upright and hobbled away as fast as she could.

The streets were dark and empty. A light glimmered up ahead, a wash of yellow that reminded her of the creature's eyes. It was coming after her. She could feel the heat of its malevolence reaching through the night, searching for her.

A sob caught at her throat and she broke into a run. The wind slapped against her as she turned the corner, catching her sodden hair and thrusting it back like a flag. The rain was a constant stream against her face, making it difficult to see, but she knew this area. Helen and she had jogged around here every morning. She could have run home blindfolded.

She pounded across the road, heading toward the footbridge that arched over the railway tracks. Her street lay on the other side. Surely the police were still there. Surely they could help her.

But would they see the evil she saw, or would they only see the police officer rather than the monster?

Maybe it would be better simply to grab her car. She'd be safe in the car. The creature might be able to outrun her, but it wouldn't outrun her old Ford with its powerful V-8.

And if it got in her way, at least she'd be able to run the bastard over.

But there were people on the bridge and an old couple climbing the narrow stairs. She looked over her shoulder. The creature was behind her, gaining fast, its mouth open in a silent scream of anger. She couldn't push past the old couple without knocking them over, and if she waited for them to get clear, she'd die.

So she ran.

Past the bridge. Past brightly lit homes that offered false illusions of warmth and safety. The creature behind her wasn't going to be stopped by lights or warmth or even locks. If any of the people in those houses offered her sanctuary, they'd die, as Helen had died. As Constable Ryan and the pizza boy had died.

The heavy thud of footsteps drew closer. Hate sizzled across the cold night, as sharp as the sound of the creature's breath. Up ahead, two bright beams of light rounded the corner. She threw up a hand to protect her eyes from the sudden glare, but the headlights died as suddenly as the sound of the engine.

She ran on, knowing the creature was gaining on her, knowing there was little she could do to avoid it. Energy began crackling across her fingertips again, but it was little more than a muted spark. She needed more than a few minutes to rebuild the energy she'd already spent, and mere sparks wouldn't be enough to stop the creature behind her.

She approached the car. There was someone standing beside it—a shadowy form that looked more a part of the windswept night than anything real or solid. She swerved away, heading across to the other side of the road, not wanting to risk endangering someone else.

The creature was close. Its breath washed heat across the back of her neck. Another sob caught at her throat, and fear flushed fresh energy into her legs. It wasn't going to be enough. It was never going to be enough. In the blustering touch of the wind, she felt the heat of the creature's launch.

"Kirby, drop!"

She did without question. She heard two sharp retorts, like a car backfiring. She felt the heat of the creature fly over her head. She heard the crunch of its body as it hit the pavement only feet away.

She saw the black liquid that leaked across the wet

concrete from the gaping hole that had once been its head.

Her stomach churned, but she swallowed against the rising bile and clenched her fist, calling to her fire once again. She wasn't out of the woods just yet, because footsteps approached. Measured, cautious steps.

"Are you okay?"

The voice was accented, but not heavily so—American, she thought. It was deep and warm, and as soothing as hot chocolate on a winter's night. It was also the voice she'd heard in the bathroom.

She shifted slightly, squinting up against the rain. The stranger stood by her right side, a black-cloaked figure holding a gun he kept aimed at the creature.

"Can you hear me? Are you okay?" he repeated, still not looking at her.

Somehow, she found her voice. "Who in hell are you?"

She felt more than saw his smile, which was odd. Helen had always been the empathic one, not her.

"What, no hysterical overtures of gratitude?" His tone was light, yet she sensed a hint of curiosity. "Not even a thank-you for saving your life?"

"Not until I know who you are and why you're here." Not until she knew if she'd jumped from the frying pan into the fire.

"You may well have done just that," he said, voice suddenly sober. "But believe me, the danger has nothing to do with me."

Anyone would have thought she'd spoken aloud, and her fear rose several notches. Energy danced across her fingertips, brighter than before, but still nowhere near full strength. Time, she just needed time.

"You won't need your weapon against me," he said softly. "I didn't save your life just to kill you, believe me."

Right now, she wasn't inclined to believe anyone. Particularly someone who'd conveniently appeared out of the darkness the precise moment that she needed help. "Then what *did* you save it for?"

"Certainly not to hold a conversation with you in the middle of a storm. You want to get up?"

"You want to tell me your name?"

Again, she sensed his smile. "Doyle."

"Doyle what?"

"Doyle Fitzgerald." He glanced down. In the glow of the nearby streetlight, his eyes were blue, but a blue so dark they were almost navy. "Is that leg stopping you from getting up?"

She shook her head and pushed upright. But pain shot up her leg and she yelped, losing her balance and tumbling back toward the concrete.

He grabbed her arm, holding her upright, his touch almost white-hot against her chilled flesh. Once again her vision blurred, and she saw not her black-cloaked rescuer but a dizzying montage of images in which a big black panther was always central.

Though it made no sense, one thing was clear.

Doyle Fitzgerald wasn't exactly human.

FOUR

Magic burned across Doyle's skin, a touch as warm as her fingers were cold. Fear flitted briefly through the vibrant depths of her eyes, though whether it was fear of him or the situation, he couldn't say. Maybe it was both.

Right now, though, it didn't matter. It was more important that they got out of here. *Manarei* usually traveled in pairs. There would be another out there in the darkness, and it would have felt the death of its mate.

Somehow, he had to get Kirby into the car without alarming her any further—no easy task, he suspected. Especially if she noticed the *manarei* was beginning to melt away.

He stepped in front of her, blocking her view of the creature. "You need those wounds tended to."

It sounded rather lame, but he couldn't think of anything else. He certainly couldn't force her into the car—not when the thrum of magic pulsed between them. Light danced across her fingertips, a gentle play of energy that lit the night with miniature thrusts of lightning. Though he'd never come across anything like it before, one thing was clear: one wrong move and that energy would be aimed at him. And that, he suspected, would *not* be pretty.

"So you're offering to drive me to the nearest hospital?" She pulled her arm from his grasp and wavered on one leg. "Why?"

"Because you're going to bleed to death if you don't get help soon." The emergency room was actually the last place he wanted to take her. There were too many people—and too many forms the *manarei* could assume.

"And you're what? The local neighborhood watch out on evening patrol? And I suppose you just happened to have a gun handy in the glove compartment?"

Implying, no doubt, that he was up to no good. Once upon a time that might have been true, but not these days. Not since he'd joined the Circle. "Listen, all I'm trying to do is save your ass." Irritation bit through his words. He thrust a hand through his hair and tried to remain calm.

She snorted softly. "Why the hell would you have any interest in saving my ass? You don't even know me."

"But I know a fine ass when I see one, and yours certainly deserves to be saved." His irritation was more obvious this time, and he took a deep breath. Damn it, why was her distrust affecting him? Although, in her shoes, he probably would have used his magic first and asked questions later.

A startled look crossed her face and, for a moment, a smile touched her lips. It transformed her features, changing them from pretty to extraordinary.

"Compliments aren't going to get you anywhere, chum."

Her tone was still tart, despite the lingering warmth

on her lips. Lips he suddenly had difficulty tearing his gaze away from.

"Tell me how you know my name, and why you're really here," she said, a slight flush invading her cheeks.

Before he could answer, a howl ran across the night. It was a high-pitched wail of distress that sounded more human than animal. The *manarei*'s mate giving voice to its grief.

Time was running out. Though he still had four silver bullets in the gun, facing a grief-stricken *manarei* was an entirely different proposition from facing one in a feeding frenzy. Given the option, he preferred to run.

Her gaze searched the night, and her voice was soft, edged with fear. "That creature had a mate?"

Doyle raised his eyebrows, wondering how she knew. "Yeah. And it's going to be a little pissed that we killed him. We have to get out of here."

"Why didn't you just say that earlier, instead of rambling on about the hospital?"

Her gaze met his. It seemed to delve right to his soul, tasting secrets he'd rather keep hidden. "I didn't want to alarm you more than necessary."

She snorted again. "Like my night hasn't been one huge, monster-filled nightmare already."

And she was counting *him* as one of those monsters, at least until she knew who and what he was— something he was in no hurry to tell her. "Can we just get in the car?"

He touched her elbow. Warmth flared, washing electricity between them. Not her magic but something deeper, something more basic. Her gaze flicked to his, startled, but she didn't pull away, didn't run.

Though only, he suspected, because the other *manarei* was still out there hunting her.

He helped her over to the car and opened the door. The lightning still danced across her fingers, stronger now than it had been before. He wondered what her magic was, and why she hadn't used it against the *manarei*.

Another scream cut across the night, closer than before. Doyle slammed the door shut and hurried around to the driver's side. The wind whipped around him, bringing with it the scent of death. *Their* death, if they didn't get out of here.

He started the engine, switched on the lights and threw the car into gear. The wheels spun on the wet road for several seconds before the car lurched forward.

"You know, you neatly avoided answering my question before."

She was leaning against the door, as far away from him as she could possibly get. Her arms were crossed, hands hidden, but he sensed this was less a defensive gesture and more an effort to keep warm. She must have been out in the rain for some time, because she looked soaked.

He leaned forward and switched the heater to full blast. "And what question would that be?"

She made an exasperated sound. "Why are you here?" she repeated. "And how do you know my name?"

The lights changed to red up ahead. Doyle braked and glanced at the rearview mirror. Though he couldn't see anything, he knew the *manarei* was out there. Its grief was so strong the night reeked with it.

"I'm here because an old witch told me to be."

"And I suppose this old witch just happened to tell you my name, as well?" Her voice was sharp with disbelief.

"Actually, yes, she did." He shifted gears and edged forward, wishing the lights would hurry up and change again.

"I see."

The tone of her voice told him she didn't. She stared out the window for several seconds. Tension rode her slender frame. *Ready to run,* Doyle thought, and he knew that if she did, she'd die.

"Look," he said, trying to keep his voice as calm and nonthreatening as possible, "I'm a private investigator. I'm working on a case that bears striking similarities to what happened to your friend tonight, and I came to investigate. That's all, nothing more."

Though this was a lie. In truth, he'd been sent out in advance of the murders, but he knew she would never believe that.

Her eyes narrowed. "Then why did you stop back there? Why come down Grice Street at all if you were going to my place?"

He shrugged. "I got lost." The lights finally went green. He pressed the accelerator and sped off.

She studied him for several long seconds. "You're a liar, Doyle Fitzgerald."

He glanced at her. Her green eyes were flecked with silver and gleamed brightly in the darkness. So pretty, and yet so full of anguish and mistrust. "I'm not lying about the reason I'm here."

"Maybe." She looked away. "And maybe you'd better just stop and let me—" She hesitated, and gasped.

The shadows moved ahead, and the streetlights

gleamed off the metal garbage can hurtling toward them. Doyle braked hard, and the car slewed sideways. The can hit the hood of the car, then bounced into the windshield, sending a web of cracks racing through the glass before rolling off into the rain-swept darkness.

Through the cracks, Doyle could see the *manarei*, eyes gleaming yellow fire as it raced toward them. He cursed and threw the gears into reverse. The tires spun, then gripped, and the car lurched backward.

But not nearly fast enough.

"Look out!" Kirby screamed a second before something heavy again hit the hood.

Glass shattered, flying everywhere. Kirby screamed again, a sound lost to the *manarei*'s howl. It reached through the large hole it had created in the windshield, claws slashing wildly. Doyle braked, but the sudden stop failed to dislodge the creature. He thrust the car into neutral, then threw a punch, connecting with the creature's jaw. The force of the blow jarred his whole arm but had little effect on the *manarei*. He might as well have been hitting concrete.

He grabbed the tire iron he always kept under car seats for emergencies like this and smashed it into the creature's mouth. The *manarei* recoiled, shaking its head, splattering Doyle and Kirby with blood. Then it snarled and lashed at him again. He thrust back in the seat as far as he could, but the claws raked his side, tearing past his coat and into skin. He cursed and hit it again.

Blue fire leapt through the night. Kirby, her hands ablaze, touched the creature's arm. The lightning leaped from her fingers and shot across the *manarei*'s body, encasing it in light. The smell of burnt flesh rent the air, and the creature howled again—this time a sound full of pain rather than anguish. Doyle grabbed his gun and scrambled out.

The wind whipped at his coat, and the rain stung his skin. He braced himself against the door and raised the gun. The *manarei* twisted around violently, trying to free itself from the web of energy that somehow pinned it to the hood of the car. Its skin was smoldering, and one large chunk near its chest had peeled away and was flapping in the wind. Kirby's power, whatever it was, would have killed anything human.

The creature looked around, eyes gleaming malevolently. Then it lunged forward, straight at Kirby. The web stretched with the creature's movement, the tendrils of power becoming thinner and thinner until, ultimately, they snapped. Doyle squeezed the trigger. The sounds of the shots were muted, lost quickly in the howl of the wind. Blood and bone sprayed through the night, and the creature dropped to the road. It didn't move.

Neither did he, not for several seconds. *Manarei*, like snakes, had been known to keep moving, to keep reacting, even after death. It was usually better to leave them completely alone, but right now he couldn't afford to do that, just in case the creature *wasn't* dead. He walked to the front of the car, gun held at the ready. He had only two bullets left. If the *manarei* was still alive after having two bullets plugged into it, then two more probably weren't going to make a huge difference.

The creature lay on the road, a huddled mass of

leathery skin that wasn't going anywhere. One bullet had torn into its brain, the other into its heart. The creature's whole body was bubbling, steaming, disintegrating. Soon there would be nothing left but a stain that the lashing rain would quickly wash away.

A gasp made him look up. Kirby had climbed out of the car and was looking wide-eyed at the creature. She covered her mouth with shaking fingers, and her face was white—too white.

He raced around the car and caught her slumping body a second before she cracked her head against the road. He picked her up and placed her back in the car. She was lighter than he'd expected—beneath the bulkiness of her coat, she was obviously little more than skin and bone.

He fastened her seat belt, then slammed the door shut and went back to look at the *manarei*. It was now little more than a bubbling, pulpy mass. One of the great side effects of silver bullets, he thought grimly. They made the cleanup a whole lot easier.

He climbed into the car and started it up again. The rain was driving in through the hole in the windshield, its touch icy. Despite this, he could feel warmth trickling down his side. He'd have to tend to his wounds—and Kirby's—as soon as possible. *Manarei* were filthy creatures, and infection was an all-too-real possibility.

He drove off, then dug into his pocket and grabbed his cell phone. After glancing in the rearview mirror to check for cops, he quickly dialed Russell's number.

It didn't ring for long. "About time you checked in, bro," Russell said. "What's happening?"

"We've two dead *manarei* and one unconscious but alive victim."

"You okay? I know from experience what nasty bastards those *manarei* can be."

"It clawed me, but it's nothing serious. Kirby's got a pretty nasty leg wound. Camille had better take a look at it."

Russ cleared his throat slightly. "That might be a bit of a problem."

Doyle glanced in the rearview mirror again. The red and blue lights of an emergency vehicle cut through the darkness, but he relaxed when he saw it was just an ambulance. Right now, the last thing he wanted was to be pulled over by the police.

"Why will it be a problem?" he said, slowing for another set of traffic lights. "What's happened to Camille?"

"Nothing. But she's done another reading using Kirby's hair. Someone's using magic to track her, and until Camille figures out how and why, she doesn't want you to bring her back to the office."

"So I hole up somewhere and wait?"

"That's the general plan, yes. But remember, she's being tracked, so you can't afford to relax."

"I gather from that you're not coming over to share guard duties."

"Nope. This pretty lady is all yours. Camille wants me to check out both Helen's and Kirby's background, then head on over to the government facility that looked after her adoption."

"I doubt whether you'll find any clues now." Doyle accelerated slowly as the lights changed to green. Between the rain and the spiderweb of cracks covering what remained of the windshield, it was difficult to see anything. He'd have to stop somewhere soon—if only because his body was beginning to go numb with cold.

"There'll be records, if nothing else. And I had a damn fine teacher when it comes to picking locks."

Doyle grinned. "Last time you tried, you set off every damn alarm in the place."

Russ snorted. "And whose fault was that? *You* were the one who was supposed to kill the alarms, not me."

"Blame Seline. It's her fault I'm not getting any practice these days." His skills as a thief were not what they'd been when she'd invited him to join the Circle some twelve years before, and she'd basically kept him on the straight-and-narrow ever since.

Not that he was altogether unhappy about that— though in many ways, life as a thief had been a hell of a lot less complicated than life in the Circle. And it had certainly been a hell of a lot safer.

"I'll give a call once we hole up somewhere."

"Do that," Russ said and hung up.

Doyle shoved the phone back into his pocket and glanced at Kirby. Her eyes were still closed and she was slumped against the door, but the tension riding her shoulders told him she wasn't unconscious.

"You want to go through your pack and see if there's anything in there that shouldn't be?"

Her eyes opened a sliver. "Like what?"

"One of my partners thinks you're being tracked by magic, so you need to go through your things." He glanced at her when she didn't react. "Now."

She studied him for a moment longer, then twisted around to grab her pack. She pulled out an odd assortment of clothes as well as, of all things, a small but cheerfully wrapped box.

"Is it your birthday?"

"Not yet." She shoved the present between her knees, then upended the pack. "There's nothing else in here."

Which didn't mean the tracker wasn't there, just that it was well hidden. He'd have to search himself—but later, when she was asleep.

"Know anywhere decent we can stay?" he asked.

She raised an eyebrow. "What's this 'we' business?"

"Like it or not, I'm all that currently stands between you and those *manarei*." Which was something of a lie—*manarei* rarely traveled in packs. They were far from sociable creatures, and he actually doubted that whoever was behind this could control more than two. But that only meant something far worse might be on her trail.

"What about the police?"

He raised an eyebrow. "Were you not under police protection when the first *manarei* attacked?"

"Yeah, but what makes you think you're going to fare any better?"

"I'm still here, aren't I?"

"Just *why* you're here is another point I'd like to discuss."

She was persistent; he had to give her that. "Later, perhaps, when we're out of this rain and you've had that leg tended to."

She regarded him silently. He could see from her thoughts that distrust was a habit, and he wondered what had happened in her life that now made her suspect the motives of everyone around her.

"Don't suppose you can suggest a good motel around here somewhere?"

She looked away. "No, I don't think I can."

He wasn't entirely sure whether she was talking about trusting him or knowing of a motel. "Then let's travel along this road and see what we find, okay?"

She didn't answer, but the lightning was beginning to flicker across her fingers again. "Kirby," he said gently, "I'm not going to hurt you. I have no intention of doing anything more than tending to your wound and guarding you from future attacks."

"I only have your word on that."

If her tone of voice was anything to go by, his word wasn't worth a dime.

"Then believe this. Whatever or whoever sent those *manarei* after you is going to be pretty pissed at their deaths. And they *will* come after you again."

She shivered and rubbed her arms. "I know." She glanced at him, eyes rich with suspicion. "And that's why I can't trust you. This whole thing may just be a ruse to gain my trust."

Killing two *manarei* was a hell of a dangerous way to gain her trust. Doyle shook his head in disbelief. "Look, you've got a pretty potent weapon at your disposal. I've seen it in action, and I know it can kill. You think I want to risk that?"

She bit her lip. Droplets of water ran down her face, shimmering silver in the warm wash of the street-lights. They looked like tears. Maybe they were.

"You make one wrong move, and I will use it," she said after a moment.

"Fair enough." He spotted an illuminated sign ahead and slowed the car. "This motel okay?"

She shrugged. "Do you really care anyway?"

"I guess not." He stopped at the motel's office and

opened the car door. Then he hesitated and glanced at her. "Wait for me. Don't go anywhere."

She shrugged. It could have meant anything. He frowned. "Promise?"

She snorted. "Bit old for that sort of foolishness, aren't you?"

He raised an eyebrow and stared at her. After a moment, she looked away, muttering, "Yeah, I promise."

He nodded, then headed inside. The motel's manager gave him a room, some advice on where to get the windshield replaced, a bottle of antiseptic and several bandages, both of which he cheerfully added to the bill.

By the time Doyle got back to the car, she was gone.

FIVE

KIRBY LEANED AGAINST A LAMPPOST AND BATTLED TO catch her breath. The night around her spun drunkenly, and she wrapped an arm around the pole. She'd pushed too hard tonight, and now she was beginning to pay for it. But the night wasn't over yet. She had to get out of this rain. Had to find somewhere safe.

She remembered Doyle's warning and shivered. Maybe he was right. Maybe there was nowhere left for her that was safe. Maybe she'd run as far as she could, and now fate was going to force her to make a stand. *If only Helen were here* . . . She bit her lip.

No amount of wishing could ever bring Helen back, so she'd better get used to life alone. Tilting her head back, she let the rain wash the heat from her eyes until her face felt as numb with cold as the rest of her. Then, resolutely, she pushed away from the pole and continued on.

In the distance, a bell dinged—a cheerful sound that seemed at odds with the stormy night. A brightly lit tram swayed along its tracks, rattling toward her. She dug into her pockets, then realized she'd dropped her purse beside the box of chicken in the doorway at home. She grimaced. She'd have to go back. Without cash or credit, she wasn't going to get very far.

She splashed on through the night, keeping to the shadows as much as possible. Doyle had probably discovered her absence by now, and she had no doubt that he'd come looking for her. It had been no accident that he'd found her on Grice Street, no matter what he said. And she wasn't inclined to trust someone so conveniently placed in a position to help her. Especially when that someone used a gun so well.

An image of the creature's bubbling, dissolving flesh flashed through her mind, and her stomach turned. Why had that happened? Why would a mere bullet make skin and bones liquefy like that? She thrust the thought from her mind. Right now, the why behind the melting wasn't so important. Getting out of this rain and tending to her aching leg were. Maybe then she could start concentrating on finding answers. Find out why Helen had been murdered.

She hurried down a side street. The wind slapped against her, thrusting cold fingers of air past her sodden clothing, chilling her flesh. She shoved her hands into her jacket pockets and wished she'd grabbed her long woolen coat when she'd had the chance. It might not have provided any more protection from the rain, but it was a hell of a lot warmer than the padded nylon raincoat she currently had on.

A car rounded the corner ahead, its headlights cutting through the darkness. She hesitated, but she knew she couldn't take the chance that it wasn't Doyle. She ducked into a driveway and hid behind a car. A dog barked furiously, and inside the house, someone yelled at the mutt to shut up.

She waited, aching with cold and the need to get moving. The lights drew close. She bit her lip and watched the car cruise slowly past. It wasn't Doyle's car or Doyle, but whoever it was, they were obviously looking for someone. Maybe even for her. Why else would they be going so slowly?

And that, she thought grimly, was surely paranoid thinking. Why wouldn't the driver be going slowly when the wind was driving the rain so hard that visibility was down to practically nothing?

She rose and moved back to the footpath. The car had parked up near the top of the street. Its lights were out, and the driver was nowhere to be seen. *See?* Kirby told herself. *He'd been going slowly because he lives here. Nothing to worry about.*

Yet the creeping sense of danger increased. She hurried down the street, away from the car. The sooner she got home, the better.

She crossed the railroad tracks and headed toward her street. Something scraped behind her. She spun, fists clenched and her heart in her mouth, but there was nothing there. She scanned the night, her stomach churning. Something *was* there, even if she couldn't see it. Its presence crawled through her, dangerous, evil.

She turned to run, but her leg buckled. She went down, hitting the pavement hard. Cursing softly, she twisted around, looking behind her again. The shadows seemed to part, disclosing a tall man with gaunt features and matted-looking hair. He looked like someone spaced out on drugs, and there was an odd sort of neediness, maybe even desperation, in his eyes. Then he smiled. His canines were long and white—the sort of canines you saw on Hollywood vampires. He was crazy—or was she? Had the crack on her head sent her imagination tripping?

Evil washed across the night, burning her skin. *This is no dream,* she thought, horror rising. The stranger snarled and leapt toward her. She screamed and scrambled backward.

From out of nowhere came a growling black mass, all sinew and power. *Panther,* she thought, and rubbed her eyes. Maybe she *was* tripping. Only the creature reminded her of the cat she'd seen when she'd first touched Doyle. He and the animal *were* connected—of that she was certain.

The cat hit the vampire hard, and the two went down in a fighting tangle of claws and teeth. The shadows seemed to close around them, momentarily hiding them from sight. When they parted, it was Doyle fighting the vampire—Doyle wrapping an arm around the stranger's neck and twisting hard. There was an audible snap, and the man with the vampire teeth went limp. He didn't move; he wasn't even breathing.

Dead, she thought, and felt her stomach rise. She scrambled over to the grass and threw up what little she'd eaten for lunch.

Footsteps approached. Kirby wiped her mouth and sat back on her heels. She didn't turn around. Didn't want to face him. His gaze all but burned a hole in her back. She clenched her fingers and waited.

"A person is only worth as much as her promise," he said eventually.

Though his voice held no inflection, his anger surged

around her. She rubbed her arms and wondered again why she could feel his emotions so clearly.

"Well, I've pretty much been told all my life that I'm worthless, so I guess that it's true, isn't it?" Bitterness crept through her words, but she just couldn't help it. He had no right to judge her, even if he had saved her life. Twice.

"At least now I know I can't trust you."

Tears stung her eyes. She blinked them away. She didn't need his trust. She didn't need anyone's trust. All she wanted was to wake up from this nightmare. "A fine statement coming from a man who's just killed someone."

"That someone was about to suck you dry and spit out the remains."

She closed her eyes and tried to ignore the chilled fingers of dread creeping through her body. She knew instinctively that tonight's strangeness had only just begun. "What do you mean? What was he? And what happened to that cat I saw?"

He made a sound that was close to a growl. "I refuse to answer any more questions out here in the rain." Exasperation sharpened his warm voice. "Get up—or do you need help?"

"I don't need anyone's help," she muttered and pushed upright. The night spun violently, and she swallowed heavily against the sudden rise of nausea.

"God grant me strength against stubborn women," he muttered.

Suddenly his arms were around her and he was lifting her up, cradling her gently against his chest. It felt safe and warm and oh-so-secure. Frighteningly so.

"Put me down," she said, struggling against the strength of his grip.

"No." His arms tightened slightly. He was holding her so close that she could feel the wild beat of his heart. It might have been her own.

"Damn it, Doyle, release me!" She thumped his chest.

His gaze met hers. Deep in the depths of his eyes wildness burned—the sort of wildness she'd seen briefly in the panther's rich blue gaze.

"I'm wet, I'm cold, and I'm running out of patience," he said grimly. "And you just punched the wounds the *manarei* gave me."

She looked at her fist. It was bloody. "Oh God, I'm sorry. I didn't know . . . You didn't tell me."

"And you didn't bother asking."

She bit her lip. No, she hadn't. This man had risked his life twice now to save hers, and the fact that she didn't know *why* worried her. But that didn't excuse her lack of courtesy. He'd earned that much, at least. "I'm sorry," she said. "And thank you for saving me."

He nodded, though amusement seemed to gleam briefly in his eyes. "Now, will you just remain still until we get to the motel?"

"I suppose I can manage that." She didn't mean to sound ungracious, but she couldn't help it. Being held so carefully, as if she were precious cargo, was doing odd things to her pulse rate.

This time a smile touched his full lips, but he didn't reply, just kept striding through the night. They reached the motel in no time. His car was parked in front of a room two doors down from reception. He placed her back on her feet, holding her arm with one hand as he rummaged in his coat pocket and pulled out a key.

He opened the door but didn't immediately enter, his gaze searching the shadows. After several seconds he relaxed and switched on the lights. Which was odd, Kirby thought. It was almost as if he could sense danger better in the darkness.

He ushered her inside and locked the door. She dumped her pack on the table and limped into the bathroom. Like the first motel, it had a window above the sink.

"Don't even think of it," Doyle said behind her.

She jumped slightly and clenched her fists as she swung around. The damnable man seemed able to read her mind. "Don't even think of going to the toilet? Why on earth not?"

He was standing in the doorway, his expression half amusement, half anger. In the light, his eyes looked bluer, richer—cobalt rather than navy. His face was a depiction of perfection, framed by thick, dark hair that even when wet somehow managed to look wild. Rather like the man himself, she suspected.

"Leave the door open," was all he said. He grabbed a couple of towels, then walked away.

Trapped by my own lies, she thought. She glanced at the window a final time and limped after him. He pointed to a chair, then moved across to the kitchenette. "There's one thing I like about Australian motels—these little kitchenettes they all seem to have."

He was making small talk, trying to get her to relax. Not something that was going to happen anytime soon.

"You don't have kitchenettes in American motels?"

"You'll occasionally find a motel that has a couple of rooms with a kitchenette, but most don't have them." He filled a small bowl with hot water. Into this he poured antiseptic.

"Where'd you get that?" She sat down on one chair and propped her leg up on a second. Blood dripped steadily onto the carpet. She frowned, wondering if she should have gone to the hospital after all.

"The manager gave it to me." He squatted down next to her, placing the bowl on the carpet. "I'm going to have to cut your jeans away from the wound."

"Cut away. They're pretty much ruined anyway."

He nodded and produced a knife from his boot. *A criminal for sure,* she thought, and she wondered suddenly about her sanity. Just because he'd saved her life didn't mean she was any safer in his presence.

"If I wanted you dead, I would have left you to the *manarei* or the vampire." He slid the knife against her skin and carefully began to cut.

She stared at him, chilled as much by his matter-of-fact tone as by what he had said. *Vampires were real?* Surely he was joking. He had to be. Vampires *couldn't* exist. They were a product of fiction, of Hollywood. They could *not* be real.

"Vampires are as real as the lightning that springs from your fingers," he murmured, peeling the remainder of the rain-soaked material from her leg.

"You *are* reading my thoughts." It should have scared the hell out of her, but given the nightmarish events of the last few hours, this discovery was definitely the least disturbing.

"So it would seem." He dunked the end of the towel

in the antiseptic wash, then glanced at her. "This will hurt."

He began washing the wound, and her whole leg suddenly felt like it was on fire. Sweat broke out across her forehead, and she hissed, gripping the sides of the chair so tightly her fingers ached. "Tell me why you're here," she all but ground out.

"I've already told you—I'm investigating a murder." Though his touch was gentle, it felt like he was pounding her leg with a hammer.

"Is Helen's death connected to your murder?"

It came out sharper than she'd intended, and he looked up. There was sympathy in his expression, as well as understanding. It made something ache deep in her heart. Which was stupid, really, considering she didn't even know this man, let alone trust him. She pulled her gaze from his.

"Yes."

"Am I?"

"Probably." He hesitated. "Someone obviously wants you dead."

"Why?" The question was more a desperate plea for understanding, and she didn't really expect an answer. Until they found the person responsible for Helen's slaughter, the answer to such a question would be little more than guesswork.

"I'd say because someone wants something you have."

She snorted softly. "That statement is *so* wrong it's almost laughable. I have nothing. Absolutely *nothing*."

His bright gaze caught hers again and something deep inside her shivered. This man saw too much, knew too much. He was dangerous on so many different levels that she should just get up and run while she still could.

"If that were true, they would not be so determined in their efforts to find you. Remember that the next time you decide to run off."

There wasn't much she could say to that, so she childishly stuck her tongue out instead. He smiled and continued washing her leg. The wounds, once cleaned, turned out to be fairly deep and a good inch long. They were still bleeding profusely.

She frowned. "Maybe you should take me to the hospital."

"Maybe." He dug into his pockets and pulled out a small, cloth-wrapped parcel.

"What's that?"

"An old witch's herbal cure-all for wounds," he said, carefully unwrapping the parcel. Inside was what looked to be little more than dried-up garden clippings.

"You're not putting that on my leg," she said.

He grabbed her leg before she could move it, his grip gentle yet unyielding. The heat of his touch burned past the coldness of her skin and seemed to sear her entire body. "This stuff works better than any doctor's needlework, believe me."

"Yeah, and pigs can fly."

Her voice was tart, and his gaze narrowed. "I will take you to the hospital if you prefer, but just remember exactly what you've seen tonight. If the *manarei* could assume the shape of a cop, what's to stop it from assuming the form of a doctor? Or even a nurse?"

She shivered and rubbed her arms. "How can something like that exist? Or a vampire? How is anything like that even possible?"

"There are more strange things that walk the Earth than you or I could ever imagine," he said, his voice edged with coldness. "What's your choice?"

Her continuing distrust was annoying him, she realized. And yet wasn't it natural, given the situation? Surely he could see that. "If my leg gets infected or I bleed to death, I'm going to come back from the dead and make your life a living hell."

He raised his eyebrows slightly. "Well, I can think of worse things. At least you'd be easy on the eyes."

Heat crept across her cheeks. "Thanks. I think."

He smiled. "Don't move while I'm putting this stuff on. I haven't got much, and I need some for my wounds, as well."

She nodded. He began packing the four claw wounds with the mix. Oddly enough, it didn't hurt. Her skin seemed to go numb the minute the mix touched it, and while the blood didn't stop, it at least slowed to a trickle. He grabbed a roll of white gauze and quickly bandaged her leg.

"Give me your hand," he said, when he'd finished.

She did. He repeated the whole process on her hand, then rose and carried the bloody water over to the sink.

"If all goes well, your wounds should be basically healed come morning," he said, rinsing the bowl and filling it again.

If they were healed by the morning, it would be nothing short of a miracle. Or magic, she thought with a chill. "You want me to wash your wounds?"

He shook his head. "I'll do it. You get out of those wet clothes and into bed."

She raised an eyebrow and didn't move. He thrust a hand through his shaggy hair and looked more than a little annoyed. "Oh, for Christ's sake, stop acting so immature. If I wanted sex, I sure as hell wouldn't be here with you. I don't find you *that* attractive."

Though she should have been totally relieved, his words inexplicably hurt. She looked away. A man with his looks could have the pick of the crop. Why *would* he waste his time on someone like her?

And why was she even worrying about it?

She frowned. "I'm not changing with you standing there watching." And yet the thought of doing just that excited her. She crossed her arms and wondered if she was going out of her mind.

"Then I'll be in the bathroom." He picked up the antiseptic, the bandages and the dried herbs, then hesitated. "You will stay in this room, won't you?"

"I promise not to leave," she murmured.

"Don't promise me anything if you don't damn well mean it," he said and walked from the room.

She shook her head. Doyle Fitzgerald was certainly proving to be a man of extremes—he could kill without a second's thought, yet he seemed to believe in the integrity of something as fragile as a promise. And she had a feeling she hadn't even begun to scratch the surface of the enigma he presented.

She rose and quickly stripped. Once she'd hung her sodden clothes over the back of the kitchen chairs to dry, she pulled a shirt out of her backpack and slipped it on. Then she dug out the present and stared at it intently. If Helen had guessed she might not be around for Kirby's birthday, why hadn't she tried to avoid that fate? It wouldn't have been the first time they'd done that . . . The toilet flushed, reminding her that she wasn't alone. She shoved the present back into the pack and climbed into bed, pulling the blankets up around her nose. Not that she really thought Doyle would harm her in any way.

Warmth finally began to creep through her body. She yawned hugely and closed her eyes, listening to the howl of the wind outside. *The wind of change,* she thought. Goose bumps raced across her flesh. What changes did the wind whisper about tonight? The urge to get up and go outside to listen was so strong that she flipped the blankets aside. But the chilled air hit her skin and knocked the fanciful thought from her mind. It wouldn't have done any good, anyway. Helen was the one who could read the nuances of the breeze, not her.

She yawned again and snuggled deeper into the blankets. But as she drifted into sleep, the wind whispered through her thoughts, speaking of changes that would affect her heart and her soul.

Speaking of power that was hers to claim—if she dared.

SHE WAS ASLEEP BY THE TIME DOYLE WALKED OUT OF the bathroom. Given her prickly demeanor, he had expected her to be nose deep in the blankets, fingers afire with electricity, waiting to attack should he decide to pounce.

To find her curled up in bed and snoring softly was definitely a surprise.

Maybe he'd misjudged her. Or maybe the night's events had simply worn her down to the point of sheer exhaustion. It was actually a miracle she was still alive. Very few people lived through the attack of one *manarei,* let alone two. Either she was very lucky or there was more to her abilities than what he'd seen so far.

He draped his wet socks and freshly washed shirt next to her clothing, then pulled on his coat to keep warm. After making himself a cup of coffee, he walked across to the table and went through Kirby's pack. Just as she'd said, there was nothing there. Nothing that even vaguely resembled a tracker. Which didn't mean that either a piece of clothing or one of the toiletries couldn't be spelled; he might be magic sensitive, but that didn't mean he could feel *all* magic. And a well-woven, well-hidden spell was a difficult find even for someone like Camille.

He drank some coffee, then dug the phone out of his pocket and called Russell.

"Hey, wild man. How's it going?" Russ said, sounding more alive than any dead man had a right to sound.

Doyle grinned. "Sounds like you've had a break-through."

"A minor one. Seems Kirby Brown and Helen Smith were dumped on hospital doorsteps as babes on exactly the same day. No trace of their parents was ever found, and both were later placed for adoption. Interestingly enough, they both ended up in the very same center for troubled teenagers as eleven-year-olds."

Kirby, at least, had never been adopted. He'd caught that much from her thoughts. She'd been shuffled around various foster homes, never staying at one for more than a few months. He wondered why. "Maybe that center is our connection."

"Camille's certain it is."

"What is she up to at the moment?"

"She's headed off to the morgue to get a look at Smith's remains."

Doyle picked up one end of the sofa, moving it around until it was positioned in such a way that he had a clear view of the door, the window, and Kirby. "Has she tried to do another reading?"

"Not yet."

He sat down and propped his bare feet on the small coffee table. "That means despite the fact that our killer seems pretty intent on grabbing Kirby, Rachel Grant could still be the next victim. You any closer to tracking her down?"

"I've got three possible addresses. And before you ask, no, I haven't checked them out yet. I might be able to run like the wind, but I can still only do one thing at a time, and Camille wants me to check the government center first."

"Then give me the addresses. I'll check them out once Kirby gets some rest."

"Is that wise?" Russell's voice held a hint of doubt. "I mean, you might lead the killer directly to Rachel Grant. Maybe that's exactly what he wants."

"I doubt it. The killer didn't seem to have any trouble finding Helen. I don't think he's sitting back waiting for us to lead him to Rachel."

"Maybe, but you might just drag Kirby into the middle of an attack."

"A risk we'll have to take. Besides, Camille was right

about her being tracked. About ten minutes after the *manarei* died, a vamp was on her tail."

"I'm gathering you've looked for the tracker?"

"Yeah. If it's under a spell of some kind, I'm not feeling it."

"What about the vamp? Did you manage to question him?"

"Didn't have the time. But I'm thinking he was a last-minute recruit or something. He was pretty scrawny—hadn't been out of the fledgling bloodlust stage that long, by the look of him."

"Not much of a problem, then."

"No." Doyle frowned and remembered the look in Kirby's bright gaze when she'd finally turned to look at him. She'd thought him a killer, a monster. And in many respects, maybe he was. He'd certainly killed the vamp without a second thought. But if he hadn't, it might have been Kirby he'd left lifeless on the pavement.

"Where have you holed up?" Russell asked.

"A motel on Bulla Road. Hopefully, we'll be left alone for a while."

"I wouldn't bank on that, bro."

Doyle smiled grimly. "I'm not." He dug a pen out of his pocket. "You got those addresses?"

Russell read them out. "Camille said to expect a call from her around dawn."

Doyle finished writing the last address on the back of the breakfast menu card, then tucked it and the pen back into his coat pocket. "I'll be awake."

Russell snorted softly. "So will I. No one warned me when I took this job that sleep deprivation was one of the requirements."

"Plenty of time to sleep when you're dead, you know."

"I *am* dead."

"I mean totally dead, not vampire dead." Doyle grinned. "Be careful when you're breaking into the building. Whoever's behind this might be expecting such a move."

"Yeah, but will they be expecting a vamp to be doing the breaking and entering? It gives me a slight advantage."

But not against magic, and Russ knew that. "Talk to you later." Doyle hung up and settled back against the sofa. The wind rattled the window frames and howled under the door. The rain pelted down against the roof, so loud it sounded like stones hitting, not water. It was certainly one hell of a storm. He was glad they weren't still in it.

He glanced across at Kirby. Her hair flowed over the pillow like wet brown silk, and in sleep her face was serene. The impish quality that was so evident when she was awake had slipped away, leaving only beauty.

He'd lied to her earlier. She was very much the sort of woman he was attracted to—not that anything was likely to happen between them. Gaining her trust enough so that she'd lower her prickly barriers would probably take longer than he had here in Australia.

Though he couldn't help wishing he *did* have the time. He had a feeling the effort would be worth it— not so much physically as emotionally. He frowned at the thought and crossed his arms, looking away. *Any* sort of relationship was nothing short of impossible right now. Damn it, he loved his job, and he wouldn't quit. But by the same token, his work was the reason he was alone. Experience had taught him that few women could cope with the fact that he was absent for weeks, sometimes months, at a time.

And why was he even thinking such things when he barely knew her? While he knew from her thoughts that the attraction was definitely mutual, they'd also told him that she wouldn't act on that attraction. Not with someone she considered little more than a killer.

He leaned back and closed his eyes. Time passed. The wind howled through the night, an eerie, almost forlorn cry. Evil enjoyed nights like this, he thought. Yet the night remained free of evil's taint, and he drifted off to sleep.

The phone vibrating against his side woke him some hours later.

He looked around quickly. Everything was as it should be, and Kirby was still curled up asleep in the bed. *Lucky,* he thought, and scrubbed a hand across his eyes. Maybe jet lag was finally catching up with him. He dug out his phone and answered it.

"Hey, shapeshifter, didn't wake you, did I?" Delight ran through Camille's sharp voice.

"No, just sitting here watching the sunrise." He bit back his yawn and glanced at the clock. It was barely five.

Camille chuckled. "You never were a very good liar. How's Kirby?"

He glanced across at her. She hadn't shifted any, but she was no longer asleep. Odd how attuned he was to her. "Awake and listening."

She flipped the covers away from her face at his words and regarded him warily. Still not trusting him, despite everything.

"I paid a visit to her friend's remains last night," Camille said.

"Russ told me you were going to do that. What did you find?"

Camille sniffed. "What I found surprised the hell out of me."

Doyle raised his eyebrows. It had to be bad if Camille was surprised. She'd been around long enough to see the worst this world could offer. "What?"

"Helen Smith died before the *manarei* got to her. She killed herself."

"She *what*?" Suicide was an unusual step for a witch to take. Most witches believed that if you took your own life, you prevented your soul from moving on, dooming it to roam the confines of Earth for time eternal. "Why would she do something like that?"

"I'm not really sure. I didn't have enough time to do a full reading on her remains, but I suspect she performed a spell of some sort. Her magic was gone, Doyle, but it wasn't ripped from her."

"But if she was able to get rid of her powers, why kill herself?"

"Better a self-inflicted death than being torn apart by the *manarei*."

True. The bastards liked their prey alive and wriggling, so they tended to work from the bottom up—ripping off toes and fingers before getting to the limbs. Shock and death would be a welcome relief in that sort of situation. "You heard back from Russ yet?"

"Not yet."

Doyle frowned. It wasn't like Russ not to report in. "You tried calling him?"

"Yeah, but there was no answer."

"If you don't hear from him by six, give me a call." Russ was still young in vampire years—forty, to be exact—and his immunity to sunlight was almost nonexistent. If it got much later than seven, he'd be in trouble.

"Will do. In the meantime, I want you to be careful. I can see some pretty bad shit headed your way in the next few hours, especially now that our killer has had time to regain some strength."

"Thanks. I needed to know that."

She snorted. "Better to be prepared, my boy."

"Yeah, right." He glanced across at Kirby as she sat up. Though she had the sheet pulled up around her, he could see the outline of her body quite clearly. He'd thought last night that she was little more than skin and bone. He was wrong. He cleared his throat slightly and looked away.

"Are you listening to me, Doyle?"

"You were talking?"

"To myself, apparently. Are you planning to hole up in that motel?"

"No. We'll be harder targets to hit if we keep moving. Besides, I told Russ I'd check out the whereabouts of the next woman on your list."

"Do that. And keep in touch."

He shoved the phone back into his pocket, then glanced at Kirby again. "You interested in breakfast?"

She shook her head. "I think I'll throw up if I eat right now."

He wasn't entirely surprised. Not after she'd walked into her home and found her friend ripped to shreds. "What about a shower?"

She raised a dark eyebrow. "You trust me to take a shower?"

He shrugged. "Believe me, I have very good hearing. You try to get out of that window, and I'll know."

"Oh."

She didn't move toward the bathroom, just continued to study him warily. Her green eyes gleamed as bright as a cat's in the light flickering past the curtains. He frowned and glanced at them. Why were the curtains moving?

"What were you talking about on the phone? Who killed themselves?" She hesitated, then added, voice lowered, "What's wrong?"

"I'm not sure." He rose and stepped toward the window. Magic stirred, its touch so sharp it felt as if he'd walked into a hornet's nest.

"Kirby, get dressed."

She didn't argue, simply scrambled out of bed and ran for her clothes. He narrowed his gaze, trying to concentrate on the flow of power. It condensed near the window, finding form, finding shape. And became the biggest damn wolf he'd ever seen.

SIX

KIRBY FROZE AND STARED AT THE CREATURE THAT had suddenly appeared before them. It was big, with a shaggy gray coat and wild yellow eyes that were somehow almost human. It looked like a wolf. It even snarled like a wolf. But wolves didn't exist in Australia—not outside the confines of zoos, anyway. Maybe this one had escaped, though that didn't explain how it had gotten past the locked door and windows and into their room.

The wolf took a pace forward. It snarled again, teeth gleaming brightly. She reached for the energy of the approaching dawn, drawing it in swiftly.

"Don't," Doyle said softly. "Wait."

"Are you crazy?" But she clenched her fists, holding the power that flowed warmly across her fingers in check.

He continued to stare at the wolf. After a moment, the animal stopped snarling, but its head was still lowered, and it looked ready to attack.

"You are under a light glamour," Doyle said softly to the wolf. "I can feel its restraints on you."

Kirby frowned. A glamour was some kind of spell. She knew that much from Helen. But why would he think the wolf was under one? And why would he think a wolf would even understand or care?

"If you attack, you will die," he continued. "You know what I am, and you know I am faster and stronger than you."

The wolf didn't move, just continued to stare at Doyle with an odd sort of intelligence in its eyes. It was almost as if it *could* understand what Doyle was saying, which meant it was a good two steps ahead of *her*.

"I can open the door and let you leave, or you can die. The choice is yours, wolf."

No one moved—not Doyle, not the wolf, not her. Energy burned across her fists, flickering wild fingers of light across the ceiling. She continued holding her power in check, even though she doubted the sanity of doing so. After several seconds, the wolf sat back on its haunches.

"Wise move," Doyle said and opened the door.

The wolf glanced at her a final time, then padded out.

Doyle locked the door and swung around. "Move. I don't think we have much time before another attack comes."

"How did that thing get in here?" She grabbed a pair of jeans out of her bag and pulled them on. She didn't bother with socks, just slipped on her still damp running shoes over her bare feet.

He'd stripped off his coat and was pulling on his shirt. He had the body of an athlete—a runner. Trim, taut and well tanned. Very nice, even with the white ring of bandages around his ribs.

He glanced at her, amusement glimmering in his eyes. Heat stole across her cheeks. "Stop reading my thoughts and just answer my damn questions," she snapped.

"I have no idea why I'm catching your thoughts so clearly, so I can't exactly stop it." He put his coat back on and swept up her bag. "And to answer your question, that wolf was sent here by whoever is after you."

She frowned. "Sent here how?"

"By magic. Whoever is behind all this has obviously recovered from their exertions last night, and that means trouble for us. You ready to go?"

"Yes." The sooner they got moving, and the sooner she got away from this craziness, the better. "Where are we going?"

"To find a woman named Rachel Grant." He ushered her through the door, then grabbed her arm and walked her down to reception.

Not taking a chance on her running, she thought with amusement. Which she would, if he made one wrong move. "Why are we trying to find this woman?"

He hesitated, his gaze considering her for several seconds. Judging her, she thought, and she wondered why it suddenly seemed so important she pass his test.

"We believe she's the next victim." He opened the reception door and motioned her through.

A chill ran through her. "Have you told the police?"

"I doubt the police will place a great deal of importance on the words of an old witch."

Another guy wandered in, his presence stopping her from asking any more questions. Doyle settled their account and chatted cheerfully with the manager. It was hard to imagine his easy grin hid a killer's instincts.

He flashed her an annoyed look, and she bit her lip,

glancing away. Killer or not, he *had* saved her life. And she'd have to remember to watch what she was thinking when she was around him.

They headed back to his car and climbed in. "The cops will pull you over with a windshield like that," she commented.

"Then that's a risk we'll have to take. I don't have the time to grab another one right now." He started the car, then reached into his pocket and handed her the breakfast menu and his phone. On the menu were three addresses. Rachel's was the first one. "You navigate."

She punched their location and destination into Google Maps, then started giving directions as he sped off. The wind whipped in through the hole in the windshield, its touch forceful and icy. She zipped up her coat and fleetingly wished she had gloves. Her hands were so cold her fingers were aching.

"Here," Doyle said, producing a pair of black leather gloves from his pockets. "Wear these. They'll be too big, but they will at least keep you warm."

She accepted the gloves with a smile of thanks and pulled them on. "What *don't* you keep in those pockets of yours?" Like him, she had to raise her voice to be heard above the wind.

"Lots of things," he said. "Like answers. Did you or Helen ever try to find out who your parents were?"

Helen certainly had, but now she'd never get the chance. Kirby blinked away the sudden sting of tears and looked out the side window. "No. Why do you ask?"

"Because we thought that was a possible connection between Helen and the other women on the list.

That maybe by searching for their past, they brought themselves to the attention of our killer."

"This list?" she said, waving the breakfast menu.

"Yes. And before you ask, an old witch named Seline did a reading and came up with those names. Helen was the first name on it."

And now Helen was dead. "But why would searching for her parents have brought such destruction down on her?"

Helen had spoken to the wind many times, but she'd never seen her murder. Kirby crossed her arms and shivered. It wasn't supposed to be like this. They were supposed to die together in a car crash years from now. Why had fate stepped in and snatched Helen away long before her time? And did the fact that it had now mean *she* wouldn't die in a car crash? Or did death still lay in her future, just in a different form?

"We don't know," he said. "All we have is four names, and a suspicion these murders have their origin somewhere in the past."

Bile rose in her throat and she swallowed against it. She didn't want Helen connected in any way to these other women, and she didn't know why. "Why in hell would someone want to do something like that for something that happened in the past?"

He shrugged. "If we knew the reason, we would probably have been able to prevent it."

She looked at him. His profile was a painter's dream, classic and stunning. "What do you mean, 'we'? Who else is working on this with you?"

He hesitated. "I work for an organization called the Damask Circle. There are three of us currently in Melbourne, trying to solve these murders."

She frowned. "But Helen only died yesterday. You were already here in Melbourne."

"Yes, because Seline, the lady in charge of the Circle, did a reading and sent us out here in advance of the first murder. She said something big was going down."

"Reading? What is she? Some sort of psychic or witch?"

"Witch," he said. "But not the witch I referred to earlier. That's Camille, who's here with me and Russell."

Russell was obviously the man she'd heard him talking to earlier. She had a feeling there was a whole lot more about his companions—and himself—that he wasn't telling. "So you have no idea who is behind all this?"

"None whatsoever." He glanced at her, eyes gleaming in the darkness. "But whoever it is seems to want you dead pretty badly. Remember that the next time you decide to run."

What could she say? She certainly couldn't deny there would be a next time, because she *did* have every intention of running. Eventually. If there was one lesson she and Helen had learned well over the years, it was to depend on no one but themselves.

She blinked back tears and looked out the side window. The rain fell in a mist, muting the glow of the streetlights and filling the silent streets with a curtain of gray. Anything could be out there, she thought. Anything at all.

She shivered again. She felt so cold it seemed to be seeping deep into her bones. Death, reaching out for her.

"He won't get you while I'm here," Doyle said softly.

She didn't look at him. Couldn't. She didn't want him to see her tears. "I'm not afraid of death." Just of being alone. Of never finding anyone who would care for her as much as Helen had cared.

Of never finding that one person who could love her as she was rather than being terrified of what she could do.

She bit her lip and watched the gray-slipped world rush by. There was little traffic on the roads and they reached Carlton quickly. She glanced down at the phone. "Turn left here," she said. "Number twenty-eight should be on your side."

He pulled into a parking space and stopped. With the headlights off, the mist seemed to crowd in, encasing them in a blanket of gray. Even the nearby gum trees looked ghostly.

"I don't like the feel of this," she muttered. There was a chill in the air that seemed unnatural. The same sort of chill she'd felt just before she pushed through her front door and discovered death had come visiting . . .

His hand covered hers, his touch flushing heat through her entire body. "Why don't you stay here in the car while I go check it out?"

"Not on your life." She withdrew her hand from the warmth of his. "I'm coming with you."

Annoyance glimmered briefly in his eyes. "It's safer in the car."

"Not if one of those creatures is out there."

"I would know if a *manarei* were out there, believe me." Yet his gaze swept the drizzle surrounding them and he frowned.

Did he sense anything? Or was it just the blanket of gray teasing their imagination? She glanced at him. Somehow, he didn't seem the type to have problems in that department.

He raised an eyebrow. "Oh, I have an active enough imagination when it matters." A smile touched his lips. "For example, I can easily imagine you actually doing something I ask."

Heat crept through her cheeks again. She looked away and crossed her arms. "I'm coming with you."

He sighed. It was a sound of sheer frustration. "Well, I guess it *is* one way of knowing where the hell you are. But you do what I tell you, is that clear?"

She nodded and climbed out of the car. The mist ran damp fingers across her skin, and she shivered. The night was quiet, hushed. The street was filled with shadows. Cars and houses loomed briefly as the fine rain swirled. Streetlights puddled light down onto the pavement, looking like forlorn stars in the night. Nothing moved. It was very easy to imagine they were the only two people alive in the world right now.

He moved to the rear of the car, then glanced back at her. "You coming?"

She cast an uneasy look at the shrouded trees, then followed him across the road. "What are you going to say to this woman if she's home?" She shoved her gloved hands into her pockets, still trying to warm them. "I certainly wouldn't open the door to a couple of wrinkled-looking specimens like us at this hour of the morning."

He shrugged. "I'm not exactly sure yet."

"Oh, great. What if she decides to call the cops? What if she's got a great, big dog and sets it on us?"

He grinned. "Dogs don't worry me."

"They worry *me*," she muttered and glanced up. "You know, you never did explain what happened to that panther I saw before."

He raised an eyebrow. "What panther?"

Anger surged through her. This man might be helping her, but in many ways, he was also treating her like a fool. "You want me to trust you, and yet you can't—or won't—answer the simplest of questions."

He looked at her. In the depths of his eyes she saw annoyance—and regret. "I'll answer your questions when you decide to stop running."

She stared at him. He wasn't just talking about running from him. She knew instinctively that he was talking about running from life—of being so scared of death that she was afraid to live. She pulled her gaze from his. She barely knew this man, and yet he seemed to understand her better than anyone ever had—maybe even Helen.

Twenty-eight was the third house along in the row of eight grand old Victorian-style terraces; she believed they called them row houses in America. Unlike the rest of the houses, number twenty-eight looked in serious need of love and attention. The picket fence was missing half its pickets, and the shoe-box-sized front garden was knee high in weeds. Wood boarded the windows on the bottom floor, and the screen door was hanging off its hinges.

She frowned. "It looks abandoned."

He opened the gate and ushered her through. "It's not. I can hear someone moving inside."

She raised an eyebrow. "You can? How?"

"Told you, I've got good hearing."

She had good hearing, and she couldn't hear a damn thing. "How can you tell if it's a human moving around inside? It might be a stray cat—or even the wind."

"It's human. Cats rarely get around on two feet." He knocked on the door. The sound seemed to echo through the silence, as sharp as thunder.

"If that's an old lady moving around in there, you've just given her a heart attack." She glanced across to the park. Nothing had moved, and no sound broke the silence. Yet something was out there, near the trees, watching them.

Doyle looked over his shoulder. "Nothing's there," he said after a moment.

He was wrong. Something was. She felt no sense of danger, no sense of doom drawing close, as she had last night when she'd stood on her front porch and watched the approaching police lights flash red through the night. It was just a sense of . . . waiting. And expectation. Neither of which made any sense.

Inside the house, something moved. Wood scraped against wood, then footsteps approached. "Yes?" The voice was high-pitched and quavery. The voice of an old woman.

He frowned. "Sorry to bother you, ma'am, but I'm looking for Rachel Grant."

"At this hour? Go bother someone else, or I'll call the police."

"Told you," Kirby muttered.

Doyle ignored her. He splayed one hand across the door but quickly jerked it away. Light glowed briefly where his hand had rested, and she saw the same symbol that had been carved into her and Helen's door. Only this time, it had two points. Doyle's gaze met hers, his expression grim as he added, "It's urgent we speak to Rachel. Is she there?"

"There's no one here by that name."

Lights appeared in the neighboring house. If he wasn't careful, he'd have the whole street down on them. But if he was at all worried by such a prospect, he certainly didn't show it.

"Do you know where we can contact her?" he continued, his voice a little louder.

"Told you, there's no one here by that name. I got the phone in my hand, you know. I'm dialing."

"Thanks for your help, ma'am." He cupped Kirby's elbow and guided her down the steps. On the way past the mailbox, he snatched an envelope that was half sticking out.

"That's theft in this country."

"It's theft in mine, too, but right now, I don't really care." He handed her the envelope. "Take a look."

She did. It was addressed to Rachel Grant. "Could be a mistake. Maybe she's just moved and hasn't had her mail redirected."

"You really think that?"

"No. But it's better than the thought of breaking into that house and seeing who's really in there. That's what you're thinking of doing, isn't it?"

He raised an eyebrow. "I see I'm not the only one reading minds here."

She rubbed her arms and looked away from the warmth in his gaze. "It doesn't take a mind reader to guess that's what you're thinking."

"But I bet you can guess what else I'm thinking."

She grimaced. "Yeah. And you no doubt can guess my answer."

"Kirby, get serious. I need to get into that house quickly and quietly. I can't do that if you're with me."

"Meaning I'm a lumbering noisemaker?"

"Lumbering, no. Far from it." He hesitated, his gaze sweeping her briefly. Her nerves jumped, as if touched by fire. "Noisy? Yes."

He opened the passenger-side door and motioned her to get in. She crossed her arms and stood her ground.

"That old lady is probably watching to see if we leave," he said. "I have no doubt she will call the cops if we don't."

"Oh." Feeling foolish, she got in. He climbed into the driver's side and reversed out, heading down the street. He turned right onto another street, then switched off the headlights and turned around, heading back. He parked several houses up from the terrace, this time on the same side of the road.

He took off his seat belt, then turned to face her. "I want you to climb into the driver's seat and keep the engine running. If anything—or anyone—remotely threatening approaches, drive off."

She frowned. "What about you?"

"I'll be okay. I'll meet you at the zoo. It's not that far away, is it?"

She shook her head, wondering how he knew if he'd never been there. He might have good hearing, but surely even he couldn't hear the zoo animals from here.

"I can't just leave you here," she said. "What if you get into trouble and need help?"

"At the slightest hint of trouble, I'll leave. It's more important right now that you keep safe. Climb out and come around to the driver's side."

She did. He was holding the door open for her. She stopped, suddenly reluctant to get any closer, though what she feared she couldn't exactly say.

For a second, neither of them moved. She stared at him, caught by the sudden intensity in his eyes—an intensity that seemed to delve right through her, touching her soul. Touching her heart. He reached out, trailing the back of his fingers down her cheek. Heat shivered through her, and her breath caught somewhere in her throat. She licked her lips and saw the heat flare deep in his eyes. God, it would be so easy to step fully into his embrace, to let him wrap the lean strength of his arms around her and keep all the demons and fear away. She clenched her fists, fighting the desire—the *need*—to do just that. It was nothing but crazy thinking. He was a stranger, and she shouldn't even be trusting him, let alone wanting him to hold her. Aching for him to kiss her. Swallowing nervously, she tore her gaze from his.

He placed a finger under her chin, raising it until her eyes met his again. "Please don't run."

His voice was little more than a warm caress in her thoughts, and it scared her.

But what scared her more was the longing she saw in the depths of his richly colored eyes—a longing that echoed through every inch of her. This man knew loneliness as intimately as she did, only he hid it a whole lot better.

"I can't promise you that," she whispered. Because this time he wasn't talking about running from life or even running away. Far from it. And in many respects, *he* was just as dangerous as whatever was out there in the darkness, watching her, stalking her.

Regret flickered in his eyes, and he dropped his hand, though her skin continued to tingle with the warmth of his touch.

"Get in the car and lock the doors. And remember what I said."

"At the first sniff of danger, drive off and meet you at the zoo," she said, climbing into the car.

He slammed the door shut, then tapped the window. She smiled slightly and hit the lock button. He gave her the thumbs-up, then walked away, quickly disappearing into the drizzle.

She leaned back and watched the misty rain eddy around her. Minutes dragged by. The silence suddenly seemed so heavy it was a weight pressing down on her, making it difficult to breathe. She shifted slightly in the seat. In the park opposite, the mist's dance quickened, as if someone—or something—had stirred it. The trees seemed to loom in and out of focus, and the feeling of being watched returned tenfold.

Lightning danced across her clenched fingers, sending jagged flashes of brightness through the night. She scanned the park, looking for some sense—some hint—of what the mist was hiding.

There was no suggestion of evil or danger. Nothing more than a sense of expectation—and warmth. She frowned. It was almost as if the mist wanted her to go over there.

She glanced toward the terraces. Doyle had told her to stay in the car, and it made perfectly good sense to do so. She could very easily walk into a trap, despite the fact that she could feel nothing dark or dangerous about the presence that waited.

Yet she wasn't going to get any answers sitting around waiting for Doyle to do all the work. She grabbed the keys and climbed out of the car.

Damp fingers of mist crept across the back of her neck, and she shivered. She flipped up her jacket's collar, then shoved her hands into the pockets and walked across the street. She stopped at the edge of the park, listening to the silence, studying the looming gum trees. Waiting, but for what she wasn't entirely certain.

A warning instinct stirred. Something approached. She clenched her fists and felt the lightning dance warmth across her skin.

Ten feet in front of her, the mist stirred, gently at first but gradually becoming more frantic. The wind had died and nothing moved in the predawn darkness, yet the mist continued to condense. Gradually, the tiny droplets of water found shape, found form. Found life.

Became Helen.

SEVEN

THE ALLEY BEHIND THE ROW HOUSES LAY WRAPPED in shadows. Doyle walked in the middle of the lane to avoid the trash cans and scattered rubbish, his gaze searching the houses for any sign of life. As a thief, he'd loved this type of setup—houses with a small, private alley behind them. It was like shopping at a supermarket. All you had to do was walk along until you found the ripest fruit to pick.

When he reached number twenty-eight, he peered over the back fence, studying the yard intently. There was no movement and, more important, no dog smell. The last thing he needed right now was some too-alert mutt giving him away.

He climbed the fence. At the back door, he splayed his fingers across the lock, feeling for any hint of magic. Unlike the front door, this one was not triggered with a spell. Yet the feel of magic was still in the air—distant fireflies that lightly burned his skin. Someone inside the house was conjuring, though what, he wasn't entirely sure.

He frowned and stepped back, studying the house. All the windows on the lower floor were boarded up. The top floors were clear, but there was no easy way of getting up there. The drain spouts didn't look as if they'd support his weight, and he didn't have his climbing gear or ropes with him. Nor was there a handy tree close by.

He turned his attention to the houses on either side. The one on the left had a balcony decorated with graceful arches of wrought iron. Perfect for climbing. He could get to the roof with little problem, then make his way across to the front of this terrace. From there, it should be easy enough to swing down onto the front balcony.

He'd have to go barefoot, though—his boots weren't pliable enough, and would make too much noise on the old tin roofing. He took them off and shoved them into the carryall pockets inside his coat, half grinning as he imagined the sort of look Kirby would have given him. But he hadn't lied to her earlier. His pockets did hold just about everything. As a thief, they'd certainly come in handy—the hidden ones more so than the obvious ones. And even now, with his thieving days long behind him, he still carried an extraordinary amount of stuff around in them, although these days it was more likely to be an assortment of charms and ready-to-use spells than the tools of his former trade.

Climbing the wrought iron proved exceptionally easy, even for someone as out of practice as he was. He pulled himself up onto the roof and followed the rows of nails across to the front of the building. On the balcony roof, he hesitated, listening. Nothing moved in the house below him, yet the distant touch of magic still skittered through him.

He peered over the edge. There was no light in any

of the windows, no sense of anyone close. Whoever was performing the magic was on the ground floor, in the back half of the house. Maybe that was why there'd been no magical lock on the back door. There'd been no need with the magician so close.

He swung down and headed for the nearest window. The windows were the old sash-and-weight style, which were usually easy to open. He reached into another pocket and grabbed a lock pick, then slid it into the gap between the two windowpanes and carefully knocked open the catch.

He slipped on some gloves, then slid the window open and looked inside. Furniture sat in the middle of the room, half covered by sheets, and several tins of paint were gathered in one corner. Rachel Grant was obviously in the process of redecorating. The question was, would she ever get the chance to finish? He had a feeling the answer was no.

He climbed into the room and slid the window shut. The last thing he needed right now was a breeze springing to life and gusting fresh air through the house. It would be warning enough to whoever was below that someone had entered.

He walked to the door and carefully looked out. The stairs were at the end of the long, dark hallway. Light rose from below, a pale blue glow that seemed to flicker in and out of focus.

Frowning, he headed toward the stairs, keeping close to the walls so there was less chance of hitting a squeaking floorboard. The buzz of magic got sharper, prickling his skin with heat. With it came a murmur. Someone was chanting. Someone whose voice was young and rich. Not the old woman who'd greeted them at the door, if she'd even been real in the first place. Somehow, he doubted it.

But whoever was casting the spell was walking the dark path, not the light. The stench of evil lay heavy in the darkness, overriding even the sharp smell of fresh paint. He hesitated at the base of the stairs, listening.

The tempo of magic increased, its touch searing. The spell was reaching a peak. The light pulsed rapidly in the darkness, its color now a sickly yellow-green touched by red—blood red. It was coming from a room down at the far end of the hall. He stepped forward, then hesitated as a shadow whisked across the brightness. Its shape was a woman's, not a man's.

There was a bright flash, then a wave of energy crashed around him, burning through his mind and sending him reeling back against the wall. He grunted in pain, every intake of breath parching his throat.

The chanting stopped abruptly, and the sense of evil left the house. Cursing, he pushed away from the wall and staggered down the hall.

And found Rachel Grant.

She was lying on her back in the middle of the kitchen floor. If the look on her face was anything to go by, death had caught her by surprise. There was a shattered teapot near her left hand and a still burning candle near her feet. The black river of tea had run across the tiles, mingling with the blood that surrounded the back of her head.

He squatted next to her, lightly touching her neck. No pulse—not that he expected any with the amount of blood on the floor. But her skin still held a touch of warmth. She hadn't been dead long. He'd missed saving her by maybe ten minutes. Ten lousy minutes.

Biting back his anger, he rose and walked across to the table. The tea in the mugs was still warm. Rachel had known her attacker—known and trusted her. Why else would she have let the woman into her house at this hour of the morning and made her a cup of tea?

He turned, studying the kitchen. The candle's small flame flickered at her feet, barely breaking the darkness. He frowned. It was a rather odd place to stick a candle, and it certainly wouldn't have provided the two women with much light. Then he saw the color of the wax—black. It was the sort of candle used in spells.

Frowning, he studied the floor. There were smudges of ash scattered around Rachel's body. Though the lines were now broken, the shape of the pentagram was still evident.

The spell he'd sensed had obviously been performed on Rachel. The question was, why? Especially if she was already dead?

He pulled out his phone, took several pictures, then dialed Camille.

"Just about to call you, shapeshifter," she said.

He moved around Rachel's body, studying a slight scuff in the ash. It almost looked like a footprint. "Hasn't Russell reported in yet?"

"No, and it's worrying the hell out of me."

"I'll head right over and check it out, then. But I've found Rachel Grant."

Camille sighed. "Dead, I take it from your tone."

"Yeah, but only just. Some woman was still performing a spell on her as I came in."

"What sort of spell?" Camille said, voice sharp. "Describe what you see."

"Rachel's on her back, the back of her head apparently caved in. Blood over the floor. Remains of a pentagram drawn in black soot. A black candle near Rachel's feet, still burning."

Camille sniffed. "That could be anything."

"The magic had the feel of the dark path. The light was blue when I came in, but then turned a yellowish green, touched by red."

"That end bit sounds like blood magic. A spell of summoning, perhaps?"

A prickle of unease stirred. He glanced around sharply. Though he'd heard no sound, he had the unsettling feeling that he was no longer alone in the house. He rose and moved back to the hall doorway. The shadows seemed to loom in on him, yet he couldn't smell, nor see, anyone hiding within them.

Even so, he lowered his voice. "Would blood magic be powerful enough to rip psychic abilities from a body?"

"Yeah, but the victim would have to be alive to do it."

"She might have been. I might have come in on the tail end of the spell."

"Possible." Camille hesitated. "Which address did you find her at?"

"The place in Carlton."

"I'll come over and have a look. It might be my best chance to figure out the exact spell being used."

"The front door has a spell on it. You'll have to counter it before I can open it."

"That shouldn't be a problem. I'll be there in ten. Don't head off to find Russ until I arrive."

He glanced at his watch. It was nearing six. Thank God it was raining. At least the clouds would temper the sunlight and give Russell more of a chance if he was stuck somewhere. "Hurry," he said and hung up.

He shoved his phone in his pocket and stepped into the hall. Through the silence came a whisper of sound— a footstep, in one of the rooms upstairs.

Maybe the woman hadn't left. Maybe she'd just relocated to a different room. But there was no smell of magic in the air, nothing beyond paint and a faint whiff of decay.

Frowning, he made his way up the stairs. Dawn's light was beginning to filter in through the windows, filling the hall with gray shadows. He stopped on the landing, listening intently. Nothing moved, yet something was definitely up here. There was an odd sort of feel to the air—a tension, a sense of expectation. The smell of decay was stronger here, too. But it wasn't the scent of age and mold so often found in old houses. It was the smell of death, of meat long gone rotten.

He edged forward. The odor seemed to be coming from the room two doors down—directly opposite the room from which he'd entered the house. At the doorway he stopped, listening again. Air stirred softly, the sound accompanied by the softest rattle. The stink had become so bad he could barely breathe. He wasn't sure if it was related to whoever was standing in that room or not, and at this point, it didn't really matter. Whoever—or whatever—was there was standing against the wall, close to the door, just like him. It left him with only one option.

He stripped off his long coat, placing it carefully on the floor, and dove through the doorway.

* * *

TEARS TRACKED DOWN KIRBY'S CHEEKS, AND A SOB caught in her throat. She knew Helen was dead, had seen her torn and bloodied remains with her own eyes— and yet here she was, smiling softly, gray eyes gentle and yet so full of mischief. Kirby wanted to reach out, to touch the untouchable—to hold her dead friend close and never let her go again. But she clenched her hands instead, frightened that even the slightest of movements would send this mist wraith scattering.

"You must stop her, Kirby." Helen's voice was as soft and as warm in death as it had been in life.

She somehow found her voice. "Stop who? Who did this to you?"

The wind stirred, rustling the leaves of the nearby gum trees and blowing away several strands of Helen's mist-spun figure. Kirby bit her lip but knew there was little she could do to prevent it. The wind was no friend of hers.

"I don't have much time and there's so much to tell you," Helen continued softly. "You are the one that binds and controls. You are the most powerful of us all. You are the only one who can destroy her."

She frowned. What she needed right now was answers, not more damn questions. "What are you talking about? Destroy who?"

"She who seeks to control what is not hers. The power of the elements—the circle of five. Two are now dead. You and one other remain. You must find her and save her. And you must find the fifth point and stop her."

How could she save some unknown woman when she hadn't even been able to save her best friend?

"We are more than just friends. And my death lies in my hands, not yours."

She stared at Helen's mist-shaped face and felt so cold her whole body began to shake. "What do you mean?" she said, her throat so restricted her question came out as little more than a harsh whisper.

"My death was my choice. I chose to die by my own hand rather than give that woman anything of mine. Now you, too, must choose your fate."

"I don't want this," Kirby muttered. "I don't want any of this." She just wanted life to go back to the way it had been, and for Helen to be real, not a creature of mist.

All of which was totally impossible now.

"Destiny creeps up on us no matter how we run, Kirby. I have learned this, if nothing else."

"But you saw the future. You saw our deaths . . ." Her voice faded. Helen had once said the wind whispered only possibilities, never certainties. It was the things people said and did that changed the paths of fate. Which was why they'd spent so much of their lives on the move, trying to outrun the death that had always loomed so large in their future.

Helen sighed. "It was my actions that sent us down this particular path, and for that, I am sorry."

"What actions?" Kirby demanded, not understanding even half of what Helen was saying.

The wind shivered through her friend's form. "I needed to find out who my parents were. I'm sorry."

For what? For wanting to know the truth? For being braver than *she'd* ever dared to be? "Did you find them?"

"No." Helen hesitated. The wind stirred again,

blowing through her form, snagging tendrils of mist and unraveling them quickly. "The wind calls me. I have to go."

"No!" Kirby reached out, but her hand slipped through Helen's form, stirring the mist and dissipating her body. "No," she repeated, dropping to her knees, her whole being aching with the pain of loss and unshed grief. "Don't go. Don't leave me!"

"You must go home. You must find the gift and say the words." Helen had almost completely faded. Only her face remained. The droplets of moisture glistened in the rising light of the day, so it looked like tears were shining in her mist-colored eyes.

Kirby frowned. "I have the gift; it's in my pack."

"That is *not* the gift I left. Find it, say the words, and complete the circle."

Her frown deepened. "What circle? What are you talking about?"

"The spell. You must complete the spell." Even as she spoke, the wind was taking the rest of her mist-spun features until all that was left was the sparkle of ghostly tears. "Fear not the cat, sister, for he will not harm you."

She meant Doyle, Kirby thought, and knew that, in this instance, Helen was wrong. Doyle might not harm her physically, but emotionally? He had the power to hurt her deeply. Irreparably.

I will always be with you, Kirby. Seek me whenever the wind calls. Take care . . .

The words caressed her mind and faded away. Kirby closed her eyes, rocking back and forth and battling the urge to scream. It wasn't fair. It wasn't Helen who should be dead, but her. Helen had lived life to the fullest, enjoying every moment, while she . . . she'd done nothing more than fake it.

Biting her lip, she sat there for what seemed like ages, controlling the pain, refusing the tears. *Not yet*, she thought. Not until she'd made sense of Helen's death and found the woman responsible. Not until justice had been done.

Eventually, she became aware of the cold touch of moisture seeping through her jeans, chilling her skin. She rose, her joints creaking in protest, and looked around. Though the mist was still heavy, the darkness was beginning to lift. In the trees above her, a magpie warbled, its melodious tones heralding the new day. Across the road, lights shone in the house two doors down from number twenty-eight. She frowned. People were waking. Doyle had better hurry up and get out of that house.

Shoving her hands in her pockets, she walked back. At the car, she stopped, her gaze going to the second-floor window. There was nothing to see but shadows, but she frowned. Doyle was in trouble. Big trouble. How she knew this, she wasn't sure. It was just a feeling—a certainty—deep in her mind. And she was just as certain that if she didn't do something to help him, he would die. Something was in that room with him, something bigger and stronger than he was. Something from beyond the grave.

Not giving herself time to think—or fear—she ran toward the house.

DOYLE ROLLED BACK TO HIS FEET, ONLY TO BE CON-fronted by a seven-foot mass of rotten flesh—something that had once been human, but now was not.

A goddamn zombie! And one of the biggest he'd ever seen. In a confined space like this, the odds of beating it weren't exactly good. The stinking creatures were faster than they looked, and strong despite the decay.

It lunged toward him, and he backpedaled fast. A fist the size of a spade hammered the air. He ducked and swung, kicking the zombie in the gut. The blow bounced off the creature's flesh and jarred his whole leg. It felt like he was kicking bricks. The zombie had to have been a boxer or bodybuilder in life to have stomach muscles that strong in death. He half wished he'd taken the time to put his boots back on. He had a bad feeling that bare feet weren't going to make much of a dent in this particular dead man.

He danced away from another blow, then jabbed at the creature's jaw. Its head snapped back, and it snarled—or smiled. It was a little hard to tell given half its mouth had decayed away. He jabbed again, but the zombie caught the blow in his fist and twisted hard. Pain burned white-hot up Doyle's arm and sweat beaded his brow. Gritting his teeth, he dropped, sweeping the creature's feet out from under it. It fell with a crash that shook the foundations of the building but began scrambling upright almost immediately. Doyle jerked his wrist from the zombie's grasp, then punched the creature in the neck, feeling flesh and muscle give under his blow. The zombie's eyes went wide and it started gasping, as if unable to breathe. Zombies weren't the brightest creatures. They were dead and didn't actually need air, but most didn't realize that immediately, if ever.

He jumped toward it, wrapping an arm around its throat and squeezing tight. The zombie roared—a sound that came out strangled and harsh. It reached back, grabbing Doyle by the back of the neck and wrenching him over its head. Doyle hit the wall with a grunt and dropped in a heap to the floor, only to feel the boards quiver as the zombie ran at him. He scrambled away on all fours, resisting the sudden urge to shapeshift. A panther wouldn't have a hope against the superior strength of this zombie. And in that form, he certainly couldn't snap the creature's neck—the only surefire way of killing it.

Fingers raked his side, seeking purchase. He rolled to his feet and grabbed the zombie's arm, twisting around and pulling hard. The creature sailed past him and landed with a crash on its back. Doyle stiffened his fingers and knifed them toward the creature's eyes. It moved, and he hit cheek instead, feeling flesh and bone give as its cheek caved in. Teeth gleamed at him in the brightening light of day.

Shuddering, he twisted, sweeping the creature off its feet again as it struggled to rise. It roared in frustration and lashed out. The blow caught the side of his face and sent him staggering. The creature was up almost instantly, arms outstretched as it sought to corner him.

He faked a blow to the creature's head, then spun and lashed out at a bony-looking knee instead. The force of the blow shuddered up his leg, and in the silence, the crack of the creature's knee shattering was audible. It didn't seem to matter to the zombie, though. It staggered toward him, arms milling quicker than a high-speed fan and twice as deadly.

He couldn't duck every blow. He was fast, but even the wind would have had trouble in this situation. The zombie's fists hit him in the ribs. Red heat flashed through him. He hissed and spun, lashing out again at the zombie's knee. This time, the whole knee bent backward and the creature howled, a sound loud enough to wake the dead—and the neighbors.

Downstairs, there was a crash, and magic burned across his skin. Someone had sprung the spell on the front door. Not Camille—she would have deactivated it first. Maybe one of the neighbors had heard all the noise and had decided to come in and see if there was a problem. If that were the case, he hoped the neighbor hadn't been hurt.

He aimed another kick at the creature's leg, but it sidestepped and caught his foot, thrusting him back. He hit the wall with a grunt, then ducked another blow. The creature's fist hit the wall instead, and dust flew. It was so damn close its reek was almost overwhelming. Gut churning, he threw another punch, mashing the creature's already bulbous nose. The creature howled. He spun, kicking the zombie in the gut, forcing it away, desperate to gain some room to move—and breathe.

Lightning seared through the room, encasing the zombie in a web of blue-white light and pinning it to the floorboards. It howled and thrashed but could not escape. The smell of burning flesh added depth to the already horrendous stench in the room.

Soon there was nothing left but a pile of ash on the floor. Kirby walked in, her gaze sweeping the room until she found him. "Are you all right?"

Though she was pale, the left side of her face was red, as if burned, and bits of dust and wood were caught in her hair.

"Are you?" he countered abruptly. "Did the spell on the door hurt you too much?"

She shook her head, but her gaze skated from his. Tears shimmered in her green eyes, and her mind was filled with pain. He winced as he stood and walked toward her. She didn't retreat, didn't move in any way. It was almost as if she were frozen by what she'd done.

I've never used the energy to intentionally kill before.

The thought whispered through him, filled with such horror it nearly took his breath away. He wrapped an arm around her shoulders. She tensed, her gaze searching his briefly before she relaxed in his embrace and rested her cheek against his shoulder.

He held her close, listening to the wild beat of her heart—a rhythm that matched his own. Her body fitted his like a glove. She felt so warm against him, so right, somehow. It was as if he'd found the other half of himself. He closed his eyes at the thought. His father had once told him he would know when he found his mate. That it would hit him like a fist to the gut—suddenly, painfully. He had a horrible feeling the old man was right.

"You had no choice but to kill it," he said. "I certainly don't think I would have survived another round with it."

He breathed deep the scent of her. She reminded him of spring—fresh and warm and rich with the scent of flowers.

She pulled back slightly, and he instantly regretted speaking.

"What was it?" Her breath washed warmth across his neck and stirred the already flaring embers of desire.

"Zombie," he said, gently picking a sliver of wood from her hair. "And dead long before you got to it."

Tears gleamed briefly in her eyes. She blinked them away and touched his cheek, her hand cool against his flesh. She must have taken his gloves off to use her magic.

"You look like shit." A smile touched her lips. Lips that looked all too warm and inviting.

"Strange," he murmured. "It's just what I feel like."

God, he wanted to kiss her so desperately it hurt, but she'd run the minute he tried. She was just starting to trust him, and he didn't dare do anything that might shatter that trust. Especially when her living or dying might well depend on his ability to keep close.

He stepped back. Sirens were wailing in the distance. They might not be headed here, but with the noise the zombie had made, they couldn't risk staying any longer. Not with Rachel Grant lying dead downstairs. "We'd better get going."

She nodded. "With all the noise I made getting in the door, the neighbors are probably awake and standing out front, wondering what's going on."

"Then we'll go out the way I came in. Through the window."

She raised an eyebrow. "The windows are boarded up."

"Only the ones on the ground floor." He caught her hand, entwining his fingers in hers. "Let's go."

He stopped in the hall long enough to put on his shoes and pick up his coat, then continued on into the other room. Pain twinged down his side at every movement, but it wasn't the sharp, excruciating pain of broken ribs. He was lucky, that was for sure.

A quick peek out the window showed lots of lights but no cops, as yet. And while there were no neighbors standing on the sidewalk, either, that didn't mean they weren't around. It was going to be a little tricky getting out, but he'd certainly been caught in worse situations during his time as a thief.

He raised the window. "Keep close to the wall," he said. "And squat down, so you present less of a silhouette."

She studied him. "You've done this before, haven't you?"

She was either very intuitive or she was reading his mind as easily as he was hers. "Done what? Been rescued by a pretty young woman from the hands of a zombie?" He gave her an easy grin. "It doesn't happen as often as I'd like, I'm afraid."

A smile touched her lips, but annoyance flickered in her eyes. "You really won't give me a straight answer about yourself, will you?"

He hesitated. If he were ever going to be honest about himself, then it would be with her, for all sorts of reasons—not the least being the attraction he felt. But right now, they simply didn't have the time.

"Force of habit, I'm afraid." He motioned toward the window. "Go, before the cops get here."

She eyed him a second longer, then climbed out the window and hunched down in the shadows. He followed her out onto the balcony, then carefully closed the window and nudged the latch closed again.

"Thief," she murmured. "You had to have been. You're too damn good at that."

He slipped the pick back into his pocket. "I could

have been a cop, you know. Cops learn all sorts of things."

She gave him a knowing look. "Yeah, right."

He grinned and slipped past her, moving to the end of the balcony. The shared wall between the two terraces jutted out several feet and would make climbing onto the next balcony awkward. At least all the windows in the neighboring house were still wrapped in darkness.

He glanced at her. "We'll have to climb around the wall to the next balcony. You ready?"

She glanced down at the ground, then back at him. Fear flickered in her eyes. Afraid of heights, he realized. "I won't let you fall," he added.

He held out his hand. She hesitated, then took it and climbed up onto the wrought iron. It wobbled under her weight, and she made a small sound of fear, grabbing for his shoulders.

He reached for her waist with his free hand, steadying her. "Look at me, not the ground," he said. Her gaze darted to his, wide and uncertain. "I won't let you fall. Believe that, if nothing else. Now, reach around the wall and pull yourself across to the next balcony."

Though she was shaking, she did as he asked, and was quickly on the other side. He followed and pushed her into the shadows as headlights speared the darkness.

"Crawl toward the next house in the row," he murmured, as the blue and red lights of the police car washed through the shadows.

"We can't climb across the balcony," she protested. "They'll see us."

"Maybe. Just go."

She did. He followed her, somehow managing to keep his gaze on the police car more than the rather fetching sight of her jeans-clad rear. The cops climbed out of the car, putting on their hats as they walked across the road and disappeared under the balcony. Doyle moved past Kirby and checked the next house. Lights were on, but he couldn't see anyone in the windows, and no one was moving around—not upstairs, anyway.

"Go," he said, catching her hand again. "Duck down under the windows when you get there."

Her expression was doubtful, but she climbed onto the railing and edged across. He followed her and pushed her forward again. They repeated the process until they reached the final house in the row.

"Now what?" she murmured.

"Now we lie down in the shadows and wait for the hubbub to die down."

She gave him another long look. "You're kidding, right?"

He shook his head and somehow managed to restrain his grin. He could certainly think of worse fates than lying down with her—even if it was for something as innocent as waiting out the cops. "Sorry, no. If we try to leave now, someone will definitely stop us. So we wait."

She crossed her arms and didn't move. "Why can't we just sit here? Why do we have to lie down?"

"Because there'll be less of us to notice. By lying down and lying still, we're a part of the shadows. Believe me, it works." He'd had many a narrow escape by doing precisely that.

"I just bet you have," she muttered. "And not all of them narrow escapes from thieving jobs, either."

She was reading his mind as easily as he was hers. Odd. He grinned and didn't refute her inference, though he'd never been a womanizer. Far from it.

"I suppose," she continued softly, "that we have to stretch out beside each other, not lie toe to head, for the same reason?"

"Afraid so." Her raised eyebrow suggested she knew he was lying. Smiling, he stretched out along the wall, then patted the boards in front of him. "Come along. I don't bite."

"I'll reserve judgment on that," she muttered, but lay down beside him— -facing him rather than the road.

To keep an eye on him, he thought with amusement. Or rather, on what he was doing. Not that he *could* do much with the cops five doors down and the owners of this house moving around downstairs.

He reached for his phone. She tensed, then relaxed when she saw it. He smiled and dialed Camille.

"Don't you be hassling an old woman," she answered, voice tart. "I'm almost there."

"I'm calling to say don't bother. When the murderer departed she left a rather large zombie to cover her tracks. I'm afraid we only just managed to escape, and the cops are crawling all over the place."

"Where are you?"

"Stuck on a balcony five doors down. We can't really move until either the cops or the owners of this house leave, and I have a bad feeling we should check on Russ before it gets too light."

"I'll head over to Russ, then. Meet you there unless you hear from me in the meantime."

"Will do. And I'll send you the pics I took." He did so, then shoved the phone away and glanced past the curve of Kirby's hip to the road. More cops were arriving. It was going to be quite a while before they could move.

He met her gaze. In the warm green depths of her eyes he saw wariness and something else—longing. Desire.

Without really thinking about the consequences, he leaned forward and kissed her.

EIGHT

HIS KISS WASN'T WHAT SHE'D EXPECTED. SHE WASN'T entirely sure what she *had* expected, but it wasn't this. There was a tenderness in his touch that was more than just passion, more than just desire. His lips burned heat through her heart, her soul, and sent common sense flying. All she could do, all she *wanted* to do, was respond.

He whispered her name, his breath warm against her lips, then he wrapped an arm around her waist and drew her close. She could feel the strength of his arousal, feel the wild beat of his heart. Knew they were an echo of her own. She touched his face, his neck, then ran her hand down to his hip. Lord help her, she wanted him as she'd never wanted another—right here, right now on the balcony. No matter how dangerous that might be or how much she might regret it later.

Seize the moment, enjoy the danger, Helen had often preached. But until this moment, she'd never truly understood what Helen had meant.

His lips left hers and moved to her neck, branding her skin with his kisses. She sighed and slipped her hand from his hip, down the outside of his jeans until she touched the hard length of him. She caressed him, teased him through the material, until she felt him quiver with need. She moved her hand away, slipping it inside his shirt, reveling in the hard, flat planes of his chest and stomach. He groaned softly, then his lips seized hers again and he kissed her urgently. He pushed up her sweater, thrust a hand under her bra, catching her nipple, teasing it, teasing her. Heat pulsed through her, and deep down the ache increased. God, it felt so good . . .

Downstairs, a door slammed and voices rose. She froze. He pulled away, his breathing harsh and fast, staring past her, his body tense as he held her close.

Footsteps clattered on concrete, moving away. A man and a woman, from their voices. Another voice broke the silence, calling to them in an authoritative tone. A cop, she thought, and she hoped Doyle was right—that the shadows would indeed hide them. She doubted the police would believe they were just an oversexed couple who couldn't wait to get home.

After five minutes or so, doors slammed and a car started up. Doyle relaxed and glanced down at her, a chagrined look on his face. "Sorry. I didn't mean for that to happen."

She studied him for a moment. "Liar."

A smile touched his lips. "While I don't mind making love outdoors, believe me, I'm not an exhibitionist. Especially when cops are among the spectators."

With his dark hair tumbling across his forehead and his smile crinkling the corners of his blue eyes, he looked so damn sexy she just wanted to kiss him again. She pushed away instead. Now that the heat between them had died a little, common sense was returning. She wasn't an exhibitionist either, but somewhere in the last few moments, both of them had almost become just that. Thank God the owners of the house had stopped them.

She thrust a hand through her hair and rolled onto her back. Lord, what on *Earth* had she been thinking? While there was no denying her attraction to this man, she knew if she took it too much further, she'd end up getting hurt. Not only was he a total stranger, he was certainly more than a thief and an adventurer. Visions of him snapping the vampire's neck flashed through her mind and her breath caught. And yet, deep down, she knew he wasn't a killer. Yes, he'd killed to protect her, but it wasn't something he'd enjoyed, of that she was certain.

What she wasn't so certain of was whether she could trust him—not with her life, but with her heart. She very much suspected the answer was no.

Or was that merely cowardice speaking?

He touched her face, gently running a finger down to her lips. She resisted the urge to kiss his fingertips and moved her face away from the warmth of his touch. "This is neither the time nor the place, and I think we both realize that."

"But the minutes did pass by rather nicely, didn't they?" His voice was little more than a throaty growl and sent shivers of warmth running down her spine. "And you and I both know it won't end here."

She glanced at him, more than a little terrified by his words. Because deep down she knew what he said was true. As much as she might deny it, as much as common sense told her to go no further, she knew they would finish what they had begun here.

But what would happen afterward? Surely a fire so quickly ignited would just as quickly be doused. It wouldn't last. Couldn't last.

Have fun and the future be damned, Helen would have said. Only she'd never been like Helen, as much as she'd tried. She couldn't disconnect her emotions from sex, couldn't have one without the other.

And the fact that she was even thinking about such things when the man in question was very much a stranger scared the hell out of her.

"I can't play this game," she murmured, looking away again. "I just can't."

He touched her chin, gently bringing her gaze to his. "I never said it was a game, Kirby."

"But what else could it be? Once this case is solved, you'll be heading home, back to America, won't you?" He didn't disagree, just watched her with that all-too-knowing gaze of his. She pulled her chin from his grip. "You don't really want someone like me."

"You have no idea what I want."

Her gaze flashed to his. "That's right," she said, an odd surge of anger rushing through her, constricting her voice. "I don't. I know nothing about you, because you won't tell me anything. You want me to trust you, and yet you won't offer me the same."

"I have my reasons—"

"Yeah, well, so have I. Now, let's get the hell off this balcony and out of here." Before she did something stupid—like give in to the desire to touch him again.

He studied her a second longer, then nodded. "Stay

here." On hands and knees, he moved back to the window. Pulling the sliver of metal from his pocket, he thrust it up between the windows, wriggling it around for several seconds. Then, as easy as that, he opened the window.

"Are you sure there are no alarms?" Surely it *couldn't* be that easy. Surely people wealthy enough to own a terrace in this part of Carlton would be wise enough to put in a security system.

"There's an alarm on the house two doors down from this one, and on the one three doors past Rachel Grant's. But there's nothing on the rest, which is why I retreated this way."

"Oh." He had to be a thief. Normal people didn't notice things like that. She certainly hadn't.

He climbed in through the window, then looked out. "You coming?"

She followed him through and looked around. She was oddly relieved to see it wasn't a bedroom, but some sort of sitting room. Antique-looking furniture filled every corner, making the place appear too crowded, too formal, for her liking.

"And mine," he said, catching her hand in his. "Come on, let's get out of here."

His fingers were warm against hers, the palms callused. Not what she'd expected from the hands of a thief. "Won't the police question us when we leave?"

"They won't even see us if we leave quietly. We'll probably have to abandon the car for the moment, though."

"I don't think walking is a good idea." Especially if someone kept sending monsters after her.

He squeezed her fingers, then released them, working his magic on the dead bolt barring their exit through the front door. He had it open in a minute flat.

She shook her head in disbelief. "Don't try to tell me you're a locksmith when you're not rescuing damsels in distress or tracking bad guys, because I just won't believe it."

He gave her that cheeky smile again, and her stomach did odd flip-flops. "You could say I've had a somewhat shady past. But it's all behind me, I promise."

"Yeah, it looks like it," she said dryly.

Smile widening, he placed a hand at her back, ushering her through the door. His touch burned into her skin, and for some reason, hurt. She frowned, flexing her shoulders, wondering what was wrong. Pain twinged, running down her spine like muted fire. Maybe she'd twisted something when the door had blown her off her feet. Maybe she hadn't felt anything until now because she'd been too scared for Doyle. Or too aroused by him.

Swallowing the thought, she moved down the steps and into the street. A crowd had gathered around Rachel's gate, watching what was happening. An ambulance had pulled up, its lights still flashing as two paramedics ran inside. But they were far too late to save Rachel—as she and Doyle had been far too late. She crossed her arms and shivered, remembering Helen's words. One more woman to go, and *she* had to save her. But how, when she couldn't even save herself? God, she was only here now because Doyle had rescued her.

His gaze swept her as he walked down the steps,

flushing heat through her body. "Make it casual," he said and wrapped an arm around her shoulders, pulling her close as they headed down the street.

"Where to now, Romeo?" she asked, voice tart. He might want casual, but right now, when her body still sang to the tune of his touch, casual was the last thing she wanted—or needed. "Right now, we disappear into this mist and get as far away as we can. Then we catch a cab and head on over to the government facility that housed you and Helen."

She glanced up at him, startled. "Why?"

"Because Camille believes that's where all this started."

She frowned. "But that was closed down years ago. What do you hope to find there now?"

He shrugged. "All I'm hoping to find at the moment is my friend, Russell, alive and unharmed."

She raised an eyebrow. If his friend was at the center at this hour, he obviously hadn't gotten in through any normal means. "He's a thief, too?"

"No. Actually, he's a vampire."

She stopped and stared at him. "A vampire?"

He glanced behind them, then nudged her forward again. "Yes. Vampires aren't all bad, you know."

They weren't? She blinked several times. Lord, it was hard enough to believe vampires were real, let alone the fact that some of them were actually on the side of the angels. "But . . . they have to drink blood to survive. How *can* he be good?"

"He doesn't take human blood."

"So he dines on animals?" Somehow, she found that even worse.

He glanced down at her, an eyebrow raised. "You eat meat, chicken and fish, don't you? What's the difference?"

He sounded so damn logical it was annoying. "But I don't actually kill them. They come in ready-to-eat pieces all wrapped in plastic. I don't have to think about where it comes from."

"Russ doesn't kill them, either. And it's mainly cows and horses he takes from."

"Oh." She wasn't entirely sure that made her feel any better about meeting this friend of his. She frowned. "If he's a vampire, how did he get into the center? Don't vampires have to be invited over thresholds? Or is that all a load of Hollywood tripe?"

"Tripe?" He grinned. "Now, there's an expression I'll have to use back home."

Right then, she didn't particularly want to think about him leaving her, let alone going back to America and whatever life he had there. She slapped him lightly in the stomach. "Just answer the damn question."

"Yes, ma'am." He guided her across the street and into the park. "When the threshold in question is private—a home, for instance—the vampire can't cross it without invitation. But if the threshold is public— say, an office, hospital or supermarket—then the vampire can cross as easily as anyone else."

"Why?"

"I don't know." He shrugged and looked at her, his gaze suddenly intense. "Some things just are, Kirby. You don't question them; you just accept."

"*You* accept," she muttered, turning her gaze from his. "I'll continue to question." It was a whole lot safer that way.

Though the mist still covered the tops of the gum trees, the drizzle was beginning to lift and, above all the gray, patches of blue were showing. They might even get a fine day. Which would be good, she thought, dragging the ends of her coat together. She needed to get warm. It felt like the chill of the last few days had settled deep into her bones.

"If you're cold, you can have my coat," he said, rubbing his hand up and down her arm.

She shivered, more from his touch than any chill. "No. I'm okay. Really," she added, when he gave her a disbelieving look. "I think I just need a coffee."

"And something to eat. You can't continue to run on empty, you know."

"I know." She looked away from the concern in his eyes. Despite the temptation to believe otherwise, she knew it wasn't real. It couldn't be. They were strangers who'd shared a mad moment of passion. Nothing more. Nothing deeper.

You're wrong. And you know it.

His thought whispered through her, its touch as warm as the wind on a hot summer evening. She certainly wasn't telepathic, and while she'd been able to catch Helen's emotions easily enough, it was never something that had expanded to anyone else—until now. That she could hear Doyle's thoughts as well as feel his emotions scared the hell out of her.

On the street ahead, yellow cars gleamed. Taxis, lined up in a row, waiting for customers. "We'll have to head back to my place sometime," she said, reminded suddenly that she didn't have any money.

"Might be safer if we didn't," he muttered. "You'll be less tempted to run without cash."

She didn't refute his statement, just crossed her arms and tried to keep warm. Though her back was on fire, the rest of her was so cold her bones were beginning to ache. They climbed into the taxi and he gave the driver the address. The center wasn't far away, and it didn't take them long to get there. The taxi stopped just shy of the locked main gates.

"Looks quiet," she said, climbing out of the taxi and studying the rows of old red-brick buildings visible behind the gates. They looked like factories—or a prison.

"It should be. It closed down a few years ago and is apparently little more than a storage facility now."

"It looks like it should have closed down earlier than that," she muttered, noting the peeling paint and cracked walls on the building closest to them. The whole place looked little better than a dump.

Had it always been like this? She couldn't say, because she had no real memories of it. She knew well enough that she'd met Helen here, and that meant she'd obviously been here for some time, but no matter how hard she tried, she couldn't remember anything else about the place. And yet she could recall every one of her foster parents. Could still recite their names and addresses. Had this place been so bad she'd wiped away all memory of it? Or had it just been so bland there was nothing worth remembering?

"Camille's van is just down the street," he said as the taxi drove off.

"What about your friend's car? Is that still about?"

Doyle shook his head and moved toward the main gate. He had the padlock undone and in his pocket in two seconds flat. "Russ doesn't need a car," he said. "Make sure you close the gate behind you."

She nodded, doing just that before following him across the damp lawn. "Why doesn't he need a car? Don't tell me the hype about vampires turning into bats is true?"

He flashed her a grin. "No, vampires aren't shapeshifters. They don't have to be, when they can run like the wind."

Shapeshifters. The word reverberated through her. She stopped abruptly, staring at his back. "That's what you are, isn't it? That panther—it was you, wasn't it?"

Tension ran through his back muscles and he slowly turned, his expression a mix of uncertainty and resignation. "Yes, it was," he said. "But you knew all along I wasn't entirely human. Your magic told you that when we first met."

She licked her lips, not entirely sure what to think now that she *had* made the connection. "You could have told me," she said softly. Could have mentioned she'd almost made love to a man who was half-beast.

"I'm still just a man, whether or not I'm in panther form. Don't get the werewolf legends confused with the reality of shapeshifters."

She thrust a hand through her hair. "I can't deal with this now." Didn't *want* to deal with it now. Her world was in the process of zooming out of her control, and her head felt like it was spinning. She didn't need this, not on top of everything else.

"You'll have to deal with it eventually," he murmured and turned away, walking toward the west side of the building.

Only if you stay, she thought. And she knew that wasn't going to happen.

He disappeared around the corner of the building, and she hurried to catch up with him. Azaleas and rhododendrons battled for space with weeds in the small garden bed lining the wall. The path was covered in moss and looked like it hadn't been swept in months. *No caretaker,* she thought, and wondered if the place was even still used as a storage facility.

He'd stopped about halfway down, his expression grim and his hands on his hips.

"What's wrong?" She stopped beside him and stared at the window. There was nothing she could see that would cause such a fierce frown.

"Blood," he said, stepping back and studying the windows on the first floor.

"There is?" She stepped forward, intent on getting a closer look, but he grabbed her arm and pulled her back.

"Careful. It's a trap."

She stared at him. "How can you tell that just by looking at it?"

"I can't. I can feel it."

"You can? How?"

"Now is not the time, believe me." Without glancing at her, he moved off down the path.

"Now is never the time," she muttered, stomping after him.

They rounded the corner of the building. About halfway along this section was an old wooden door. Standing in front of it was a woman. Though she had gray hair and, from a distance, looked reasonably old, her multicolored sweater was so bright you almost had to squint to look at it. To complement this, she also wore black leather pants and red sneakers. A woman who didn't care about the opinions of others, Kirby thought with a smile.

The woman glanced up as they approached, a smile creasing her lined features.

"About time you got here. I can't get this damn lock to open." The woman's bright gaze swept past Doyle, fixing on her. "You'd be Kirby, then?"

Her blue eyes were luminous, almost electric. Not a woman who missed much.

Kirby nodded. "You're Camille?"

"That I am." She swatted Doyle's arm, then stepped to one side, out of the way. "Get a move on. We can't stand out here all day, you know."

"You could have spelled it open," he said, voice dry as he squatted in front of the lock.

"I could have, but that would have let whoever placed those spells around the front of the building know another witch was near."

Kirby crossed her arms and watched Doyle work on the lock. "Are you sure your friend is inside?"

"Something is," he said, as the lock clicked open. "I can hear it scuffing around."

She frowned. Did vampire's scuff? Somehow it didn't fit the image she had. "It could be a trap."

"It could be," he agreed, rising. "Which is why you'll wait out here."

"I'm not—"

"You are. We need someone to watch for security patrols. You're it."

She bit her lip. It made perfectly good sense for her to remain out here, and they both knew it. Problem was, she didn't want to be left alone in this place. Something about it spooked her. But whether it was forgotten memories finally surfacing or something else, she wasn't entirely sure.

Camille patted her arm, fingernails painted purple and glittering in the pale morning light. "Don't worry, dear. Whatever they're using to track you, it's not with you now. You're safe."

Doyle's glance was sharp. "Her backpack is the only thing that's not with us, and I checked that last night."

"You did?" Kirby said.

He gave her a half-apologetic glance. "Yeah, sorry, but I had to double-check, given I can sense magic and you can't."

Camille nodded. "The spell might be layered deep, though. I'd get rid of the pack, fast."

"But I packed it myself. Believe me, nobody put anything in there that I don't know about." Then she remembered Helen's words and a chill ran through her. If her friend hadn't left that gift for her, who had?

"The spell might be on the pack itself. As there's no immediate way to discover the truth, it would be better to abandon it." Camille glanced back to Doyle. "You ready?"

He nodded, his gaze meeting Kirby's. "Stay here. Don't go anywhere and don't run." *Warn me like this if you hear or see anything. Don't yell, and don't enter the building.*

His thoughts were firm but warm as they whispered

through her mind. She stared at him for several heart-beats, wondering if she *should* take this opportunity to run. His blue gaze narrowed slightly.

Don't, he added, mind-voice more forceful this time.

She nodded. He opened the door and ushered Camille inside. Sighing, Kirby leaned back against the wall. The chill of the bricks pressed into her back, easing the fire a little. Her gaze skated across the nearby buildings and settled on the perimeter fence. Bottlebrush and flowering gums lined it, the bright red and gold of their flowers flashing like fire in the fog. For an instant, a memory surfaced—Helen and her, weaving through the trunks of the trees, running in fear. She closed her eyes, trying to remember just what—or whom—they'd run from. But the memory slipped back to the recesses of her mind. She swore and opened her eyes.

Her gaze drifted across the buildings, coming to rest on the third of the five that sat opposite. Like the one beside it, it had been partially destroyed by fire and the elements, and vandals had covered it with graffiti. But the building was theirs—that was where they'd stayed.

She pushed away from the wall. She would see anyone approaching this door from over there, and she could use the shadows crowding the entrance porch to hide in if anyone did walk by. Besides, she had a very bad feeling she *needed* to remember what had happened in this place.

She headed for the third dorm. If she remembered right, the doors were half glass. Maybe she could peer in and jog a few more memories loose.

She was close to the main entrance when she noticed the doors were actually open, and she stopped abruptly. Inside, someone whistled tunelessly, and memories beckoned.

She knew that tune. Had heard it often when she was a little girl stuck here in the darkness.

Clenching her fingers, she walked past the ramps and up the steps, heading inside.

NINE

DOYLE STOPPED. MOTES OF DUST DANCED SLUG-gishly in the light filtering in from the skylight above them, but it did little to lift the shadows that filled the corridor. Boxes and broken bits of furniture lined the walls, and the whole place smelled of age and decay. No one had been through here in a very long time. No one human, anyway.

"Can you smell him?" Camille whispered softly.

He nodded. "Three doors down."

"Magic?"

"Two doors down." Its echo was so sharp his skin burned with it. "It's got the same feel as the magic that was being performed on Rachel Grant."

Which had to mean there was something here to find; otherwise, why bother setting a spell in this wasteland?

Camille grunted and pushed past. She stopped near the door, studying it for several seconds. Magic stirred, but this time it felt clean, sunshine compared to rain. Camille, battling the spell with one of her own. After several seconds, she gave a satisfied sigh.

"Looped it," she said, "so we can get past without triggering it. And it'll still feel set to the caster."

"Good." He hurried to the third door. The scuffing had stopped. No one moved inside, no one breathed. And the only person he could smell was Russell.

Warily, he stepped inside. The room was another wasteland of decay and boxes. Dust-caked windows lined the far wall, filtering brightness into the room— brightness that could kill his friend. Russell was lying in one corner, half in the shadows, half out, his hands and feet tied by wire and tape covering his mouth. Sweat beaded his forehead, and his skin looked red, as if sunburned.

Doyle swore. "Camille, get your van and bring it around the back. The gate is open."

She hurried off. He took off his coat and flung it over his friend, protecting his uncovered skin from the sun's rays. Then, tucking his hands under Russell's shoulders, he dragged him back into the safety of the shadow-filled corridor.

He ripped the tape off Russell's mouth. As he began unwinding the wire from the vampire's hands, expletives fell thick and fast into the gloom.

"Tell us what you're really feeling," Doyle said, amused.

"When we catch the bitch," Russell muttered, "she's going to get a taste of her own medicine."

Doyle flipped the wire into the rubbish behind him, then shifted to undo the wire around Russell's feet. "Meaning she's a vamp?"

"No," Russell snapped, rubbing his head. "Meaning I'm going to hit the witch over the head and kick her in the gut and groin a few times, just like she did to me."

"*Tsk*. That's no way to treat a lady."

"This is no lady we're dealing with, believe me."

He rose and offered Russell a hand up. "It's unlike you to let anyone sneak up on you. What happened?"

"A goddamn spell. I was looking through the files in some boxes, and suddenly I couldn't move. Then she appeared from nowhere and clubbed me."

Doyle raised an eyebrow. "Which suggests she didn't know you were a vampire. Otherwise, she might have staked you."

"True," Russell muttered. "I guess she figured it out pretty quickly, though, because she was cackling when she dragged me into the sunlight."

"Did she take the files you were looking at?"

"Yeah. But I did manage to get a look at a couple of them first."

Doyle glanced around as Camille approached. She offered Russell some sunburn cream and patted his shoulder, a look of relief on her face.

"And?" Doyle prodded Russell.

"One was Rachel Grant's file. Like Helen, she'd been put up for adoption as a baby, but her adoptive parents were killed in a freak storm. A tree went through the roof and crushed them in bed."

"How old was she when this happened?" Camille asked, frowning.

"Seven."

"Too young to have gone through puberty," she murmured. "Talents don't usually appear until then— unless they're freakishly strong. What happened to Rachel after that?"

"None of the relatives wanted her, so she came back into government care. She was farmed out to a series of foster parents, but she never lasted with any of them. The records state she was classed a 'difficult' child and she ended up in this center."

"Like Helen," Camille said. "It's looking more and more like this place is the connection."

"And the second file?" Doyle asked, although he had a pretty good idea who that second file was about.

Russell glanced at him. "Kirby Brown. She was never adopted, and there's no mention of why. She stayed in several long-term foster homes, but ended up here at eleven."

"And this is where she and Helen met," he said, wondering about the strong bond between the two of them. It went far deeper than mere friendship. If he were to believe her thoughts, it was almost as if they'd been spiritually bonded—something that usually only ever happened between twins.

Camille raised an eyebrow. "Has Kirby said much about this place?"

He shook his head. "No. I don't think she can actually remember much about her time here." Which was odd, considering she seemed to be able to remember everything else about her past.

"Then you'd better start trying to jog her memories, because I've got a feeling the answers are locked in the past and what happened in this place." Camille glanced back at Russell. "Nothing else in those files? None of the other names on the list?"

"There might be. I didn't get a chance to go through the rest of the files."

"And now the witch has them. Damn," Camille commented.

"Nothing's ever easy when it comes to tracking evil,"

Doyle said. "Do you want to continue checking the boxes?"

Camille shook her head. "Waste of time now. If there *was* anything else here, she would have taken it."

"And she now knows we're hunting her," Russell said. "We need to find the remaining two women."

They also needed to uncover just *how* Kirby was connected to all this. Was the witch merely after power, or was there something deeper going on? "Have you found anything more about that symbol she's been carving on the doors?"

"I'm doing an online search through the Circle's library. It's going to take time."

The problem was, time was running out. And with Kirby on the killer's list, he wanted this case solved as soon as possible.

He glanced at his watch. Half an hour had passed. They wouldn't be able to reclaim the car just yet. "Do you think it's safe for me to bring Kirby back in yet?"

Camille hesitated. "I'd rather not take the chance. And to be honest, if the killer is concentrating on finding you and Kirby, then maybe Russell and I can catch her unaware."

It was a good plan, but he wasn't happy about using Kirby as bait. Too many things could go wrong—like her running. He had to catch some sleep sometime, and sooner or later she *would* take advantage of it.

"What's your plan, then?"

"First we get our sunburned friend somewhere safe and out of the light, then I'll continue searching for that symbol. You and Kirby can go on hunting for our final victim. If you have no luck, Russ can go out again tonight."

"Did you get those photos I sent you?"

"Yes, but I haven't had much of a chance to look at them yet." She patted his arm. "Now, you'd better go find that girl of yours. She's wandered off again."

He frowned. "No, she hasn't."

Camille raised an eyebrow. "Are you doubting an old woman? She wasn't at the door when I drove up."

"Maybe not, but she's close."

"She has a pretty distinct smell if you can still catch it above the dust and decay in here," Russell commented, eyeing him with amusement. "A little smitten with the girl, are we?"

"No." He was well past being smitten. "I can read her thoughts, and I have no idea why."

Russ raised his eyebrows. "She telepathic?"

"No, and neither am I—as you know."

Russ snorted. "Yeah. It's easier to draw blood from a stone than it is to reach through your thick skull."

Doyle grinned. "At least it stops you from putting improper thoughts in my head. Like the time you tried to get me—"

"Enough," Camille said, frowning. "What other talents has she got?"

"Energy," he said. "It races across her fingers like lightning, and she can cast it like a net."

Camille's frown deepened. "Drawing down lightning is usually the provenance of a storm witch, and Kirby certainly isn't one of those. She has a completely different energy output."

"Could it be some form of elemental magic?" Russ asked.

"Maybe, but elementals are extremely rare. Besides, air elementals are merely the conduit for the energy.

They rarely have enough control to weave something as intricate as a web." Her expression was thoughtful. "Let's get back to the office. Doyle, keep in regular contact."

"I will."

He followed them from the building. Camille opened the van's back doors. The van had been fully lined with sun-blocking material. You could never be too careful when a vampire was part of your team.

Russell dove in and Camille slammed the door shut before he started to sizzle. "I think I know what that symbol being carved on the door is," she said. "And if I'm right, we could be in real trouble. I'll call and let you know in a few hours. In the meantime, keep that girl of yours safe."

"I will, don't worry."

She climbed into the van and drove off. He shoved his hands into his pockets and headed across to the third building to find Kirby.

Office furniture lined the walls where once there had been two long rows of beds. Kirby stopped in the middle of the dorm, her gaze going to the fourth window from the remains of the back wall. That was where her bed had been. Helen, when she'd finally arrived at the center, had slept next to her. Damn it, why couldn't she remember this place, when everything else was so clear?

She sniffed, and the smell hit her—age and mustiness, mixed with the pungent scent of ammonia. Memories stirred, as did her fear. She retreated a step, then stopped. Running wasn't going to help anyone. If something had happened in this room, she needed to remember it. The answer to why Helen was murdered could lie anywhere, even in something as innocuous as memories long locked away.

The whistling was coming from the ruins of the back of the dorm, from what had once been the nurse's quarters. She took a few more steps forward, then stopped. "Hello?"

The whistling cut off abruptly, and a soft whirring filled the gloom. Two seconds later, a man in an electric wheelchair appeared in the doorway, his berry-brown face fixed into a scowl. "And what would you be doing here, girlie?"

His voice was as flat and lifeless as his brown eyes, and it sent a chill up her spine. She knew that voice. In the past she had feared it.

She again resisted the impulse to run. "I'm . . ." She hesitated, uncertain whether she should really be talking to this man. Surely if she'd once feared him, it had been for good reason. "I stayed at this center for a while. I'm just trying to find a friend I met here."

Why she lied, she wasn't entirely sure. She certainly wasn't going to get much information about her past by inquiring about someone else, and yet instinct suggested it was better than mentioning who she was. Though she had no idea why this would be dangerous, she trusted her instincts. They'd saved her too often in the past to ignore them now.

The old man's gaze narrowed, and he rolled a little farther into the room. He was scrawny, with thick, steel-gray hair that looked silver in the morning light. He had a clipboard on his lap, and his hands were long and thin. The hands of a piano player, she thought.

The hands of a molester.

Images hit her, thick and fast. *Oh God,* she thought, swallowing back the bile that rose in her throat as pictures and sounds swelled around her. Suddenly she was an eleven-year-old again, lying in bed, wide-eyed and fearful, listening to the sounds night after night. Cries of pain, odd grunting, the rough squeak of bedsprings. Not her. He'd never touched her. Didn't like her green eyes—they were fey, he'd once told her. Dangerous. But he'd touched Helen, and he'd touched others, here in the long nights of darkness.

His frown deepened, and he rolled forward some more. She retreated. She couldn't help it. Her memories had too strong a grip, and it felt like her fear was going to stifle her.

"You were one of the kids who lived here?" His free hand clenched briefly.

Get out, instinct said. *Run.*

She nodded. If he got any closer, she'd throw up all over him—all over his overalls and shiny brown shoes.

Shoes he'd always kept on when he'd lain on top of Helen. Fighting horror, she retreated another step.

I'm here behind you, in the shadows, Doyle said, his mind-voice filled with such anger it burned through her like a flame. *I won't let him hurt you. Question him if you want to.*

I don't want to remember this. The man is a monster.

Yes, he is. But he may also hold some answers. I think you need those answers, and not just to solve Helen's death.

She bit her lip and crossed her arms. The chill in

her body was so strong she was beginning to shiver. But he was right. The past, and this man, had to be faced if she wanted to find answers.

"You've got green eyes," the man in the wheelchair said suddenly. "Fey eyes, like a cat's. I've seen them before. Seen *you*." He hesitated. "You're one of *them*, aren't you?"

Fear mingled with the anger in his dead brown eyes. She frowned, wondering why. "One of who? What are you talking about?"

"One of them bitches that did this to me." He slapped a hand against the wheelchair and rolled a little closer.

His scent surrounded her—cigar smoke and whisky. The same smell that had haunted her nights, all those years ago. Her stomach roiled. "I have no idea what you're talking about."

He snorted. "You and those other four. You did this to me. You broke my back, made me dead from the waist down."

Dead from the waist down was nearly punishment enough, she thought, and rubbed her arms. "Me and what four? I have no idea—"

"Them witches. You formed a circle and smashed me like I was nothing more than one of your stupid dolls. All of you bitches deserve what's coming to you."

He hawked and spat at her. The globule barely missed her toes. She stepped back again, watching him closely, another chill racing through her spine. "Did *you* kill them? Are you responsible?"

Maliciousness mixed with the fear in his brown eyes. He wasn't responsible, she realized, but he knew who was.

"How could five children possibly throw a man your size around?"

"Magic," he whispered. "It surrounded me, a shield of energy I couldn't see. But I could feel it. Oh God, could I feel it . . ." His voice drifted off, and for a moment the terror of that night showed in his eyes.

She felt no sympathy for him. One night hardly made up for the many nights of hell this fiend had given Helen and the others. "So you killed them? And tore their bodies apart afterward?"

He snorted. "I didn't kill anyone. Look at me. I'm a goddamn cripple. I don't pose a threat to anyone these days."

"Yet you know who is behind these murders, don't you?"

"What if I do, girlie? What are you going to do? Beat the information out of me?" He grinned maliciously, revealing yellow-stained teeth. "Might like that, you know. Don't get touched by many women nowadays."

"*She* might not beat the information out of you," Doyle said, his voice flat and yet somehow ferocious. He moved out of the shadows and stopped beside her. "But I'd love to take a crack at you, let me assure you."

Doyle twined his fingers around hers. The warmth of his touch flushed through her, and while it didn't completely erase the chill, it made her feel infinitely safer.

The old man's face went pale. "Who are you?" he whispered hoarsely. "What right have you to threaten me like that?"

"What right did you have to molest eleven-year-olds? I should wring your scrawny neck just for that."

She touched his arm with her free hand, trying to calm him. It felt like she was touching a tightly coiled spring. It wouldn't take too much to provoke an attack, of that she was certain. Just as she was certain he *would* tear this man apart if he provided the slightest excuse—because of what he'd done to the others. Because of the hurt he'd inflicted on her.

No one had ever cared for her that much. No one. Tears stung her eyes. She blinked them back, then said, "Tell me what you know, or you can tell the police. Your choice."

The old man's glance darted between the two of them. "I don't know much," he muttered.

"Then tell us what you do know," Doyle said. His voice was little more than a scratch of sound—almost, but not quite, the growl of a big cat.

She studied him for a minute, wondering if perhaps he was going to become the panther right here in this room. She wasn't sure if she was ready to see that— wasn't sure if she'd *ever* be ready to see that.

He glanced at her, blue eyes narrowed. *Give me credit for a little control. I am not a beast who takes the shape of a man, you know.*

Sorry. It's just your voice . . .

I only mean to scare him—for now, at least.

"Got a visitor last week," the old man said into the silence. "Said she used to stay here in this cabin. She wasn't one of my—" He hesitated, his gaze flicking from her to Doyle. "She said she wanted revenge on the witches, just like me."

"What are you talking about? We never—" She bit back the rest of her words. If she couldn't remember attacking the caretaker, how could she say they'd never attacked anyone else?

"Do you know this woman's name?"

He hesitated. "Felicity Barnes."

"And you recognized her?" she asked, surprised. After all, they'd all been barely eleven when they were here with this man. Surely they'd changed in the years since.

"No. But I checked the files afterward, and she was here." He sniffed. "She offered me money."

His sly look implied they should be doing the same. Doyle's fingers twitched against hers. He might be controlling his beast, but she had a feeling it was a struggle.

"I'm offering you life," he ground out. "Give me a description of this woman."

The old man's hand twitched and the wheelchair jerked backward slightly. "Petite little thing, she was. Brown hair, gray eyes, boyish figure. Nothing remarkable."

Heat flashed in his eyes. Felicity Barnes's boyish figure had excited him, Kirby realized, feeling sick again. God, if they had indeed been responsible for putting him in the wheelchair all those years ago, why hadn't they just finished him? Why had they let this monster live?

Doyle's thoughts touched hers again, offering comfort, offering warmth. She took a deep breath and tried to keep calm. "What did she want you to do?"

"Nothing. She just wanted to look at the files, that's all."

"Our files are still here?" she asked, surprised. Surely they should be tucked away somewhere safer.

The caretaker snorted. "This *was* a government-run facility."

And it had been a safe environment. Until he'd come. Until Mariel had come. She blinked. Who in the hell was Mariel?

"Do you know which files she wanted?" Doyle asked.

"The witches' files, what else? Three of them, there was."

"Why?"

"Photos. Last known address, stuff like that. This place was closed down not long after them bitches attacked me, and all the kids here scattered. Makes tracking them down a little hard."

But track them down she had. And not only killed them, but ripped their remains to shreds. Or at least, had ripped Helen to shreds. Rachel had died in a more dignified manner. Her stomach twisted, and bile rose in her throat. *I'm going to be sick . . .*

She wrenched her hand from Doyle's and raced outside, barely making it to the garden to the left of the door.

When she'd finished, she leaned back against the cool brick wall and closed her eyes. She didn't want to do this. Didn't want to remember the past—especially if it was going to reveal more horrors like the caretaker. And it *would* reveal more; of that she was certain.

But as Doyle had said earlier, it was time she faced the past. For Helen's sake. And for her own. She'd spent too many years in retreat, afraid to trust, afraid to live. Part of the reason why had now been revealed, but she couldn't stop, not until the whole truth was out. Helen had once said their future lay locked in acceptance. It was only now that she realized Helen had meant acceptance of the past, of what had happened, and what they'd done.

But just what, exactly, *had* they done?

She wasn't sure, and that scared her. What could five prepubescent children have done to this Felicity Barnes that she now exacted bloody revenge all these years later?

Footsteps approached. Doyle walked through the doors and stopped. "Are you okay?"

She didn't open her eyes. Didn't want to see the caring in his eyes that she could feel in his thoughts. It was a lie. It had to be. No one could care for her—especially a man who was still such a stranger.

"I'm fine," she said, her voice a little sharper than she'd intended. "Is the caretaker still alive?"

"Scared out of his wits, but yeah, he's still alive." His gaze swept over her, a heated touch she felt rather than saw. "I'm not a cold-blooded killer, Kirby. I'm not an animal. I'm just a man."

No one who could assume the shape of a panther was *just* a man. She felt an insane desire to laugh at the thought and crossed her arms, trying to hold it back, trying to hold in all the pain. It didn't work, and a sob escaped.

"Come here," he all but growled.

Wrapping a hand around her arm, he pulled her toward him. His touch was gentle yet firm, and she made no effort to resist. Couldn't resist, in fact. That one sob had broken the dam wall, and she felt so weak her knees were shaking. She fell into his embrace, sobs racking her body, her tears soaking his shirt.

He didn't say anything, just held her tightly as all

the pain, all the fear of the last few days, poured out of her. Even when the sobbing had eased, she remained in his arms, finding strength in his strength, finding comfort in the warm flow of his thoughts through her mind.

After a while, she sighed softly. "Thank you," she murmured into his chest.

His smile shimmered through her, as warm as sunshine. *Anytime you want a chest to cry on, I'm here.* Out loud, he said, "Feeling a little better?"

He caressed her hair, his touch running warmth to the pit of her stomach. She looked up, saw the heated look in his eyes, and felt an insane desire to rise up on her toes and taste the sweetness of his lips again. But *that* had nearly gotten them into trouble an hour ago, so she pulled away instead. His hand slipped from her back to her hip and rested there, warming the base of her spine.

"I'm afraid I've soaked your shirt," she said, plucking at the wet material.

His smile touched his eyes and made her heart stutter. "It's drip-dry, so don't worry." He brushed some hair away from her cheek, his touch trailing heat against her skin. Then he froze, and his grip on her waist tightened slightly. "What the hell . . . ?"

He turned, thrusting her behind him. Fear rose in her throat, and lightning warmed her fingertips. "What—"

She got no further. A chill ran through her, and for an instant, her vision blurred. Suddenly she was seeing inside the dorm, inside the nurse's quarters where the old man was checking numbers and ticking them off on his clipboard. A small figure cowled in black appeared behind him, its face little more than a rotting skull.

Death, she thought with a shiver. But it wasn't there for them.

Inside the dorm, the caretaker began screaming.

TEN

MAGIC BURNED ACROSS HIS SKIN. IT HAD THE SAME foul flavor as the trap he'd sensed in the other building and the magic he'd felt at Rachel Grant's. She was getting rid of the evidence, he thought, as the caretaker's screaming reached fever pitch.

He stepped forward, but Kirby grabbed his arm. "She'll kill you," she murmured.

Images streamed from her mind to his—a figure cowled in black, wearing a death mask. Long, thin hands from which flames sprung, surrounding the old man. Fire burning through the air, *through the old man*. His screams clashing with the howl of the inferno before dying abruptly.

The searing touch of magic flashed again, and the figure was gone, leaving only a burning wreck that had once been a man.

"Not a man," Kirby murmured. "A monster."

Doyle turned away from the door. The old man was dead, but the flames still burned. If the alarms in the building were still working, they would no doubt go off soon. They had to be out of here before the fire department arrived.

He caught Kirby's hand and squeezed her fingers gently. There were tears in her eyes, and he could feel the pain in her thoughts. As much as she'd hated the caretaker, as much as she might have wished him dead, she hadn't wanted him to die in such a manner. She was a gentle spirit, despite everything she'd faced as a child.

"We have to go," he said, tugging her forward when all he really wanted to do was take her into his arms again.

"Where to now?" she asked, making no attempt to remove her fingers from his as they quickly made their way toward the main exit.

"Breakfast for me, and hot coffee, at the very least, for you." Though her fingers were warm against his, he could feel the trembling running through them. Whether it was a reaction to what she'd learned, the old man's death, or something else entirely, he wasn't sure.

"No," she said, a smile touching her lips as her bright gaze flashed to his. "I meant what's our next plan of attack? Do we try to find the next name on that list of yours?"

He hesitated at the gate, checking to make sure there was no one around, then motioned her through. "There's nothing else we can do." Even though they hadn't exactly been successful in getting to these people before the killer did.

"We *have* to stop her before she gets to the third victim," she said.

"We will." He touched her back lightly and guided her across the road. "The caretaker spoke of the five of you forming a circle and surrounding him with magic. Any idea what he was talking about?"

She shook her head, her thoughts troubled. "It's like there's this big brick wall in my mind. I can't remember anything . . ." She hesitated, taking a shaky breath. "Helen told me that I was the one that binds. She said the killer seeks to control the power of the elements—the circle of five."

A chill ran through him. Helen was dead. She couldn't possibly have told Kirby anything. Was the killer playing games? "Helen said this? When?"

His voice was sharper than he'd intended, and she bit her lip, her face pale. "In the park, when you were in Rachel's house. It wasn't Helen, just her spirit. She's one with the wind now."

Her voice faded, but images skated from her mind to his, fractured reflections of what had happened, and what Helen had said. He relaxed a little. No wraith in league with evil could be *that* convincing. "She didn't explain what this circle was? Or why the killer is after the four of you?"

"She said there was five of us," she corrected, rubbing her arms. "The killer is one of the five."

"*What?*" He stopped, pulling her around to face him. "Are you sure about that?" God, that meant that if Camille's list was correct, they'd had the name of the killer all along. Only Felicity Barnes's name wasn't on it, so where did she fit in?

Her face was troubled, her green eyes silvered with tears. "Helen was sure."

And because it was Helen, she believed it. While he'd never been one to trust the word of ghosts, he *did* trust Kirby's judgment. "Did Helen say anything else?"

She hesitated. "She said that I had to find the fourth point and save her. Then I had to stop the fifth."

"You won't be stopping anyone. You'll be tucked away somewhere nice and safe."

Her gaze searched his for a second. "I'm the only one who can stop her. Helen told me that."

"Well, Helen's wrong. Camille's a damn powerful witch, and Russ and I aren't a bad backup team. We've handled a lot worse than this, believe me."

She didn't. He could sense the doubt in her mind, the fear. Despite everything, despite what she was feeling—albeit unwillingly—she still didn't trust him. Or rather, didn't trust his ability to keep her safe.

Perhaps, given her past, that was understandable, but it was also damned annoying. "What more do I have to do to prove myself to you?" he added, his voice holding an edge.

She turned away, but not before he saw the sheen of tears on her cheeks. He took a deep breath. "I'm sorry—"

She held up a hand. "Forget it. Let's just go get that coffee."

Her voice was flat. Emotionless. The total opposite to her thoughts, which careened chaotically from wanting to trust to desperately needing to run from him and everything she was feeling.

He wasn't the only one who'd been hit by the emotional club, but it appeared he was the only one who really understood it. He had to give her time to get used to him, to get used to what she was feeling, or she'd run for sure. And now that he'd found her, he didn't want to lose her.

They headed down the street and eventually found a small coffee shop that was just opening. He guided her inside, chose a table in the back close to the rear exit and ordered them both breakfast and coffee.

She did little more than pick at her toast, but at least she was trying. He was hungrier than he'd thought, and he wolfed down his eggs and bacon. Settling back in the chair, he picked up his coffee and watched her over the rim of his cup.

Heat crept across her cheeks. She brushed the hair out of her eyes, then met his gaze. "Stop it."

He raised his eyebrows. "Stop what?"

"Looking at me that way . . . like I'm some sort of luscious bun you can't wait to devour."

He grinned. "Well, you're certainly the tastiest morsel I've tried in a long, long time."

"Yeah, like I believe that."

He shrugged. Nothing he said right now would make her believe otherwise. She was looking for excuses to keep him at a distance. He put his coffee back on the table, then crossed his arms and leaned forward. "Do the names Marline Thomas or Trina Jones mean anything to you?"

She frowned. "No. Why?"

"Because they're the other two women on Camille's list of possible victims. If your ghost is right, then one of them is the killer."

Her frown deepened. "But the caretaker said it was a Felicity Barnes who asked him about our records, so where does she fit in?"

"I don't know," he admitted. And it was damned frustrating.

She sipped at her coffee for a moment. "Helen told me that she'd tried to find out who her parents were, and that's why we were involved."

"It could be." Maybe their killer worked for the government department responsible for adoptions. Why else would Helen have been killed *after* she'd begun her inquiries, and not before? "Had you?"

She shook her head, grimacing slightly. "I've never wanted to."

If she had, she might now be dead, right alongside Helen. He reached out and clasped her hand. "Why not?"

"I don't know." She hesitated. "I guess it stems from anger. I mean, they abandoned me. They left me on the doorstep of a hospital and walked away. Why would I ever want to find people who could do that to a baby?"

"They might have had good reasons—"

"To leave me on the steps? To not even give me a *birth* certificate?" She wrenched her hands from his. "Do you know what it's like to always be alone, knowing there is no one—*no one*—you could really turn to when . . ."

She broke off, but her unfinished sentence whispered through him, sharp with pain and memories. *When the bad things happened.* She was right, of course. He could never know what it had been like for her, but he *could* imagine. For the last ten years he'd been alone, away from his family, and it had certainly provided an insight. And while he'd had friends and the occasional lover to fill the void, it just wasn't the same.

And she'd spent nearly her entire life with that feeling. "At least you had Helen once you reached that facility," he murmured lamely.

She looked down at the table. "Yeah. I guess I did."

He watched her a minute longer, then resignedly got out his cell phone and dialed Camille. He quickly filled her in on what had happened at the facility as well as what the ghostly Helen had told Kirby.

"I was afraid of this," Camille muttered. "That circle being carved into the doors has to represent an elemental circle."

"Which is?" He pulled the phone away from his ear so Kirby could hear. The old witch had a loud voice, and it would carry across the table easily enough.

"It was thought for a long time to be little more than a myth, but we've been doing some research and our findings are saying otherwise." She sniffed. "An elemental circle is the combination of five elements— fire, water, earth and air. The fifth element is strength, but it's more commonly known as the binding element. The binder is the most important element of all, because without one, the others cannot unite."

"It sounds like a pentagram."

"It isn't. A pentagram is just used to perform magic or to protect. An elemental circle is a *force*."

"Why would one of the five be killing the others, if they need each other to work this circle?"

"She's not just killing them, she's sucking their abilities from them. Maybe she tasted the power once and now hungers for it all. But, this time, she wants all the elements under her control." Camille's voice was grim. "But that could only happen if either she is the binding element, or she consumes the binding element."

His gaze met Kirby's. The caretaker had said they'd formed the circle to attack him. That's when it had started, all those years ago. But why wait until now to attack? It didn't make any sense. "One of the two remaining names might be the killer, Camille."

"Maybe," Camille growled. "And maybe not. I'll take Trina Jones. You two try to find Marline Thomas. Russ can search for the mysterious Felicity Barnes."

"You got addresses?" He pulled a pen from his pocket and grabbed a table napkin, quickly jotting them down as Camille read them out. There were close to fifteen possible locations. They weren't going to get through them all today.

"Kirby wants to head home and grab some money and clothes, then we'll head off."

"Don't go back to your car. Leave whatever is in her bag right where it is. Safer that way for you both."

He frowned. "Someone will report it as abandoned."

"So? You didn't actually rent it, did you?"

He glanced at Kirby. She'd raised an eyebrow, a knowing gleam in her eyes. "Well, no." And he'd worn gloves when driving, so they wouldn't find his prints. But they'd find Kirby's. And they'd find her backpack.

"Believe an old witch when she says it's best not to go back to that car. If our murderer saw you in Rachel Grant's house, she's had time to set a trap. Kirby's probably got a car. Use that."

He hadn't thought of that. He raised an eyebrow in query, and she nodded.

"Keep in contact, shapeshifter. Hourly reports."

"Will do." He disconnected and tucked the phone away. Kirby picked up the list, studying it. "The third address is actually not far away from my place."

"Then we'll head to your place and continue on from there." He motioned the waiter for the bill. "Tell me, why are you so desperate to go back to your place? It's not just for money, is it?"

She bit her lip and looked away. "Helen told me to go. She said it was urgent."

Doyle frowned. "Why?"

"She said I had to find her gift, that the gift I had wasn't the one she'd left." She hesitated. "Which made me wonder if perhaps that gift contained the tracker you were searching for."

"It might." He hadn't felt any magic emanating from it, but then, the woman behind all this was obviously very adept at magic and could easily have shielded a tracking spell from casual examination. "Is there anyone else likely to have left you a gift?"

She shook her head, a smile touching her lips. "No boyfriend, if that's what you're asking."

He wasn't, but it was still nice to have it confirmed. "Did you open the present in your pack at all?"

"I haven't had the chance."

"Probably just as well, given it might contain more than just a tracker." He'd have to contact Camille and get her to check it out. If that present *did* contain some form of magic, it would need to be diffused. She might also be able to use it to trace the magic back to its source. "Why did Helen leave you a gift?"

"My birthday is tomorrow." Her voice broke slightly, and she took a deep, shuddering breath. "Hers would have been, too. She was always talking to the wind and reading our futures. She must have known—"

Her voice broke again. He placed a hand over hers.

"Did Helen say why you needed to find her present so urgently?"

"She said I needed to say the words and complete the circle." Kirby grimaced. "It doesn't really make much sense."

It did if there was some sort of spell involved. He stood. "Ready to go?"

"No." She grimaced and rose. "And won't it still be a crime scene?"

"More than likely, but we should be able to get around that."

Her face went pale. "You're not going to hurt anyone, are you?"

"Of course not." Irritation edged his voice. "I'm a reformed thief, not a killer."

"I'm sorry. I didn't mean—" Her voice faded and she bit her lip, looking contrite and confused and so damn cute all he wanted to do was hug her.

Instead, he took her hand and led her outside. They caught a cab but stopped at the top of her street, far enough away that any cops who might be watching the place wouldn't immediately recognize Kirby. She climbed out as he paid the cabbie, but didn't move when he joined her on the sidewalk.

"There's a cop car out front." Her voice was little more than a whisper, and was filled with horror. Not because of the cops, he suspected, but because of the memories evoked after she looked at the house they guarded. "I suppose they're looking for me."

"More than likely. And it's only been a couple of days since the murder. They probably haven't finished their investigation yet." He clasped her fingers and squeezed them gently, then turned to study the house.

Aside from the officers in the car, police tape barred the front door, which was closed. Which probably meant that there weren't any other officers on site at the moment—although he had no doubt they would be back later in the day to search the scene yet again, hunting for the smallest of clues. But as Camille said, they were looking in all the wrong places. There was nothing in any procedural manual that would ever prepare them for something like magic—or the *manarei*.

The cops out front *did* mean they couldn't go in that way, even if he did take them out temporarily. "Does the garage provide access to the back of the house?"

She nodded. "But there were bits of Ross all over the kitchen. I can't . . ." Tears glimmered again, and she bit her lip.

He wondered why she was so determined not to show any emotion, to hold it all inside. Had some nut in her past enforced the impression that it was better that way?

"Close your eyes, then. I'll lead you through."

She glanced at him and nodded. "I guess I can manage that."

"Good. Wait here while I go deal with the officers." He hesitated. "What's the name of the local newspaper?"

"*The Moonee Valley Leader.* Why?"

"I need a cover story."

"Oh. Be careful."

He smiled, raised her hand and kissed her fingers. "Always."

A pretty blush crept across her cheeks. He resisted

the impulse to kiss her more thoroughly, then pulled his phone out as he made his way down the street. He sent Camille a quick text, giving her a rundown on the present and asking her to check it out; then he plucked one of her ready-to-go potions from an inner pocket and held it loosely in his free hand. Once he was near the car, he hit the phone's record button. The passenger's-side window was halfway down.

The cop raised an eyebrow as Doyle stopped beside the car. "May I help you?"

"Officer, Mike Jones from the *Moonee Valley Leader*," Doyle said, and held his phone closer to the half-open window. "I was just wondering if you could give us an update on the events here. Are you any closer to discovering the murderer?"

The officer grimaced. "I'm sorry, sir, but I'm afraid I can't comment."

"I've talked to the neighbors, and several said it looked like the bodies were torn apart." He crushed the charm as he spoke, and felt a tingle against his palm as the magic activated. "Is that true?"

"Again, I'm sorry, but if you want more information, you're going to have—"

The rest of the sentence was cut off as Doyle threw the crushed remnants of the charm into the car. Blue smoke immediately began to fill the cabin, and Doyle stepped back as a few tendrils curled out through the half-open window. The last thing he needed was to be caught in the spell's immobilizing net. Neither cop stood much of a chance—the spell was designed to work fast and it would hold them for about ten minutes. He hoped that would be long enough to get Kirby in and out of her house.

He went back to collect her, then led her into her backyard via the unlocked garage door. Birches lined the boundaries, casting dappled shadows across the tiny patch of grass. Azaleas brightened the corners of the yard, providing cheerful splashes of yellow, red and orange through the shade.

"Pretty," he said, meaning it.

"Thanks." She plucked a key from under the mat and glanced at him, a smile touching her lips. "And don't tell me that's a dumb place to keep a key, because I already know it."

"I wasn't going to mention it." Besides, for most professional thieves, door locks were the least of their problems. It was things like pressure pads, heat and motion sensors and all the other varieties of alarms available these days that provided the worry. "But you could at least try somewhere more original."

"Like what? The potted plant?"

"Actually, if you have to leave a key, then sticking it to the back of something like a leaf is a damn fine hiding place. Most amateurs don't think of that."

"And most professionals don't bother?"

"Something like that." He took the key from her and opened the door. "Ready?"

She nodded. He caught her hand, ducked under the crime scene tape and led her into the kitchen. It was as if he'd walked into a slaughterhouse. Seeing the pictures was one thing, seeing the reality another. Granted, there were no body parts lying about, but blood was still splashed everywhere, and the outlines of where they'd found the different pieces of humanity littered the floor.

No wonder she had been so fearful to confront this all again. While he was no stranger to the various faces of death, even he found this sickening. He quickly guided her through it and up the stairs.

"You can open your eyes now," he said once they were out of sight of the mess below.

She did so, taking a deep breath in the process. "Thank you."

He nodded and touched her cheek, lightly thumbing away a tear. "Any idea where Helen might have hidden this present?"

"In her room, I'd presume." She stepped away from his touch and entered the room to the right of the stairs.

It had a moody blue-and-gray color scheme—odd colors for a woman, but fitting for a storm witch. He glanced across the corridor to the other room. Yellows, reds and creams. The colors of summer and the sun. Kirby's room. He resisted the temptation to go and look. Instead, he watched as she opened the wardrobe.

"She usually kept things she wanted hidden in with all her shoes," she said, getting down on her knees.

"Wait, don't touch anything." He knelt down beside her and swept his hand through the shadows, searching for any indication of magic. "Clear," he said, sitting back on his heels.

She leaned forward, pulling out various boxes and shoes, but in the end found nothing. She sat back, her shoulder brushing his arm as she contemplated the wardrobe.

"What about the storage space up top?" he said, pointing to the shelf above the hanging space.

She wrinkled her nose.

"Helen was short, like me. She usually settled for lower hiding places."

"We can't stay here long," he reminded her softly. "This is still an active crime scene. More cops could arrive at any minute."

"I know." She took a deep breath, then climbed to her feet. "You check up there. I'll check her drawers."

"Deal." He rose and began pulling everything out of the top of the wardrobe. There was nothing there that even remotely resembled a present. He shoved it all back and headed over to the bed. Kneeling down, he looked under it. There, in the darkness, a gaily wrapped present sat waiting.

"Found it," he said, reaching out. Magic tingled through his fingertips, but its touch was warm, muted. Nonthreatening.

He held it out to her, but she didn't take it, just regarded it warily. "Are you sure it's from Helen? Maybe it's another gift from our murderous friend."

"There's nothing evil here. I wouldn't let you touch it, otherwise." Although he hadn't felt anything in the first one, either.

"Oh." She swallowed heavily, a bright light in her eyes. "You hold it for me. I have to get some clothes and stuff."

"Aren't you going to open the present? Especially given what Helen said?"

"I can't. It's not my birthday until tomorrow."

"I don't think—"

"It's bad luck," she said, then all but ran out of the room.

Hiding her tears, he thought. He waited in the hallway outside her room, sensing her need to be alone, however briefly.

When she finally came back out, there was no sign of the tears he'd glimpsed. She was wearing a long black coat similar to his and holding an overnight bag. He took it from her and checked to make sure there was nothing resembling anything magical in it, then dropped the present inside. "That all?"

She hesitated. "I need my wallet. I can't keep letting you pay for everything."

"And you can't exactly run if you haven't got cash or credit cards, can you?"

She didn't deny his accusation. He sighed. "Where did you leave it?"

"It's in my handbag, which I dropped near the front door when I came in last night."

"I'll go get it. You wait here."

He gave her the overnight bag and headed down the stairs. Her handbag was where she'd said, zipper open and the outside covered in white dust. He squatted, carefully nudging a finger into the open compartment— and felt the sting of magic burn through him.

He yanked his hand away and quickly upended the bag. The contents fell out, littering the carpet. Wind stirred, raising the hairs along the back of his neck. Something was coming. Something bad.

He grabbed her car keys, then rose. The air shimmered and flexed, half forming the shape of a hand. The wind keened into the silence, battering at him, as if trying to force him away.

Watching the energy-forming hand, he stepped back.

And fell into darkness.

ELEVEN

THE HIGH-PITCHED HOWL FILLED THE AIR, AND GOOSE bumps chased down Kirby's spine. She froze, listening to the sound and wondering what in hell was coming after them now. Then, as abruptly as it started, the sound stopped.

But the silence that followed was in some ways more frightening.

"Doyle?" She leaned over the banister and tried to look down. She couldn't see him, but that didn't mean he wasn't there. She couldn't see her handbag or the front door, either, and she knew the front door, at least, would be there.

Doyle? she queried tentatively. Still no response. And the wash of warmth that she'd come to associate with the odd connection forming between them was gone, leaving her feeling suddenly bereft.

She bit her lip, then picked up her bag and slowly edged down the stairs. Lightning streaked across her fingers, sending jagged edges of light flickering across the walls.

"Doyle?" she repeated, hesitating halfway down. Still nothing. Her handbag was lying near the door, contents scattered across the carpet. Her car keys didn't seem to be among them, although the wallet that held her credit cards and driver's license was.

Where the hell was he?

She edged down the remaining stairs and stopped again, listening. Nothing moved. The silence seemed so intense it was like a hammer, battering at her.

With her heart thumping somewhere in her throat, she edged toward the front door. Why had he tipped everything out of her handbag? Something glinted in the morning light, catching her eye. She bent, frowning. It was a small silver coin etched with a star. It was nothing she'd ever owned—or seen—before.

Even as she watched, the coin began to dissolve, until there was nothing but a small patch of black dust staining the carpet. Some form of magic, obviously, meant to capture or kill *her*. And Doyle, who could sense the presence of magic, had somehow been caught by it.

Fear shot through her, and her stomach churned. God, if he was hurt or dead because of her—because of his stupid insistence that he had to protect her— she didn't know if she could ever forgive herself.

She picked up the wallet, then rose and stared out the front window for a moment. She had to try to find him, but how? She could no longer hear the warm whisper of his thoughts, and she didn't want to think about the implications of that. He *wasn't* dead. She had to believe that, if nothing else, or panic might set in.

She turned, her gaze skating past the blood and outlines in the living room. Her car keys were missing, but Helen had a spare set on her key ring. Only trouble was, they were probably hanging on the key holder near the refrigerator, and to get them, she'd have to go past all the gore in the kitchen.

Not something she wanted to do, but she had very little choice. They couldn't keep using taxis to get around. It would cost them a fortune.

She took a deep, calming breath and headed into the kitchen. Her stomach churned, threatening to revolt as she edged past the thick, dark pools, smashed crockery and taped outlines. Snatching the keys from the hook, she ran for the back door and out into the yard, where she was violently sick.

After a while, she rinsed out her mouth with water from the outside tap and resolutely headed into the garage, opening the door just in time to see more cops pull into her driveway.

"Well, well, well," a cold voice said into the silence. "It looks like my little trap caught the cat rather than the mouse."

Doyle rolled onto his back and rubbed his eyes. He felt as though he'd been picked up and thrown around like some rag doll, and given the howl of the wind before he'd stepped into nothingness, maybe that impression wasn't far off.

Beyond the speaker's whisper of breath to his left, he could hear the rustle of leaves and a bird's piping tune. The air was an odd mixture of smells—sweet and fresh, free of the usual fumes that were associated with city living, and yet touched by a muskiness usually linked with damp basements. He flexed his fingers. Concrete met his touch—cold, wet and just a little slimy.

"I know you're awake, so stop your foxing. I'm not coming anywhere near you, if that's your plan."

The voice was rich and soft—the same voice he'd heard performing the spell at Rachel's. He opened his eyes. A square patch of sunlight swam before them, framing and shadowing the face that stared down at him. A face that was thin and long and crowned by short, dark hair. Felicity Barnes, he thought, and wondered if it was her real name or an assumed one. Wondered if this was her real face or a disguise. The slight wash of magic suggested it was the latter.

"What do you plan to do?" he asked, his gaze sweeping his surroundings. The room was circular and fully concrete. By the look of it, it was an old tank of some kind.

"With you? Nothing. You're not what I intended to catch at all."

For which he had to be extremely thankful. Though in some respects, Kirby was probably better equipped to deal with this situation than he was. At least her lightning could have blasted a way out.

"You can stay here and rot," the woman continued. "I'm certainly not going to waste my strength on the likes of you."

Now that his eyes were getting used to the darkness, he could see her features more clearly. Her face was extremely gaunt, her eyes protruding and ringed with shadows, and her mouth little more than a slash of pale blue. Blood magic was sucking her dry, he thought. Maybe that was why she was killing the rest of the circle. She wanted power without cost.

But was this her real image, or was she merely showing him what he expected to see? If she was powerful enough to control two *manarei* and bring the King Kong of all zombies to life, then surely the blood magic could not have sucked her *this* dry. Not yet. Because the face he was seeing now was close to death and would not have the strength to conjure a rabbit, let alone control two of the most dangerous creatures ever to walk this earth.

If he got closer, he might be able to see through her veil, see her real features. He tensed, getting ready to spring to his feet.

She laughed. "Don't even think about it, shifter. This lid will be slammed in your face if you so much as twitch in my direction."

He didn't relax, just watched her through slightly narrowed eyes. "Where am I?"

"Way, way out in the country on a farm owned by friends. They've gone overseas and won't be back for months. By then, you'll be well and truly dead."

Not if he had any say about it. He still had his phone. He could feel it, digging into his side. "We *will* stop you, you know."

She snorted softly. For an instant, the veil fluttered, revealing cold blue eyes and a wisp of light brown hair.

"I doubt it," she said, amusement heavy in her voice. "All you've done so far is chase your tail. You don't know who or what you're even looking for."

"No," he agreed. "Unlike you, we don't work for the government and haven't had access to their computers and records."

She might have been a damn powerful practitioner

of the black arts, but her acting skills were nonexistent, because she twitched, telling him his guess was right. All they had to do now was find out if either Trina or Marline worked for the department that looked after kids, and they had their killer.

"Too bad you're locked in this water tank and can't tell anyone, huh, shapeshifter?"

He wasn't locked in yet. There was still a chance . . . if he was fast enough. He reached for his alternate shape, getting ready to change and spring. "Anyone egotistical enough to stand around and mock potential victims will make a mistake, sooner or later."

He shifted shape and sprang toward her in one smooth motion. She yelped and pushed back, and the lid arced downward. He caught the rim of the tank with his claws, scrambling desperately to get up. The lid crashed down on his head, stunning him, but he managed to hang on, his back claws scraping against the concrete as he tried to find purchase. She stepped forward, hands raised, fire burning across her fingertips. He snarled and slashed at her desperately, catching hair and cutting skin. She screamed, and fire leapt toward him. He dropped into the darkness, shifting shape as he fell. Crouching, he stared up at the hatch. It glowed white-hot, and for an instant, the air shimmered with heat. The fire would have killed him had it caught him.

The metal soon cooled, and darkness returned. Something heavy hit the hatch, and the metal, weakened by the fire, bowed slightly.

"Don't hope for escape, shifter. The hatch is locked, and there's a rather large rock sitting on top, ready and waiting to crush you should you have anything in those pockets of yours that might cut through metal. There's also a spell set to kill whoever tries to shift this rock in any way." She hesitated. "I hope you die a slow and ugly death, shifter. Goodbye."

Footsteps moved away. He waited until he heard the distant roar of an engine, then got out his phone and dialed Camille.

"I was getting worried about you, Doyle. Been more than an hour, you know."

"I know. Listen, we got caught by a spell over at Kirby's. I'm trapped in a water tank out in the country somewhere, and Kirby's alone at her place. You want to go get her, then come rescue me?"

"How the hell did you, of all people, get caught by a spell?"

"Stupidity." The last place he'd expected a spell to be set was in a handbag, though now that he'd had time to think about it, it *did* make sense. Kirby would have had to come back for her purse sooner or later. "It was just lucky I breached the spell and not Kirby." Because if it *had* caught her, she might be dead, not just trapped.

Camille sniffed. "I'll do a locating spell, then go get Kirby. Do you think she'll still be at her house?"

"God knows." He might be able to read her thoughts, but he didn't understand her well enough just yet to guess what she'd do when she discovered he was gone.

"I'd better do a locator on her as well, then."

"Just make sure you get to her first," he said. "Felicity Barnes, or whatever her real name is, will have guessed she was at the house with me. She's probably on her way there right now."

"Be patient, shifter. We'll get to you both."

Patience was one thing he usually had plenty of, except when it came to someone he cared about being in danger. He hit the wall in frustration, then began prowling the confines of his concrete cage.

KIRBY RUBBED HER EYES WEARILY. IT FELT AS IF THERE were a madman running loose in her head with a jackhammer, and the pain was so bad that she was in serious danger of throwing up all over the police station's worn gray carpet. What she needed was darkness, painkillers and coffee, and not necessarily in that order. But what she needed most of all was to get out of this place and find Doyle. She had a niggling sensation that he was in some sort of danger, and she had to get out of here and find him before real trouble hit. Yet getting out was the one thing that didn't look likely to happen anytime soon.

For the last three hours she'd been stuck in this box they had the cheek to call an interview room, answering endless questions about the events of the last twenty-four hours. It was obvious from the detectives' expressions and their repeated questions that they didn't believe her—that they knew she was lying. But what other choice did she really have? She couldn't tell them the truth. They wouldn't believe that any more than they believed her now.

She rubbed her eyes again, then looked up as the door opened. One of the two brown-suited detectives that had been questioning her came in and sat back down. He slid a coffee across the desk, then leaned back in the chair, regarding her quizzically.

She wrapped her hands around the foam cup in an effort to keep them warm and returned his gaze evenly. She had nothing to hide, except a truth he just wouldn't believe. And they couldn't hold her here forever, not without charging her with something. She just had to be patient. Just had to hope Doyle was okay.

"Tell me again," he said, voice monotone, bored. The total opposite of what his sharp brown eyes portrayed. "What happened when Constables Dicks and Ryan took you to the motel?"

She sighed. "I've told you that five times already. Do you want me to lie? Would you believe me if I did?"

"What I want is for you to tell me the truth."

"I have," she said, resisting the temptation to look away.

"And you have no idea what attacked your friends and the two constables?"

"No." She hesitated, swallowing. "I told you, I heard a strange noise, then the screaming started, and I just got out of there."

"And you've been on the run ever since?"

She raised an eyebrow. "Wouldn't you be?"

A hint of amusement touched his expression. "Maybe. So why go back to your house?"

"I told you, I'd left my purse back there."

He regarded her steadily, his brown eyes cold. Not buying a word, she thought with a chill.

"We spoke to your neighbors. They reported you being accompanied by a tall, dark-haired man."

She silently cursed the old biddy across the road. Chelsea had appointed herself the local neighborhood watch, and there wasn't a thing that went on that she didn't know about. Shame the old girl hadn't been on guard duty the night the *manarei* had attacked, she thought bitterly. Maybe Helen would still be alive.

"Did you ask her if she was wearing her specs at the time?"

The detective didn't bite, merely continued to regard her. "Were you at the house with a man?"

"Damn it, why is this even important? Something killed my friend and your constables, and you're sitting here questioning me about whether or not I went back to the house with a man? How much sense does that make?"

She slammed a hand down on the table. The sound rebounded sharply, ringing through her ears. She licked her lips, wondering why she suddenly felt so light-headed. Lack of food, perhaps.

The detective raised an eyebrow, the only sign he even noticed her outburst. "Did you know Helen Smith was insured?"

She blinked. "Yeah? So?"

"Did you know you were the major beneficiary of that policy?"

His implication took several seconds to sink in. Her gut churned, and she clenched her fists around the coffee cup so hard the sides collapsed and the hot brown liquid spouted everywhere.

She ignored it, ignored her burned hands, and stared at the detective. "You think that I . . . ?" Her voice shook with the fury she was barely controlling. "For money? For a few lousy dollars?"

"It's more than a few lousy dollars." His voice was dry. He regarded her for a second longer, then leaned across to the cabinet near the door and snagged some paper, offering it to her. "It's close to half a million dollars."

"I wouldn't care if it was a million. Or two. Or even three. I'd rather have Helen than any amount of money, believe me." She snatched the paper from him and wiped her hands.

"And yet you were in serious trouble financially, weren't you?"

Only because she still had three clients owing her for work she'd done on their houses, but there was nothing unusual about that, not in the building trade. "Last I heard, that wasn't a crime."

"But a half a million dollars would set you up financially, wouldn't it?"

She thrust her hands under the table, hiding the heat that was beginning to dance across them. Heat she was tempted, so tempted, to let loose. "If you're going to charge me, then charge me," she said, her voice so low and tight with anger it was little more than a harsh whisper. "If you're not, stop asking me stupid questions, get off your fat ass and start looking for the real killer. Because she hasn't finished yet."

He raised the eyebrow again, seemingly unmoved by her hostility. "She? What makes you think the murderer is a she?"

Kirby cursed silently, realizing then that he was goading her intentionally. She sat back in her chair. Pain twinged down her spine, but she ignored it and regarded the detective stonily. "I have a fifty percent chance of being right, don't I?"

"Yes, you do," he said. "But we both know you

know more than what you're saying. And you *will* tell me, Miss Brown. Eventually."

"If you're going to lock me up, you owe me a phone call." Who she'd call she wasn't entirely sure. Doyle was missing, and she had no idea how to get in contact with his friends. Or even if they'd be willing to help her.

"I have no intention of locking you up. Not yet, anyway. I do, however, recommend police protection."

She snorted. "Fat lot of good it did me last time." Besides, the last thing she needed right now was the weight of more deaths on her conscience.

"It's in the interest of your own safety." He looked around as the door opened and a blue uniformed officer stepped in, handing him a sheet of paper. He read it quickly and looked up, his expression grim. "Seems you have some high-powered friends somewhere, Miss Brown. I've been ordered to release you immediately."

"Yeah, right," she said, not believing him for an instant. The only person in power she knew was the janitor at the local municipal offices.

"You keep in contact and let us know where you're staying, or I'll have a warrant out for your arrest and your ass back in this station so fast your head will spin."

She blinked at the anger in his voice. "Then I *am* free to go? You're not kidding?"

"Not in anything I'm saying," he said, stony-faced. "Officer Duncan will escort you to the front desk. Collect your things and leave a contact number."

She rose quickly, then hesitated. What if the person who arranged for her release was the killer? What if she was walking out into another trap? "How will I keep in contact with you? Should I just ring the station?"

He handed her a business card. "I want to know where you're staying, Miss Brown, and I want a number where I can reach you at any time."

She nodded and followed the younger officer from the room. Five minutes later she was outside, blinking at the bright summer sunshine. It wasn't warm, not by a long shot, but at least the rain had finally cleared. Maybe summer would arrive back in Melbourne after all.

"About time they released you," a sharp voice beside her said. "This concrete gets a bit hard on old bones after a few hours, you know."

Kirby jumped and spun, calling to the fire as she did so. Only the voice belonged to a woman she recognized—Doyle's friend Camille. She was perched on the planter box at the base of the steps, silver hair gleaming in the sun, her expression a mix of amusement and curiosity.

"Scared you, huh? Because that's a pretty impressive play of energy you have dancing across your fingers."

Kirby clenched her fists and extinguished the lightning. "Did you arrange for my release?"

Camille smiled. "I called in a favor or two." She hesitated, her sharp gaze darting around. "We'd better get you out of here. Come along, dear."

She hopped off her perch and marched down the street. Kirby glanced briefly at the police station and saw the brown-suited officer watching her from a window. She stared at him for a second, then turned and followed the old woman. Right now, she trusted Doyle's friends to keep her safe more than she trusted the police.

"Where are we going?" she asked once they were in Camille's beat-up van and driving toward the city.

"We aren't going anywhere," Camille replied. "I gotta hunch I might be tagged, so I'm going to create a few illusions and drop you off at the nearest car rental."

"Why? I've got a car. I don't need another."

"Yes, you do. Your car's probably been booby-trapped, just like your handbag was. The killer certainly has had the time to do it. So you'll rent a car and go find Doyle."

"He's safe?" she said, a huge sense of relief sweeping through her.

"Madder than hell, but yeah, he's safe." Camille cast her a sly grin. "You've got yourself a good man there, you know."

"He's a thief," she muttered. She pulled her gaze from Camille's, heat creeping across her cheeks. "And he's not *my* anything. I barely even know the man." And yet here she was, trusting him, and trusting his friends. Why? She wasn't entirely sure, and that scared her more than the heat that simmered between her and Doyle.

"What he may have been in his life isn't what he is, remember that," Camille said. "And sometimes you don't have to know someone to love him. Sometimes love is just predestined."

Kirby rolled her eyes. "Yeah, right. Two souls fated to meet through time and the ages, and all that crap."

Camille's smile was wry. "Not one ounce of crap involved, believe me. Especially in his family."

She looked away from the old woman's knowing gaze. Part of her *wanted* to believe that such a thing as predestined love could exist, if only because it would mean that there might be someone out there for her, that she wasn't fated to spend the rest of her life alone—a fear that had been with her for as long as she could remember. A fear that even Helen's presence in her life hadn't eased.

But if she did let go, did take the chance and give in to the attraction she felt for Doyle, she was more than a little certain she'd end up getting hurt. In some ways, he reminded her of Helen. He seemed to like walking the edge, courting danger. He didn't seem the type to want to settle down, and that was the one thing she wanted above anything else. Stability. A place to call her own. "What's so special about his family?" she said eventually.

Camille laughed, a short, sharp sound of amusement. "Ask him sometime about his dad and his granddad." She glanced in the rearview mirror. "There's an address in the glove compartment, along with a satnav. Find Doyle, then hide somewhere safe for the night. Tell him to contact me when you're settled."

Kirby opened the glove box and found both the satnav and address. "What about the woman we're supposed to be looking for? Shouldn't we be trying to find her before the murderer does?"

"For the moment, it looks like the murderer has set her sights on you. Russell and I will continue the search tonight, and we'll see what happens after that."

She tucked the two bits of paper into her pocket and noticed Camille looking in the rearview mirror again. Tension ran through her. "Are we being followed?"

"Maybe. There's a large white car that appears to be mighty interested in where we're going." The old woman's voice was vague, her attention more on the mirror than on the road. She reached into her pocket and withdrew what looked like a string of diamond-shaped beads. "Take these."

Kirby did. They felt warm against her skin and pulsed slightly, as if alive. These were no ordinary beads, obviously. She frowned. "What are they?"

"A shield, of sorts. It won't work for more than a couple of minutes, but that's all you're going to need."

"Why do I need a shield?" She clenched her fingers around the string of beads and felt the sharp edges cut into her palm. An odd tingle of electricity ran through her.

"Because you're going to get out of the car and walk away as if you had all the time in the world."

Her frown deepened. "But isn't that a little dangerous? If we are being followed, they'll see me, plain as day."

"Not with that shield, they won't. It'll warp your appearance long enough to fool whoever's following us."

She glanced down at the beads clenched in her hands. Odd that something so incongruous could do magic powerful enough to change a person's appearance, if only for a few minutes. "When am I going to do this?"

"I'm going to run the next red light and do a quick left. I remember seeing a small café on my way to the police station. Walk down there, get yourself a coffee and a seat, and don't move for a good ten minutes. By then, I should be well clear."

Camille had slowed the van as she was talking, but the minute the lights ahead changed to red, she flattened the accelerator. The scream of the tires mingled with abuse from scattering pedestrians as she sped through the light and into the next street.

"I'm not stopping long," Camille muttered, "so grab your bag and get ready to jump."

Kirby undid her seat belt, the beads and her bag gripped in one hand and the other braced against the dash. The van slid to a stop. She wrenched open the door and clambered out—and barely had time to slam the door shut before the old woman was off again, burning rubber as she disappeared up the street. She had to have been a race car driver sometime in her life, Kirby thought as she headed for the café. She'd barely made it inside when a white sedan thundered past.

"Teenagers," a woman in the shop muttered. Kirby wondered what the woman would say if she knew one of those teenagers was at least sixty. After ordering a coffee, she sat down at a table near the back of the café and got out her phone, dialing directory assistance. Within a couple of minutes she had the number of the nearest car rental agency. She called them, got their address and made arrangements to rent a car.

An hour later she cruised down the Calder Freeway, heading toward Gisborne. According to the address she'd entered into the satnav, Doyle was being held on a farm sitting on the outskirts of the small township, close to the Macedon Ranges foothills.

Which didn't exactly make sense. If the woman was

powerful enough to transport someone Doyle's size so far, why was she bothering to kill the circle? Surely her powers were greater than all of theirs combined. And why leave Doyle alive? It was odd—especially since her actions up until now suggested she had no qualms about killing. Kirby drove through Gisborne, then slowed, looking for the right road. She turned right, and the asphalt gave way to dirt and dust. If there were any guards on this farm, they'd see her coming a mile away. She bit her lip and slowed, watching the numbers on the roadside mailboxes. They slowly climbed, as did the road. The gums huddled closer, casting deep shadows through which the occasional beam of sunlight danced.

Eventually she found number thirty-eight and pulled off the road, squeezing the small Honda behind the wattles that framed the driveway with a haze of yellow. After locking the car, she made her way toward the gate. It was chained and padlocked. She climbed over it and walked up the deeply rutted driveway. Cicadas sang around her, their noise almost piercing.

She wiped the sweat from her forehead and glanced skyward. Trees sighed in the breeze, but despite this, it suddenly felt a hundred times hotter up here near the mountains than it had in the city. She wished she had a drink. Her throat felt so dry it was aching.

A house appeared through the trees up ahead. It was long and ramshackle in style and looked somewhat forlorn. She slowed, wondering if anyone was home. Wondering if there were guards—or dogs. But nothing moved. The curtains were drawn across the windows, and no clothes fluttered on the washing line. She walked on carefully. No dogs barked or emerged from the shadows.

Where was Doyle? Surely he couldn't be in the house. It didn't look strong enough to contain a gnat, let alone a fairly ingenious thief. But if he wasn't in the house, where was he?

Doyle? she queried tentatively.

Warmth rushed through her mind, its force so strong it knocked her several steps backward.

Kirby? What in hell are you doing here? There was both relief and anger in his mind-voice. He obviously didn't want her here—or at least, he didn't want her in the line of fire.

And that annoyed the hell out of her. *I'll turn around and leave, if you prefer.*

No! He hesitated, and his sigh shimmered through her, a breeze so cool when compared to the heat of his mind's touch. *No. I'm sorry. It's just that the rock on the top of this tank has been spelled. It might be safer to call Camille in.*

Camille's busy, so you're stuck with me. Now, where are you?

In an unused water tank of some kind. One with a big rock sitting on it, if that's any help.

Her gaze swept the small clearing. No tanks this side of the house, or anywhere near what she could see of the big old shed behind it. He had to be on the other side, then.

Have you heard anything moving about?

No. The only sounds I've heard are noisy bugs and the occasional bird. That doesn't mean there isn't something here, though. Our murderous friend is not one to leave things to chance.

An understatement if ever there was one. She approached the house cautiously, trying to hear beyond the high-pitched call of the cicadas. A chill crept across her skin and, for an instant, her vision blurred. The world seemed to spin briefly, and she had to thrust a hand against the side of the house to remain upright. The dizziness eased, but her throat felt as rough as sandpaper, and no amount of swallowing seemed to help. She swiped at the sweat dripping down her forehead and wondered if she was coming down with something.

You okay? Concern shimmered down the link between them.

She nodded, then remembered he couldn't see her. *I'm just a little light-headed. Lack of food, probably. I'll be there in a sec.*

Just be careful. The cicadas have gone quiet.

She looked around. The sudden hush felt almost threatening. Another chill ran through her, and this time it was more fear than anything else. *I'm okay. I can protect myself, you know.* But she wondered who she was trying to convince—him or herself.

She pushed away from the wall and headed past the front of the house. Three tanks came into sight, one close to the house and two others near the shed. The one farthest from the house had a large rock perched on one end. She certainly wasn't going to be able to move *that* rock by herself. She'd have to draw on the energy of the day and the earth to help her.

Just don't do so when you're standing close, Doyle warned. *It's been set to explode the minute anyone tries to move it.*

Warning heeded. She turned the corner. *Found you.*

But the words were barely said when she came nose to stomach with the second-biggest dead guy she'd ever seen.

TWELVE

HER SCREAM FROZE SOMEWHERE IN HER THROAT, AND for an instant all she could do was stand there and stare up at him. He was monstrous. Not as big as the zombie that had attacked Doyle, but damn close.

Fear shot through her—not hers. Doyle's. *Kirby, run!*

His mental shout unlocked her limbs. But before she could react, the zombie threw a punch, his fist smashing into her jaw. It sent her flying backward. She hit the ground hard and her breath whooshed out, leaving her gasping. Blinking back tears, battling to breathe, she looked up to see the zombie launch at her.

She yelped and rolled away. The zombie hit where she'd been only seconds before, and the ground literally shook. He screamed in frustration and lashed out again, fingers clawing the air inches from her face. She scrambled farther away and called to the energy. It burned through her body, flashing jaggedly across her fingertips before she launched it toward the zombie.

Pain surged through her mind, and again her vision blurred. Suddenly there were two zombies burning up in front of her. Two pairs of flaming hands fighting the force of her net, trying to reach for her.

She scrambled backward, even though her net seemed to be containing the zombie for the moment. But there was no easy escape from the stench of the dying zombie's burning flesh, and her already churning stomach rebelled again. She threw up in the grass and felt like she was going to die. The madman in her head had obviously found some friends to help him, and the pounding was mixed with a weird buzzing that hurt so intensely she could barely see.

Kirby! Damn it, answer me. Doyle's mind-voice seemed hollow, as if it were coming from a million miles away.

She looked up, barely able to make out the water tank that trapped him. She felt so weak her whole body was shaking. She couldn't walk up there. She didn't have the strength to even stand right now.

Move to the back of the tank.

There is no back. It's round. For God's sake, tell me what's wrong!

I don't know. She blinked, but it didn't seem to help her blurry vision.

Can you see the rock at all?

I can see the hatch it's sitting on.

Face it, then move to your left. The buzzing was getting louder, becoming a tunnel of noise that was closing in around her. *Quickly.*

She closed her eyes and took a deep breath. Then she reached for the fire again. It burned through her, almost wild and uncontrolled. She clenched her fists, somehow restraining it, and opened her eyes. The water tank had become three white blobs dancing erratically on the hill above her. She blinked again, and the three became one, a blob of white surrounded by a darkness that was quickly closing in on her. She launched the pent-up energy, then the darkness encased her, and she knew no more.

THE SIDE OF THE TANK EXPLODED INWARD, SHOWERing Doyle with chunks of rocks. Concrete dust billowed, filling the small tank with a choking cloud that made it difficult to breathe. Coughing, he battered away the worst of the missiles and shifted shape, diving through the hole Kirby had created. It was a tight squeeze, even in his panther form. He pushed through, skinning his shoulders against the jagged sides of the hole, then ran down the slope to the house.

Smoke trailed skyward, and the smell of burning flesh stung the air. But the zombie was still alive, pulling its burning body along the ground, reaching with blackened claws toward Kirby. She wasn't moving, wasn't protecting herself in any way.

Fear shot through him. He didn't know what was wrong, but the warmth of her mind's touch had become an inferno of confusion and darkness.

He shifted shape, grabbed the zombie by the leg and wrenched it back and away from her. The creature snarled—a sound filled with anger and pain. It twisted and threw a punch. He ducked past it and grabbed the creature by the throat. Flames danced around his hand, burning his skin. He ignored them, shifted his grip, and snapped the zombie's neck sideways. Bones shattered, and the burning creature went limp.

He dumped the body on the ground and ran across

to Kirby. Kneeling, he felt for a pulse. It was racing, and her skin was hot, as if the energy she controlled was burning her up from the inside.

Let it be just a fever and not something more serious. He picked her up and ran for the house. She felt so hot he might well have been cradling a fire, not a woman. He had to get her cool, and fast, before she started convulsing.

He ran up the back steps and along the veranda to the door. Setting her down momentarily, he picked the dead bolt and carefully opened the door. No alarms sounded, and in the large living room–cum–kitchen beyond, there didn't appear to be any sensors. If the run-down state of the furniture and fittings was anything to go by, the small farm was little more than a holiday retreat. Which meant, with any luck, that they wouldn't be disturbed by nosy neighbors.

He picked her up again and kicked the door shut behind him. Light peeked past the drawn curtains, flushing a hazy brightness through the dusty room. He headed left, following the hallway, moving past several small bedrooms and a laundry before he found the bathroom.

He stripped off her coat and boots, then found the plug and began filling the bath with cold water. He dumped her in, clothes and all, fearing the fever and knowing the extra few minutes it would take to strip her could push her into convulsions.

Grabbing a towel from the cupboard under the sink, he wet it and quickly began wiping her heat-flushed face. She moaned, batting weakly at his hands, struggling to rise out of the water. Though her eyes were open, there was no life in their green depths, no awareness. She was delirious, fighting on instinct alone.

He held her down lightly and continued to wash her face. Lightning flickered across her fingers and jumped to his hands, webbing across his flesh. It felt like electricity but did little more than singe the hair on his arms. She must have spent most of her energy on the zombie and getting him out of the tank. For that, he was extremely grateful. In her present condition, she could have killed him without even realizing it.

But if it wasn't the energy she controlled causing this fever, then what was?

He didn't know, and it worried him. She'd been all right only a few hours ago. It had to be something serious to come on so fast.

He continued to wash her down, holding her head above the water once the bath had filled. Her struggles eventually ceased, only to be replaced by shivering. He touched her face, gently brushing away the wet strands of hair from her cheeks and lips. Though her skin was still hot, the heat was nowhere as fierce as before. Time to get her out.

He dragged her free of the water and stripped her down, quickly toweling her dry—a task he would have enjoyed any other time. But it was then that he discovered the reason for her fever. Her back was a mass of infected, swollen cuts—cuts that looked to have come from claws rather than a knife. The *manarei*, he thought, and swore savagely. Using her powers must have exacerbated the fever, made it flare hotter and faster. If he didn't clean the wounds quickly and stop the infection running through her body, she might die. He'd seen it happen before, and with people far stronger than she.

He ignored the thrust of fear and wrapped the towels around her. She *wouldn't* die. He wasn't going to let her.

There were two bedrooms downstairs, but the beds looked older than Camille and had little more than moth-eaten comforters covering them. Guessing the main bedroom was in the loft, he carried her up the stairs and was relieved to find that the bed there had both blankets and pillows. He flipped back the blankets and placed her stomach-down on the bed. The wounds were scabbed over, but red and bulging with infection. Why in hell hadn't she told him about the wounds? Frowning, he headed back downstairs and raided the cupboards until he'd found everything he needed.

Cleaning her wounds was a hell of a job. He was glad she wasn't conscious enough to feel any of it, though wisps of agony skittered through his mind— ghosts of the pain she'd be in if she were awake.

Once he'd cleaned the worst of the infection from her wounds, he packed them with what was left of Seline's healing herbs and wrapped them in bandages. He tucked the blankets tightly around her so she couldn't thrash around, then headed back downstairs to clean up. There was nothing much more he could do for her right now, other than to keep her fluid levels up and hope he'd caught the infection in time to save her.

* * *

THE FEVER BROKE CLOSE TO MIDNIGHT. IT WAS SOMEthing Doyle felt rather than saw—just a sudden easing in the troubled rush of pain running from her mind to his. He brushed the sweaty strands of hair from her closed eyes, running his fingers down to her lips. Her skin no longer felt consumed by fire, and her cheeks and mouth had a more healthy, rosy glow.

She stirred at his touch, murmuring softly, and reached with one hand for him. He caught her fingers, kissing them gently, then wrapped his hand around hers and held it close to his heart. He ached to do more. Ached to strip and lie under the covers with her, hold her lithe body close to his. But he didn't think he had the strength to touch her, hold her so close, and resist doing anything more. He wasn't made of stone, and the image of her naked body still hovered bright in his mind whenever he closed his eyes.

Besides, if ever they *were* going to make love, then the first move should be hers. It couldn't happen now, when she was still half delirious after the fever. It would have to be a conscious decision on her part; otherwise she'd still have excuses to run. And if it *did* happen, he wanted her aware of the commitment he was making to her with his touch and with his body.

As for his heart—he smiled wryly. *That* had been committed from the time he'd picked up her photo and stared into her incredible green eyes.

And to think he'd spent years insisting that lightning could not strike thrice in one family. How wrong he'd been! His old man would no doubt fall over with laughter when he found out.

He leaned forward, brushing a kiss across her sweet lips, and knew it was time to catch some shut-eye himself. Even as uncomfortable as it was lying on top of the blankets, fully clothed and aching with the need to make love to her, he knew he would sleep. Years of living on the wrong side of the law had trained him to catch rest whenever he could.

At least they should be relatively safe from discovery here in the old farmhouse. Felicity, or whatever her real name was, had said the owners were overseas, so they weren't likely to suddenly drop in. And if Felicity had the keys, then she was no doubt looking after the place for them, which implied no relatives. He'd moved Kirby's rental car into the shed, out of sight. As long as they kept the lights off, they shouldn't draw any attention from the neighboring farms, and he doubted Felicity herself would come back until she thought he was dead.

They were probably safer here than they would be anywhere else. Surely this was the one place Felicity would not think to look for them. Or so he hoped.

Closing his eyes, he went to sleep.

Movement woke him sometime later. He lay on his side, facing the windows. Outside, the wind had picked up again, and the nearest trees tossed and groaned. The old house creaked in response, shuddering slightly under the impact of the oncoming storm.

The bed shifted, and he turned around. Kirby climbed out, her pale skin almost ghostly as she padded naked out of the bedroom.

"You okay?" he asked softly.

She didn't answer him, and her thoughts were distant, almost sleepy. Frowning, he rose and followed her down the hall. She hesitated in the living room, then headed for the back door, battling to open it.

Sleepwalking, he thought. But why was she attempting to go outside? He reached past her, unlocking the door. She showed no awareness of his presence, and though her eyes were open, it was obvious she wasn't seeing anything beyond whatever images filled her dreams. He grabbed his coat to wrap around her once the dream had ended and followed her outside.

Sure-footed as a cat, she walked down the steps and out into the wildness of the night. The wind spun around her, snagging her warm brown hair and playing with it wildly. She raised her hands, as if reaching for the wind, then laughed, a soft sound of pleasure that sent a shiver of desire running through him.

She moved down the hill, a slender apparition barely visible in the darkness. He followed her past the black patch of grass that was the remains of the zombie, to the trees. There she sat cross-legged on the grass, staring up at the tossing trees.

Communing with the wind, he thought. He stopped behind her, watching the goose bumps chase across her pale skin, wishing he could hear what the wind was telling her. Wishing he knew why this was happening. She wasn't a storm witch, and talking to the wind was not something she'd been able to do before now. He knew that from her earlier thoughts and words.

She raised her hands again, as if reaching for someone. Sorrow ran through her, through him, and he knew without looking that there were tears on her cheeks. Maybe it wasn't the wind she was talking to after all. Maybe it was the ghost of her dead friend.

The wind played about her again, briefly including him in its wild dance. For an instant he heard the song—a gentle, melodious sound of love. Then it died, and Kirby collapsed sideways to the ground. He tucked his coat around her and carried her back inside.

She snuggled back under the blankets and sighed contentedly. He caressed her cheek, wondering if she'd remember her nocturnal journey in the morning. Wondering if she'd remember what the wind and her dead friend had told her—and whether she'd pass that information on to him.

He glanced at his watch. It was barely three o'clock, and he really needed to get some more sleep. But that wasn't going to happen just yet, especially if he tried to lie down beside her. Good intentions were all well and good, but right now he wanted her more than he'd ever wanted anyone in his life. Time, he thought, for a shower. A very *cold* shower. He bent and kissed her cheek, then headed into the bathroom.

KIRBY DREAMT OF WARMTH AND DESIRE. IT WRAPPED around her, pressed heat against her, providing a security, a tenderness, she'd never felt before.

She sighed and turned toward it. An arm wrapped around her, pulling her close. Breath whispered against her skin, sleepy and warm. Lips sought hers, lips that were tender yet sensuous. Lips she just wanted to keep tasting forever.

Desire ached through her, and in that instant, she fully woke, realizing with shock that it was no dream. She was indeed lying in bed and kissing a man. And she was naked to boot.

Her breath caught in her throat, and she pulled back abruptly. *We couldn't have,* she thought, not daring to open her eyes. Surely she would remember if she and Doyle had made love . . .

"I would certainly hope so," he said, his voice gravelly and sexy as hell.

She opened her eyes. His face was inches from hers, blue eyes filled with mischief, warmth and desire.

"How are you feeling this morning?" he asked.

"Fine." A little on the weak side, maybe, but that was probably due to lack of food more than anything else. She touched his smooth cheek, running her finger down to his chin. "You've shaved."

He was also fully dressed and lying on top of the covers, rather than underneath. Relief ran through her, though it was touched by an odd sense of disappointment.

His sudden grin sent another shiver of desire through her.

"I thought I'd better," he said. "Didn't want to give you whisker burn, if I ever got the chance to kiss you again."

She raised an eyebrow. "What made you think you were ever going to get another chance?"

"You're a woman. I'm a man. We're in a dangerous situation, and we're mutually attracted." He brushed a stray lock of hair from her eyes, his touch flushing warmth down to her toes. "The odds are on my side, you know."

"Pretty damn sure of yourself, aren't you?" she muttered. Trouble was, they both knew he was right.

"Sure of myself, yes." He stared at her for a moment, blue eyes intent, his thoughts suddenly troubled. "But sure of you? *That* I'm not."

It was pointless to say anything. Not when she was as unsure of herself as he was.

He caught her fingers and kissed them lightly. "Happy birthday, by the way."

Her birthday. Helen's birthday. This certainly *wasn't* the way she'd imagined she'd be spending it. Nor was he the person she'd thought she'd be spending it with. She bit her lip and blinked back the sting of tears.

"I haven't got you a present," he said, and rose swiftly from the bed. "But I can make you breakfast."

She blinked at his abrupt departure. "Great. And thanks."

"Your bag is in the bathroom. Don't get those bandages wet if you decide to wash."

Bandages? She glanced down and saw that she was indeed wrapped in bandages, from just under her breasts to her waist.

"Why am I wearing bandages?" she called after him.

"Long story. Get dressed, and I'll explain."

She cursed him silently but didn't move, for the first time taking in their surroundings. If they were in a hotel, it was certainly the dustiest hotel she'd ever seen. And the furnishings were so old and worn they looked ready for the dump.

She looked up, saw the pitched roof and the strings of cobwebs trailing the length of the room and frowned. If she didn't know any better, she'd swear they were inside the old farmhouse. But that didn't make any sense. Surely it would be too dangerous. Their murderer would come here, if only to make sure that Doyle was still in her trap.

She climbed out of bed and walked across to the window, peering out. Trecs swayed beyond the roof of the veranda, and on the ground to her left was a patch of black soil in a sea of yellow-green grass. *Zombie remains*, she thought with a shiver. They were definitely at the farmhouse, then.

She wrapped a blanket around herself and headed down the stairs. Doyle turned around in the kitchen as she entered the living room.

"Nice outfit," he commented, eyes bright in the hazy light. "I especially like the teasing flash of thigh as you walk."

She blushed and tugged the blanket around her. "Why are we still here?"

He turned away, stirring the contents of a bubbling pot. "Why are you not getting dressed?"

"Because I want answers."

"You'll get them when you get dressed."

He moved across to the freezer and opened the door, then hesitated and met her gaze. Heat trembled between them, burning through every part of her. She knew that if she so much as breathed his name right now, he would take her in his arms and make love to her, right here in this dusty old living room. And while she ached for his touch, she wasn't ready yet to give in to desire. Wasn't ready to trust that completely. So she tugged the blanket closer and remained silent.

He sighed. "I'm not made of stone, Kirby. I've made no secret of my desire for you, and right now, you're not making it any easier for me to keep my distance."

Her blushed deepened. "Sorry," she muttered and retreated. God, what had she been thinking? She'd only been with two men in her life, and both times it had been an uncomfortable experience. She'd certainly never been relaxed enough with either of them to parade around semi-naked. Yet here she was, draped in nothing but a blanket, padding about in the presence of a man she barely knew.

Maybe she'd lost some brain cells somewhere in the last twenty-four hours.

She found the bathroom. By the time she'd cleaned up and dressed, the smell of toast was drifting through the air, making her stomach rumble.

She headed back out and sat on one of the stools near the kitchen counter, sniffing the air appreciatively. "Smells good."

"Thank God for canned food and freezers," he said, sliding a plate of baked beans and toast across to her. "Remind me to leave some money behind for our unknowing hosts when we leave."

She raised an eyebrow. "A considerate thief?"

He smiled. "Always." He motioned with his fork to her plate. "Eat. You need to regain your strength."

She ate, discovering she was hungrier than she'd thought. He offered her a second helping, and she demolished that as well, feeling a whole lot better for it.

"Thank you," she said as he replaced her empty plate with a cup of coffee. "Now, answers, if you don't mind."

He sipped his coffee for a moment, leaning back against the sink and regarding her steadily over the rim of his mug. There was a touch of accusation in his gaze, and heat crept across her cheeks, though she wasn't entirely sure why.

"Why didn't you tell me about the wounds on your back?" he asked.

She frowned for a second, then remembered the

manarei attacking her as she'd tried to flee over the fence. "To be honest, I forgot. It was my leg that hurt, not my back."

"The wounds got infected and could have killed you. Next time, mention it."

A shiver ran through her. She hoped there never would be a next time. "What's that got to do with the reason we're still here? Shouldn't we go before Felicity gets back?"

"She left me here to die, so I don't think she'll be back for a while. It's too obvious."

She raised an eyebrow. "So we're here because it's safe?"

"No, we're here because you collapsed with a high fever, and I had no other choice but to stay here."

And he'd been worried about her, really worried. The thought warmed her. Maybe he wasn't just attracted in a physical sense . . .

"It's way beyond physical, and I've already told you that."

He had? When? She stared at him, more than a little troubled by his words. How could *any* emotion be real after little more than twenty-four hours? "Doyle, we barely know each other."

He shrugged. "Sometimes you don't have to know to care."

Care, not love. She looked away for a moment, inexplicably hurt by his choice of words. "Your boss told me I should ask about your father and grandfather."

"The old witch should mind her own business."

"Does that mean you're not going to tell me?" She

sipped her coffee and regarded him steadily over the rim of the mug.

He sighed again. "My father asked my mother to marry him after knowing her for precisely ten minutes. My grandfather waited a whole hour before he did the same with my grandmother."

She grinned. "You're kidding."

He shook his head. "Of course, in my mother's case, she thought my father was crazy, and at one stage she asked her brother the policeman to threaten him. But in the end she came around."

"And your grandmother?"

"Shoved my grandfather in the car and headed for Las Vegas as fast as her old Ford would go."

Her grin widened. "So this sort of insanity runs in your family, huh?"

"Apparently so." He considered her for a moment, then said, "Do you remember what happened last night?"

She blinked and wondered why he had suddenly changed the subject. It was almost as if he didn't want to talk about his family, but why? "No. What happened last night? I thought you said I had a fever."

"You did, but it broke around midnight. At three, you were up and talking to the wind."

A sense of dread ran through her. She wasn't a storm witch, and the wind had never talked to her before, so why would it be doing so now?

"Can you remember any of it?"

"No." She hesitated. Images ran through her mind, fractured remnants of dreams that had assailed her during the night. The wind had not featured in any of them, but Helen had.

She frowned. "I dreamt about Helen. Dreamt that I was dancing with her in the wildness of a storm. She talked to me."

Even though it sounded crazy, he appeared to take her dreams seriously. "Can you remember what she said?"

She sorted through the memories, trying to catch fragments of conversations. "She was trying to warn me about something—or someone. I'm not sure. And she said I had to open the present and perform the spell tonight, at midnight."

"Did she say why?"

"No. All she said was that I must complete the circle." Kirby frowned. The coldness was back in the pit of her stomach, and she was beginning to wish she hadn't eaten so much. "Why would she be asking me to perform a spell? I've never had anything to do with magic, even when she was performing it."

He hesitated. "Camille went to the morgue and checked out Helen's body. Her magic was gone, but unlike our killer's other victim, it had not been ripped from her but rather spelled away. Maybe Helen's final gift to you *is* her magic."

"No." She wouldn't—*couldn't*—accept such a gift. "Surely something like that is impossible." Yet life, time and again, had shown her *nothing* in this world was impossible.

Then the realization hit, and horror rushed through her. Oh God, *no!* Helen had died because of *her*. Had died because she'd spelled her abilities away and had nothing to protect herself against the *manarei*.

"It was Helen's choice—Helen's decision," Doyle

said. "There was nothing you could have done to prevent it."

His thoughts wrapped around her, offering sympathy and strength. She thrust them away angrily. "I could have been there. I could have stopped her."

"If you had been there, you'd be dead as well," he said, his voice sharp. "All you can do now is make sure Helen's sacrifice doesn't go to waste."

She swiped at the tears on her cheeks. He was right. She knew that deep down. But right now, she just wasn't ready to accept any of it, particularly the gift her best friend had died to give her.

"I don't want to do this," she muttered.

"You have no real choice now."

"Maybe." She looked away from the understanding in his eyes. She wasn't ready to accept that yet, either. "What now?"

"Right now, we're going to join the hunt for the remaining members of this elemental circle of yours."

His tone was still a little sharp. Maybe he'd heard her thoughts. "Camille didn't have any luck uncovering the whereabouts of the two women or tracking down Felicity Barnes, then?"

He shook his head. "I was talking to her earlier this morning. They've eliminated several past addresses for both women, and have a couple to go."

"And Felicity Barnes?"

As she said the name, an image ran through her mind—a skinny girl in jeans and a red sweater, brown hair tied back in pigtails, blue eyes ablaze as she chased her and Helen through the trees.

Not Felicity, but her best friend, Mariel, who liked to tear the wings off bugs. Mariel, who could make dead things come to life. She was their killer—of that Kirby was suddenly certain. The only trouble was, there was no Mariel on Camille's list.

"Camille's list obviously isn't entirely accurate," Doyle commented. "The fact that you're not on it proves that. And Mariel could easily have assumed another identity."

She nodded and rose. "Then let's get going." Because she had a feeling time was running out—for them, and for the next victim.

He didn't move. The window behind him threw his features into shadows, but his eyes gleamed blue fire. There was concern in his gaze and in his thoughts. "Are you really feeling okay? You were so sick yesterday, maybe you shouldn't push it today. It might be better—"

"Don't even suggest it," she interrupted. "I'm not staying here alone while you gallivant about looking for the next victim. Helen said I had to find her, and find her I will."

"Damn it, will you just listen to common sense for a change? I'm sure Helen never meant for you to run yourself into the ground."

"Helen *died* to keep me safe," she retorted. "I couldn't live with myself if I did anything less."

"You are the most annoying, aggravating, pigheaded woman I have ever met." His voice was so low, his words were little more than a soft growl.

She smiled sweetly at him. "And you love me for it."

He shot her a look that could have meant anything and pushed away from the counter. "We'll come back here tonight. I still think it's the safest place to be right now. And if you have to perform that spell tonight, then there's less likelihood of us being disturbed here."

She followed him out of the house, not wanting to think about the spell right now. "You have the new list of addresses?"

He locked the door and handed her the list and car keys. "I'll open the gate. You bring out the car."

She did. While he relocked the gate, she pulled the list out of her pocket and studied it.

Seven addresses—three for Marline Thomas, four for Trina Jones. Which of the two was the girl she had to save? It could take all day to check these damn addresses, and the feeling that they had to get to the fourth member of the elemental circle was growing more urgent.

The writing blurred briefly, the addresses merging into one. She blinked several times, wondering what was going on, then thrust back against the seat as one address seemed to leap off the page at her. Suddenly she wasn't staring at a piece of paper, but at a single-story, red-brick house. In the distance, a clock chimed, ten times. Confusion ran through her. It wasn't even nine yet . . . was she seeing the future? Or merely hallucinating? The vision blurred again, shifting closer.

In the shadows that loomed close to the house, a *manarei* crept. From the house came a soft humming—a sound that echoed through the fog, opening a window to the past. *Trina,* she thought, remembering the taste of her terror, the shaking of her hand, as the younger Trina had clasped her fingers and completed the circle. Remembering the force that had thrummed between them, through the other girls, to her, filling her until she was one with the elements, a being of energy, not flesh.

Trina, who had trusted her only at Helen's urging, was about to be torn apart by a creature sent from hell.

Unless they got there first.

THIRTEEN

DOYLE HAD BARELY CLIMBED INTO THE CAR WHEN Kirby sped off. He cursed, thrusting a hand against the dashboard to stop from being smashed against it, then grabbed his seat belt.

Her hands were clenched around the steering wheel, knuckles white. She drove too fast around a corner, and the car slewed on the gravel road, forcing him to grab the dash again to keep from being flung against her. There was fear in her thoughts, in her expression. What the hell had happened in the few minutes they'd been apart?

"Kirby, ease up a little and tell me what's wrong." He touched her knee. Her gaze jumped to his, eyes wide and filled with horror.

"I can't ease up. We don't have much time." She hesitated, barely even braking as she swung onto the main road. "I had a vision. Trina Jones, who lives in Port Melbourne, will be attacked by a *manarei* at precisely ten o'clock this morning unless we get to her first."

He didn't doubt her, just grabbed his cell phone and dialed Camille.

"Two phone calls in a matter of hours. This is something of a record, shapeshifter."

"We've got a problem, Camille. In just over an hour, Trina Jones of Port Melbourne will meet death at the hands of a *manarei*."

"*Goddamn it*—how do you know this?"

"Kirby saw it."

"You believe her?"

How could he *not* believe her? "Yes. I left my gun in my car, too, so bring some weapons with you."

"I will, though I think we have only a couple of silvers left."

"Then we'll have to make every shot count, won't we?" He glanced at Kirby. "How long will it take us to get there?"

She chewed her lip briefly. "Maybe an hour, depending on the traffic."

"It'll probably take me about the same, given I have to find the damn place," Camille said. "I'll meet you out front."

They made the trip in silence. Once they neared Port Melbourne, he grabbed his phone, brought up Google Maps, and guided Kirby through the maze of side streets until they reached Trina's. She stopped the car several houses up and looked at the clock in the dash.

"We've got five minutes. Camille doesn't appear to be here yet."

"No." He studied the small, red-brick house. Several large trees dominated the front yard, surrounding the house with shadows and providing perfect cover for the *manarei*. He glanced at her. "You stay here. I'll go scout."

"You can't confront a *manarei* without any weapons. Wait for your boss."

"We haven't got the time, and I'm not going to confront anything. I'm not that stupid."

"Then I'm coming with you."

She reached to undo her seat belt, but he placed a hand on hers, preventing her. He was so close to her that her breath washed warmth across his mouth. All he had to do was lean forward a little, and her lips would be his to claim.

"No." He watched the sexual awareness grow in her amazing eyes. Could feel it in the link between them, but it was a heat muted by caution. She wasn't ready yet to fully trust him, and it was more than a little worrying. Just because his father and grandfather had happy endings didn't mean he would. "You're on their hit list as well, remember, so you *will* stay right here. If I smell a *manarei,* I'll retreat."

She stared at him for several seconds, her expression troubled. "Be careful." She hesitated, then touched his face, briefly caressing his cheek. "Please."

Heat shivered through him. He forced a grin. "Being careful is the motto us thieves live by. I won't be long." Lord, it would be so easy to pull her close, to taste her lips once again. Easy, but the wrong thing to do right at this moment. He pulled away. "Please stay here."

She didn't reply, and her thoughts told him she wasn't happy. He didn't care about that. Her staying safe and alive was far more important.

He climbed out of the car and motioned her to lock the door. *At the first sign of trouble, you get out of here, okay?*

At the first sign of trouble, I'll come running. I'm not leaving you to face one of those things alone, so just forget it.

Damn it, he didn't have the time to stand here and argue, and the tone of her thoughts told him it was an argument he wasn't likely to win, anyway. Short of tying her to the car, there wasn't much else he could do.

I'll call if I need help. Just don't get out of the car before then, okay?

Okay.

Though her reluctance to agree was evident in her mind-voice, he had no real choice but to trust she'd do as he asked.

He headed toward Trina's house. The wind stirred, tossing his hair and murmuring through the two large gum trees in the front yard. He sniffed the air, but he could smell nothing beyond the warmth of freshly baked bread. He glanced at his watch. If Kirby's vision was accurate, the *manarei* had three minutes to get here.

He hesitated in the shadows filling the driveway. Someone inside the house was vacuuming, but it was a noise muted by the pounding thump of music. It would be useless ringing the front doorbell. Maybe he should check around the back.

He walked down to the gates and whistled softly. No dog came bounding up to greet him, so he went through. The music was louder back here, the beat so heavy it seemed to thump through his body. The yard was a sea of knee-high grass and weeds. Pines huddled along the rear boundary, throwing vast shadows across the rest of the yard. A perfect place for evil to hide, though as yet, he could smell nothing but dampness and mildew.

He ducked past the windows and moved to the far end of the house. Like the backyard, the narrow gap separating the two houses was a mass of weeds and shadows. As hiding places for evil went, it was even better.

He leaned a shoulder against the fence and waited. Minutes slipped by, and the thump of music abruptly died. Through the sudden silence came the sound of humming—an old disco tune he vaguely remembered but couldn't name.

Down the road, bells began to chime the hour. He glanced at his watch. Ten o'clock. Why wasn't Camille here? The last thing he needed right now was to face a *manarei* weaponless . . .

The foul touch of magic burned across his skin. Halfway down the side of the house, the air began to shimmer and sparkle, until it became a shower of golden lights. Through this, a shadow formed—became a *manarei*, eyes gleaming like freshly drawn blood in the shadowed half-light.

He reached into his boot and withdrew a small knife. It would be as useless as a toothpick against the creature, but right then, it was all he had. The *manarei* stepped free of the sparkle, and the shimmering air died away. It sniffed for several seconds, then it snaked its head around, glaring at him and hissing in anger.

"Care to play?" he said, waving the knife before him, as if it were a stick and the *manarei* nothing more than a playful dog.

The creature leapt. He waited until the last moment and slashed at the *manarei's* snarling, snapping jaws before diving away. He hit the ground and rolled quickly to his feet, spinning to face the monster.

It wiped a claw across reptilian lips, smearing black

blood across its leathery cheeks. "I will gut you with that little stick." The *manarei*'s voice was thick, its words barely understandable. "Then I will consume what little brains you have."

"Try it," he muttered, watching its tail rather than its eyes. When a *manarei* attacked, its spring came from its powerful hind legs. Usually, the tail was the first indicator of an impending attack.

Its tail lashed, and a split second later, the *manarei* launched itself. He held his ground again, cutting the knife across the creature's eyes before ducking under its claws and rolling away.

The *manarei* snarled in frustration. It hit the ground and sprang again, almost catlike in its agility. He scrambled to his feet, slashing desperately with the knife, then ducked away and spun, kicking the creature in the gut. It caught his foot and tossed him forward. He sailed through the air and hit the ground nose first, sliding through the weeds and skinning half his face.

The air screamed again. He rolled away and called to his alternate shape. In panther form, he leapt onto the reptile's back and bit deep into its neck. Blood gushed, thick and hot, its taste like acid in his mouth. The *manarei* screamed and reached back, grabbing him by the scruff of the neck and pulling him off. He slashed with his claws, tearing into the creature's face, but it tossed him away as if he were nothing more than a lightweight ball. He hit ground feet first, felt the tremor of the earth through his pads and looked up to see the *manarei* pounding toward him. He twisted around, saw the closeness of the trees and leapt for the nearest branch, scrambling up into the deep, dark recesses of the pine.

The creature snarled and pounded the trunk in frustration. The whole tree shivered. He dug his claws into the branch. *Manarei* weren't the best climbers, and right now, this tree was all that stood between him and certain death.

Where the hell was Camille?

Another tremor ran through the old tree, stronger than before. The *manarei* was thrusting its weight against the trunk, trying to bring it down. Doyle looked up. The top of the tree was beginning to rock ever so gently.

He shifted shape again and wrapped his legs around the branch, holding on for dear life. The tree began to sigh, pine needles rustling, as if stirred by the gentlest of breezes. The branch he was sitting on vibrated to the tune of the *manarei*'s pounding, jarring his spine. Not even a tree as old as this pine had the strength to withstand the might of an enraged *manarei* for long.

He reached to his left, plucking pinecones from the nearest branches, and began bombarding the creature. This did little more than seriously annoy it, but right then, that was exactly what he wanted. An enraged creature was more likely to stay put and not remember the woman it was sent here to capture. As long as *he* stayed out of its way, everything should be okay.

The *manarei* howled its frustration, then sunk its claws into the trunk and began to climb.

He dropped the remainder of the cones and scrambled to his feet. "You're not supposed to be able to climb, you bastard!"

The creature merely grinned, revealing long rows

of gleaming teeth, and continued to climb. Doyle shifted shape once more and worked his way farther up into the tree. But he was running out of room—and tree—fast. The branch beneath him snapped, and suddenly he was falling. Branches caught at his fur, tearing deep. He twisted, slashing wildly with his claws, trying to regain some purchase but catching only pine needles. He heard the guttural laugh of the *manarei* and the fetid warmth of its breath wash over him. Felt the air vibrate as the killing stroke closed in.

He twisted desperately, throwing himself to the right, away from the creature—away from the tree. He heard a sharp sound, felt something sting past his ear and the warm rush of blood, then he was hurtling uncontrolled toward the ground.

He twisted again, somehow managing to get feet first before he hit the ground, but the impact shuddered through him. For an instant, it felt as if every bone in his body had shattered.

He shifted shape and collapsed onto his back, eyes closed and mouth dragging in air. Death had come far too close, and for the first time ever, it had truly scared him.

Maybe because for the first time in his life it actually mattered whether he lived or died—because this time, he had something to lose beyond his life.

"About time you got here," he muttered, when he could.

"I've told you before not to tease them," Camille said, her voice sharp. "It's your own damn fault it got so close in the first place."

He opened his eyes. She was standing close by his

side, a gun clenched firmly in two hands and aimed toward the tree.

"Did you kill it?"

She gave him a scathing look. "Of course I killed it. I can shoot a damn sight better than you, boy. Now get off your butt. There should be another one of those suckers around here somewhere."

He rose slowly. Every muscle protested, making him feel a hundred years old. "Did you bring me a weapon?"

She pulled a gun from the waistband of her leather pants and handed it to him. "You've got two shots, I've got one. That's it, so make them count."

"I will." He checked the gun, then swiped away the blood running down his neck. Camille's shot had nicked his ear, but it could have been far worse had she not risked the shot and the *manarei* had gotten hold of him. "You'd better get inside that house and grab Trina. I'll keep watch—"

He stopped. Magic touched him, the same sharp, foul sensation as before.

Inside the house, someone began screaming.

KIRBY WAS HALFWAY DOWN THE DRIVEWAY WHEN her vision blurred. Suddenly she was inside the house rather than outside. In the rear of the house, in a room warmed by the summer sun, a *manarei* was creeping toward its unknowing victim. Fear clutched her heart and squeezed tight, and for several seconds she couldn't even breathe.

Then she was running up the steps, fingers alive with energy that she launched at the front door. It crashed open, but the sound got lost in the high-pitched screaming coming from the rear of the house—screaming that abruptly died. The glass surrounding the door shattered, sending deadly-looking slivers slicing through the air. She raised her hands to protect her face and ran through the entrance.

"Trina!" she screamed. The only reply was a whimper of fear—a sound she felt like echoing.

She pounded down the hall, her footsteps resounding on the wooden floors. She saw Trina on the kitchen floor, scrambling backward, one arm bloodied and dangling uselessly.

She saw the *manarei,* claws gleaming a bloody red in the morning light streaming in through the kitchen windows.

"Hey, reptile!" she shouted, sliding to a stop just inside the doorway. Its head snaked around, eyes narrowing when it saw her. She didn't give it time to think or react but raised her hands, drew in the energy of everything around her and unleashed it. "Fight this, you bastard!"

This time, the lightning didn't come from her fingers. It erupted from the floorboards and spun up the creature's body, binding it as it burned. The creature howled, fighting the energy that held him captive. Pain shivered through her, adding fuel to her already agitated stomach. But the energy itself couldn't kill a *manarei*—she'd learned that the hard way last time— and she didn't have the strength to contain it for very long. The madmen in her head were beginning their pounding with renewed vigor.

She ran to Trina's side. Her face was pale, skin clammy, gray eyes more than a little vague as they met Kirby's.

"Who are you?" she asked, her voice shrill, almost childlike.

"A friend from the past," Kirby said. *A friend you may not want to remember.* "Can you get up?"

Trina nodded, but her movements were weak, and she seemed unable to find any purchase on the floor tiles. Swearing softly, Kirby tucked her arms under the woman's shoulders and hauled her upright. Trina whimpered and went limp. Grunting under the sudden impact of her weight, Kirby gritted her teeth and struggled to keep them both upright.

The *manarei's* snarl made her look up. The net was flickering, its power fading. She reached desperately for more energy, and for several seconds the net flared brightly. Then the pain in her head kicked in full strength, and the net continued to fade. There was nothing more she could do to hold it. The *manarei* wrenched an arm free, its claws slashing the air, a chilling indicator of what it intended once it escaped.

Fear surged, threatening to stifle her. She had a minute, maybe less, to get out of here. The energy was fading fast, trickling away from her control as quickly as the time. She began dragging Trina from the room.

She'd almost reached the hall when the *manarei* partially broke free. Red-hot knives of agony tore through her brain, and she gasped, dropping to her knees, unable to hold herself up, let alone Trina. Tears filled her eyes, but it was the pain in her head that blurred her vision. She couldn't see. Didn't need to. The air seemed to scream with the *manarei's* fury.

She called desperately to the fire, but the knives dug deeper, burning white-hot through her entire body. She gasped, doubling over, pain pounding through her head and body. She couldn't move, couldn't even defend herself, much less Trina . . . *Trina*. Who was one of the five and had a power all her own.

"Trina," she croaked. "You have to wake up. You have to help me."

The other woman groaned. She was close to unconsciousness, but if she gave in completely, they'd both die.

The *manarei* screamed again. It was close, so close, to getting free.

She grabbed Trina's hand, squeezing hard as she slapped her face. Trina's eyes flickered open and, in that instant, energy surged between them, as fierce as the answering rumble from the ground. It was a rumble that became a roar so powerful the entire house began to shake and sway. *Earthquake,* she thought, and knew it wouldn't save them. Not unless the earth itself opened up and swallowed the creature whole . . .

She closed her eyes. Doyle's image swam before her, his blue eyes rich with warmth and caring—something she would not now have the chance to explore. *And for that, I'm sorry . . .*

The rumble died away. A door slammed open to her right, and footsteps approached. She sensed, rather than saw, that it was Doyle. But he stopped just beyond the room and, for several seconds, there was only silence.

Then he said, "Kirby, are you hurt?"

Relief swept through her, so intense it snatched her voice away. He was okay, and so was she.

"Damn it, answer me. Are you hurt?"

His voice was sharp with anger and concern, but right then, she'd never heard a sweeter sound. She shook her head, but even that small movement sent the madmen in her head into overdrive.

"The *manarei*," she ground out. "What happened to it?"

"If there's any sort of justice in this world, it's halfway to hell by now."

There was amusement in his voice, but why? She forced her eyes open and saw the reason. Half the room had been destroyed, and where the *manarei* had been standing there was a gaping, jagged hole. The earth really *had* opened up and swallowed the creature whole. Trina's doing. Thank God she'd managed to keep her conscious!

"Camille?" Doyle said. "I need your help in here."

Boot heels echoed across the floorboards. Doyle knelt beside her, something she felt rather than saw. Her vision was still blurry, and the pounding ache in her head was so bad she felt like throwing up.

"I thought I told you to stay in the car," he chided softly. Warmth brushed across her cheek as he thumbed away a tear.

"I thought I told you to call for help if you ran into a *manarei*."

His smile shimmered through her. He touched her hand, fingers twining around hers. "Touché. Are you able to move? We really have to get out of this house in case the rest of the place falls down."

She nodded carefully. Given the intensity of the quake that had shaken this place, there would no doubt be cops and ambulances on the way. The last thing she needed right now was another three-hour session with disbelieving police officers. "What about Trina?"

"We take her with us," Camille said from the doorway. "She's unconscious, so I'll splint her arm once we're safe."

Doyle grunted. "Don't suppose you've got anything in your magic box to cure a psi-blinding headache?"

Psi-blinding headache? There was a technical term for this sort of pain?

"Not on me, no." Camille said, her sharp voice close. "I have something back at the office, if you want to follow us."

"Is that safe with the murderer still on the loose?" Doubt echoed through his soft tones.

"Got no other choice. We can't exactly take either of them to the hospital right now, can we?"

"No."

"Then just make sure neither of us is tailed."

Doyle picked Kirby up and cradled her close. This time, she simply enjoyed the warmth of his arms around her, the tight sense of security that ached through her heart. She blinked against the day's sudden brightness, her eyes watering again. She swiped a hand across her eyes, but her vision was still blurred. His face was little more than a wash of skin and dark hair. But she didn't need to see him when his arms were wrapped so tightly around her, and his scent—a rich mix of muskiness, pine and masculinity—tingled across her senses and warmed her deep inside.

"Have I ever mentioned the fact you smell nice?" She leaned her head against his chest and listened to the rapid pounding of his heart. It was a rhythm matched by her own.

His laugh rumbled through her. "No, I don't believe you have. And this is a rather strange time to mention it."

"Hey, I might not get the chance to say it later."

His arms tightened briefly. "You'll have as much time as you want. I'll make sure of it."

She closed her eyes, not ready to confront the emotion so evident behind his words and in his thoughts. Nothing had ever come easy to her, so why should something as elusive as love? Especially now, when her whole world seemed to be tearing apart.

If he was following her thoughts, he didn't say anything, just opened the car door and placed her carefully inside. She kept her eyes closed. The darkness seemed to ease the pounding in her head a little.

He climbed into the driver's seat and started the engine. She listened to the rumble of traffic passing by and drifted off into a semi-sleep, only to jerk awake when the sound of the engine ceased. Blinking, she looked at the clock on the dash. Only twenty minutes had passed. It had seemed like hours.

The warm sunshine had given way to shadows. Around them, slabs of gray concrete stood like silent sentinels in an empty, filth-ridden world. A place where demons roamed, and the dull puddles of brightness provided by the lights dotted haphazardly across the roof did little to provide an air of safety.

For an instant, her fear surged. *Where the hell are we?* She blinked again, and their surroundings became a parking garage. Yet she had an odd feeling that what she had seen she would see again. Sometime in the near future, fate and she would meet in such a place.

Doyle's hand closed over hers. "You feeling any better?"

She carefully shook her head. "I feel like I'm going to throw up."

"That can happen when you overextend your psychic strength," he commented. "You want to be carried again?"

"I'm not an invalid. I can walk." Besides, if she risked another five minutes in his arms she might not want to leave.

"I wouldn't mind," he said softly.

She didn't answer, just got out of the car. Helen would have called it cowardice. She called it caution. She wasn't going to commit to anything she wasn't certain about, and right now that included Doyle.

The air smelled stale and was perfumed with the rich scent of rubbish and urine. Beer bottles decorated the far corners, scattered about like abandoned toys. "Nice section of town to have an office," she muttered, rubbing her arms against the chill in the air.

He shrugged and cupped her elbow, gently guiding her toward the elevator. "Most of the building has been converted to a shelter for the homeless. Our offices are on the top floor, and the rent pays for a lot of the meals."

She raised an eyebrow as he punched the button for the eighth floor. "So this Damask Circle of yours actually has offices here in Melbourne?"

"We have offices everywhere. Evil doesn't stick to a single country, you know."

"I guess it doesn't." Though it was something she'd never been forced to think about before now. "So, are we going to stay here rather than going back to the farmhouse tonight?" Disappointment twinged through her at the thought.

He leaned a shoulder against the wall and regarded her thoughtfully. The left side of his face was grazed, and blood had formed dried-up rivulets down his neck. But if he was in any sort of pain, she couldn't feel or see it. Maybe shapeshifters had a high tolerance to such things.

"Would you rather stay here?"

There was so little emotion in his words and expression, one would have thought he was asking the time of day. But she knew it was the very last thing *he* wanted. She also knew that he'd do it for her if she asked. It was a thought that was oddly warming.

She raised an eyebrow. "And how would you steal your kisses if we stayed with your friends?"

"I didn't exactly steal them the last two times." His voice was dry, and amusement glittered in his bright eyes. "Besides, there'll be plenty of time to worry about that once you're safe."

His dark hair was falling in unruly waves across his forehead, and a smile teased the corners of his full lips. Too sexy for *her* own good, she thought, and pulled her gaze from his.

Did she want to stay here? Part of her said yes; part of her said no. The only thing she *was* certain of was the fact that whatever was happening between them— whether it was merely a passing fancy or something more permanent—it wasn't going to be stopped by the presence of others. And in many respects, staying with his friends was the coward's way out.

Under any other circumstance, she might have grabbed at the chance *not* to be alone with him. As Helen had noted many a time, cowardice was her middle name. But it just wasn't a good move, tactically, for them all to be in the same place. At least if there were two groups, the murdering witch after her and Trina would have to expend a lot more time and energy to find them. And in doing so, with any luck she'd give them the chance to find and stop her.

"It's safer if we remain apart," she said eventually.

His smile crinkled the corners of his bright eyes again. "Admit it—you like being with me, don't you?"

Heat crept through her cheeks. "I will admit to nothing more than feeling safe with you."

"Well, that's a damn good start." He pushed upright as the elevator stopped and the door opened. "After you." He motioned her forward with a gracious sweep of his hand.

As they traveled upward, she wondered why her words seemed to please him so much. They certainly hadn't committed her in any shape or form. Frowning, she walked out of the lift. The corridor beyond was a bright, sterile white. Blinking at the light's harshness, she hesitated and rubbed a hand across her eyes. The brightness had invigorated the madmen in her head again.

He touched her elbow, lightly guiding her toward the only door visible. It opened before they got there, revealing a broad-shouldered, brown-haired man she would have classed the "all-American boy" type except for his eyes. They were a warm, rich brown, at once inviting and yet somehow chilling. This was a man who knew death more intimately than most.

"Russell, Kirby," Doyle said by way of introduction.

Her hand got lost in the big man's grip. She tried to ignore the little voice reminding her that this man was a vampire, a drinker of blood.

"Only animal blood," Russell said, his voice as rich as his eyes and oddly soothing.

"Oh great," she muttered. "Another one who can read my thoughts. Just what I need right now."

Russell grinned. "I promise not to play about in your mind."

She snorted. "Yeah, well, I guess if I'm trusting the word of a thief, I might as well trust the word of a vampire."

Russell threw a grin over the top of her head. "I've got the feeling she's not exactly sure of you yet, my friend,"

Doyle snorted. "Ain't that the truth."

Though his words were aimed at his friend, his gaze found hers. For the first time, she saw that he was annoyed by her refusal to trust him completely. Even hurt by it. She looked away, troubled by the thought, and brushed past the big vampire. The office beyond was a mess—desks littered with paperwork and files, bins overflowing with takeout containers, bookcase lined with empty beer cans and stained coffee cups.

"You've been in Australia how long?" she asked, raising an eyebrow as she glanced around.

"A week," Russell said, bolting the door shut after them. "Give or take a day."

She shook her head in amazement. They'd made this much mess in a week? "Another week and this place won't be livable."

Russell shrugged. "Another week and hopefully we'll be out of here."

His words reminded her of just how little time she had with Doyle. She bit her lip, blinking rapidly. Yet she refused to think about what such a reaction might mean. If she did, she'd have to admit what she felt, and she was far from ready for that.

Doyle touched her back, guiding her toward another doorway. "The boss in the interview room, Russ?"

"Yeah, tending to Trina."

Doyle opened the second door and ushered her through. This room was shadowed, the only light provided by several flickering candles. But it was cleaner than the first and smelled of lime and lemongrass rather than old burgers. Trina was lying unmoving on the large table that dominated the center of the room. Maybe she'd passed out.

Camille was standing next to Trina, bandaging her arm. "That headache still bad?" she said, without looking up.

"Yeah." Kirby walked around the other side of the table. Trina's skin was almost translucent, her gray eyes closed. Even so, she looked nothing like the child Kirby had seen briefly in her vision. Her hair was blond, her face was rounder, and there was a bump near the bridge of her nose, suggesting she'd broken it at some point. They could have passed each other on the street and never known it. "She going to be all right?"

Camille nodded. "She lost some blood, but I've given her some herbs to help with that. She's lucky, because the *manarei*'s claws didn't hit anything vital."

"What are you going to do with her now?"

"Keep her safe from the murdering witch, obviously." Camille finished bandaging, then stood upright, pressing her hands against her back and stretching. Bones cracked in the silence. "Kirby, you stay here and watch the girl, and I'll go find you some herbs for that head-ache. Doyle, you come with me. I need to talk to you."

The old woman whirled and departed. Kirby raised her eyebrows. "Is she always like that?"

"Abrupt and full of energy, you mean?" A smile crinkled the corners of his eyes again. "No. You've hit her on a mellow day. Usually, she's much, much worse." He hesitated. "Just call if you need anything. I'll be in the next room."

She nodded and watched him walk away. He left the door slightly ajar, and she wondered why he seemed so reluctant to leave her alone. Surely the witch wouldn't get them here, in a room eight stories up, with no win-dows and only one exit. A chill ran through her. But anyone who could use magic to control and transport the *manarei* probably wasn't going to be daunted by a lack of entry points.

She pulled a chair close to the table and sat down. Trina was beginning to stir, her eyes moving under her closed lids and her hands twitching. Dreaming . . . or remembering? Kirby crossed her arms and waited. Time ticked slowly by. The candles flickered and danced, casting warm shadows across the walls. In her mind's eye, they became ghostly figures dancing to some un-known beat, heralding in darkness and death. *Her* death, if she wasn't very careful.

She rubbed a hand across her eyes, trying to shake the growing sense of dread. It was just tiredness, just imagination, nothing more.

"You," a voice said into the silence.

She started and opened her eyes. Trina was staring at her, eyes wide and filled with fear.

"You're okay," she said, forcing a calmness into her

voice that she certainly didn't feel. "You're with friends."

She might never have even spoken, for all the notice Trina seemed to take.

"I know you," Trina said, voice low but edged with hysteria. "You . . . you killed Felicity Barnes!"

FOURTEEN

"WHAT'S THE PROBLEM?" DOYLE ASKED, DROPPING down onto the chair behind Russell's desk.

Camille propped a hip on the edge of the other desk, her expression grim. "We've been doing some more research into this elemental circle of Kirby's."

He accepted the coffee Russell offered with a grunt of thanks and tried to ignore the niggle of fear in his gut. "And?"

"According to legend, the circle was one of the most powerful forces of nature to evolve during the dawn of time. It's said that the gods themselves split the force into five elements, to protect the Earth and all its species. It's also said that if the elements were ever rejoined as one, the Earth itself would be torn apart." She grimaced. "Granted, that's not likely to happen, but joining the elements of earth, air, fire and water *would* certainly create a dangerous force of energy."

He frowned. "Not that dangerous, given that Kirby apparently *did* join the circle when she was eleven. All it did was put a monster who deserved death into a wheelchair."

"Not exactly true." Russell tossed a folder across to him. "I've been digging around in old newspaper articles. Eighteen years ago, a very centralized quake hit Melbourne. It happened in the dead of night, in the midst of a freak storm, and the only place to be hit was a certain government facility caring for unwanted teenagers. One building was partially destroyed, and a child was killed. Several other children were injured, as well as a nurse and a caretaker who were in the building at the time."

He opened the folder and flipped through the reports. There were images of destruction and terrified children. Kirby wasn't among them, though why he thought he would recognize her he wasn't entirely sure. He dropped the folder back onto the desk.

"So what you're saying is that she caused this quake by forming the circle?"

Camille nodded. "But because she was one of five, the power was, in a sense, muted—or at least controlled. But imagine that power all placed in one body."

"It would be damn near unstoppable," Russell intoned. "And that's what we're facing, buddy boy."

"Not yet, we're not. Kirby and Trina are still alive." And would remain that way, no matter what the cost—or what he had to give up.

"Yes," Camille agreed. "But two others are dead, and while Helen managed to thwart the witch's plans to grab her power, Rachel Grant did not. I have no doubt this is the reason she was able to summon and control two pairs of *manarei* as well as the zombies. No witch, light or dark, could perform spells that strong so close together without suffering some side effects." She shuddered. "No wonder Seline was so determined to stop this."

Doyle rubbed a hand across his eyes. There might

have been three of them, but the odds, it seemed, were decidedly on evil's side. "Have we any idea what abilities she's stolen?"

"Given what happened inside Trina's house, Trina is obviously earth, and it would have been her power that caused both quakes. From what Kirby has said and what we've discovered, it seems she is the binder, so that leaves fire and water."

"The witch tried lashing me with fire when she locked me in that water tank," he murmured. "So she's definitely got that one. What power does water give her?"

Camille shrugged. "She could call in ice and freeze. She could change the course of any nearby water."

"And Kirby? Can she do anything more than call a web of lightning to her fingers?" Because if she couldn't, she was seriously outgunned.

"There's not much known about binders, because they're extremely rare." Camille's expression was one of annoyance. She *hated* not knowing. "In theory, she should only be able to use the power of all the elements when they are bound together, but it's obvious she can draw energy from everything around her."

"What about the wind?" he asked.

Camille frowned at him. "What about it?"

"Well, she sleepwalked the other night, and when I questioned her about it the following morning, she said she talked to Helen through the wind," he said. "And she's said that Helen used to read their future in the wind's whispers. I didn't think that was something storm witches could do."

"It's not—but it *is* something an air element could do. Which would explain why she was number one on the witch's list. Air is perhaps one of the most powerful elements, because a person cannot live without it." Camille frowned. "I wonder what she did with her powers? It's a damn unusual thing to do, I'm telling you that."

He sipped his coffee for a moment, remembering the words of a ghost. "Is it possible to gift your powers to someone else?"

"Not usually. I've seen it happen once, but the two people were related. Why?"

"I think that's what Helen intended to do when she stripped her powers. She wanted to give them to Kirby."

"What?" Camille's voice was gratingly sharp. "Why would you say that?"

"Because her spirit still roams this Earth—"

"Well, it would, wouldn't it?" Camille interrupted harshly. "She killed herself, after all."

He ignored her and continued. "Helen has talked to Kirby twice now that I know of. She wants Kirby to perform a spell of some sort tonight, and she left a box that tingles with magic."

"Good or bad?"

"If it was bad, I would have destroyed it. You know that." He hesitated. "Have you had the chance to look at the other gift that was left for her?"

"Yeah. It wasn't only a tracker, but another transport spell. It was well shielded, which is why you couldn't sense anything."

"Were you able to trace the magic back to its source?"

"No. The witch is too cunning for that. The minute I tried, the spell disintegrated."

Doyle scrubbed a hand across his eyes. Luck, it

seemed, wasn't on their side at the moment. "Kirby and Helen aren't related, so why would Helen think she could transfer her powers?"

"We don't know that they aren't," Russell said. "They were left at different hospitals when they were born. Their birth certificates simply have 'unknown' when it comes to the name of their parents. They *could* be related, for all we know."

Camille's gaze cut back to him. "Doyle, are you going to let her perform this ceremony?"

"Yes." If only because Helen's abilities might be her last hope of survival if the Circle failed her.

"Then you're going to have to do a protection circle." She twisted around and grabbed a paper and pen. "You do know how to do that, don't you?"

"How to make them, and how to destroy them. You can't feel magic and not know the ins and outs of it, Camille."

"Good." She handed him a note. On it was an address and what amounted to a grocery list of magical ingredients—everything he needed to make a circle of protection, and a little bit more.

"Go to the bathroom and clean yourself up, then head out and get that stuff," she continued. "Russell, you keep digging and see if you can find the identity of the kid that was killed in the quake. After that, see if you can find anything else on this Felicity Barnes or Marline Thomas. One of them has to be the killer—I'm sure of it."

Doyle stood, tucking the note into his jeans pocket. "Keep an eye out, you two. The wicked witch from the west hasn't had much trouble finding us so far."

"Don't you be telling *this* old witch her business. Get out of here, before I'm tempted to box your ears."

He grinned and glanced toward the interview room. Kirby was as safe here as she would be anywhere. Even so, he had an odd feeling that he didn't dare leave her side long or all hell *would* break loose and claim her. He headed quickly out the door.

KIRBY STARED AT TRINA FOR SEVERAL SECONDS. She'd killed? Was that why she'd locked those memories so far away?

Just for an instant, the fog stirred. Once again she felt the thrum of power flooding through her, through the room, until the whole world seemed to be buzzing with energy. She saw the earth itself rise, dancing around Trina's feet, as if in exultation. Heard the clash of thunder and the icy thrust of rain lashing through walls, through *them*—right through them, as if they were beings of energy, not flesh. But the daggers of ice and water cut the others. Cut the caretaker. Then the buildings began to collapse, trapping the very people they were trying to save . . .

Tears stung her eyes. She raised a hand against the horror, and the memories momentarily fled. "It was an accident," she whispered hoarsely, her stomach churning. "I didn't mean for her to die. I just wanted to stop *him*."

Trina edged farther away. "You forced us to join hands. You and that other one—Helen. You did something to us, made us feel the power, the energy. Made the earth tremble at my feet."

"No, that was all of us." She'd never had the power

to stir the earth or call to the rain and the storms. It had come from the circle itself, from the power of the five of them. "It wasn't me."

It was fate that had loaded the weapon and placed them all in that one place. All she'd done was aim the gun and pull the trigger. Did that make her a murderer? She didn't *know,* and it scared the hell out of her.

"You killed her," Trina continued, her soft voice edging closer to hysteria. "It's your fault, not mine. I didn't want any part of it."

"Would you have rather suffered the attentions of the caretaker night after night?" she snapped back, suddenly angry. "It was you and the others who pleaded with me and Helen to do something—to somehow stop him."

"Kill *him,* not the others. I saw her, you know. Saw her squashed, saw the blood . . ."

Trina's voice faded. Kirby closed her eyes, but there was no escaping the images now. The old dormitory walls hadn't been built to withstand the force they'd summoned that night, and a good half of the building had collapsed, trapping many children still in their beds. Felicity had been one of them.

Felicity, who'd been Mariel's best friend and co-conspirator.

"*You* killed her, not me!" Trina intoned shrilly into the silence.

You killed . . . The words seemed to echo through the silence. Guilt washed through Kirby—guilt that was both old and new—and yet surely she couldn't bear the entire burden herself. She may have been the one who called the power into being, but she was still only one of five. She opened her eyes, staring at Trina's fear-stricken face. Saw the haunted look in her gray eyes, the edge of madness lurking close.

They'd all been terrified that night. They'd raised a power that shook the very world around them, and because of that, a child had died and many more had been injured.

She'd coped by wiping out the memory of that place and pushing the pain, the guilt and the images of destruction so far back into the recesses of her mind that even now, when it mattered most, she still couldn't remember everything that had happened. And she'd retreated, not so much mentally as physically, afraid of taking a chance lest she hurt anyone else.

Helen, who'd also been a part of that circle, had reacted completely the opposite. She became a wild child, afraid of nothing, willing to push the limits in all that she did.

Trina, it seemed, had spent her years seeking someone else to take the burden of her guilt, and if the look in her eyes was anything to go by, she hadn't been all that successful. She wondered how intimately Trina knew the local psychiatric wards. She had a feeling the answer might be very.

"It was an accident," she murmured softly, firmly. They hadn't meant to kill anyone but the caretaker, and had failed even in that. But they did stop him and, in the end, maybe that was the one fact they all had to cling to.

"How many lives did we save that night, Trina? I can remember you saying that you'd rather kill yourself than have that man touch you again. How many of the others felt like that, do you think?" Helen had, which was what had moved Kirby into action in the first place.

"We killed—*you* killed," Trina whispered hoarsely. "That power . . . it ate me, you know. Swept through me like I wasn't even there, like I wasn't even real. It was horrible . . . *horrible*. And it was you who did that to me. You and her."

The madness was brighter in her gaze. Her eyes were wide, staring, as if she was seeing the past rather than the present. Maybe Kirby's sudden reappearance, combined with the *manarei*'s attack, had snapped whatever tenuous hold Trina had on sanity.

Camille swept into the room and moved toward Trina. "Now, don't go making a fuss," she said, her normally edgy tones gentle, almost calming. "I just got that arm of yours all neatly fixed."

"Who are you?" Trina thrust away from Camille's hand, sliding down to the far end of the table. For the first time, she seemed to take in her surroundings. Her face went white, and her fear became something Kirby could almost smell. "Why am I here? Who are you people?"

"Trina, calm down," Kirby said.

Trina made a violent chopping motion with her hand. "*You* calm down! Better yet, you go to *hell*. I want to know what's going on!"

"Need some help?" Russell said, his large frame filling the doorway.

Camille sighed. "Afraid so. Calm her down. Better yet, put her to sleep."

"Don't you touch me!" Trina cried. She teetered on the edge of the table, watching Russell with wide, frightened eyes.

Russell didn't move, just narrowed his gaze slightly. Trina gasped, then her gaze went blank, and she slumped to the table. Camille caught her before she could hit her head, and she made sure her injured arm wasn't taking the weight of her body.

Kirby glanced uneasily at Russell. "You did that? How?"

"Mind control. It's an ability most vamps have, in varying degrees of strength. I merely calmed her fears and put her into a trance. She'll remain that way now, until I suggest otherwise."

She eyed him warily. "You did promise to keep out of my mind, you know."

He grinned. It was oddly boyish and very charming. "And I always keep my word. Especially when that someone is a friend of someone I care about."

"Good," she muttered and rubbed her eyes, wondering again at the sanity of trusting a vampire. "Where is Doyle, by the way?"

"Gone shopping," Camille said, voice sharp enough to nail wood to a wall. "That headache still bad?"

She nodded, though in truth, it had ebbed a little. Camille muttered something under her breath, then walked across the room to the urn and filled a mug with hot water. Into this, she tipped what looked like dried-up leaves.

"Drink this tea. It'll ease the immediate effects of the headache. I'll make up some more that you can take with you."

Kirby accepted the offered cup and sniffed it warily. It smelled faintly of lemongrass and lime, but there were other scents mingled among those two that she knew but couldn't name. Helen had used them sometimes in the past.

Camille sat opposite her. "Did Trina say anything? Did she remember anything that might help us?"

Kirby sipped the tea, finding the taste wasn't as bad as she'd expected. "Not really. But she did shake loose some of my memories. It can't be the real Felicity Barnes who's working for the government. Felicity died that night we formed the circle."

Camille raised an eyebrow. "So you can remember that now?"

She nodded. "Part of it. I have no idea who Marline is. She certainly wasn't one of the five. There was a Mariel, though."

"Marline and Mariel are awfully similar names," Russell commented. "Maybe when you did the reading you just got the spelling wrong."

"Possible," Camille muttered. "Quite possible. Anything else?"

Kirby took another sip of tea, considering all the bits and pieces that had floated through the fog in the last day or so. "Mariel was a witch. She could make dead things come to life."

"*What?*"

She nodded. "Both Helen and I saw her do it on several occasions. She used to kill bugs, then bring them back to life." And make the dead things chase them. She shuddered, remembering again the horror of it all. But in many respects, if it weren't for those bugs, neither she nor Helen would have discovered the full potential of their abilities. "It wasn't a trick, either."

Camille and Russell shared a glance. "At least that explains the zombies," Russell said.

"Yeah, but it's an ability that usually runs in families and has to be taught. These kids were all orphans."

"Helen and I figured out how to use our abilities," she said. "Why couldn't Mariel?"

"She could have taught herself to raise small things like bugs easily enough. There's not much skill needed for that. But raising anything larger requires finesse. It can sometimes take half a lifetime to refine the skills needed to raise something as large as a human."

"I hear a *but* in all that," she said, when Camille hesitated.

"That's because there *is* a second option. It involves invoking the spirit of the dead and drawing them into your body—making them a part of your world, and you a part of theirs."

A chill ran through her, and her hands began to shake. She set the tea down and clasped her fingers under the table. It didn't stop the growing feeling of dread, however. "Felicity Barnes, the girl who died in the quake that hit the night we raised the circle? She was Mariel's best friend. Mariel swore she'd get her back, no matter what it took or how long it took."

Camille cursed. "Did you ever see her do it?"

"No. We were all separated for a few months after the quake, shifted to various other homes or into foster care. Helen and I only remained together because we ran away."

"Damn." Camille looked at Russell. "Try doing a search for Mariel Thomas and see what you come up with. I've got a feeling she and Felicity Barnes might now be one and the same."

Russell nodded and moved back into the other room. Kirby stared at Camille incredulously. "Meaning Felicity's spirit might be living in Mariel?"

Camille nodded. "If she's only recently performed the summoning, it would certainly explain the sudden need for revenge."

"But . . ." Her voice faded. She swallowed some tea to ease the dryness in her throat and tried again. "How is something like that possible? Felicity died eighteen years ago! Don't try to tell me her spirit has been hanging about all that time waiting to be resurrected."

"It depends. Some spirits move on and get reborn. Some remain on this Earth, compelled to right some wrong. And a very few are swept into a void some might call hell, destined to remain there for eternity unless recalled by the forces of darkness." Camille hesitated, her blue eyes sympathetic. "Where do you think the legends of demons come from? They are merely twisted souls who have been in that void for a very long time."

Kirby rubbed her head. She was having a very hard time taking all this in. Witches she could cope with. After all, Helen had been one. Vampires and shapeshifters she could learn to handle. But a void containing dead spirits who became demons was going a little too far beyond comprehension. "I don't think I can handle all this right now."

"You might have no choice," Camille said, her voice still sympathetic and yet holding a hint of steel.

"You have to know what you're facing in case the rest of us fail."

She closed her eyes. She didn't want to think about them failing. Didn't want to think about Doyle dying while trying to protect her. She'd sworn eighteen years ago to never be the cause of another death. If it came down to a choice between his life and hers, there would be no contest.

She sipped her tea, but all it was doing now was agitating her stomach. She put it back on the table half-finished. "Why would anyone in their right mind raise the spirit of a person who'd been dead for eighteen years?"

"She may not have been in her right mind, and if Felicity's spirit is in her, she sure as hell won't be now."

She stared at Camille for a second, a chill chasing down her spine. "What do you mean?"

"I mean it's pretty obvious that this woman is not just after the power of the circle. She wants you all to suffer, as Felicity must have suffered when she was crushed all those years ago. All you have to do is look at the way she killed Helen and the way she attempted to kill Trina. And remember, Felicity's spirit has had eighteen years in hell to plot its revenge."

"Oh great, so I have two nuts after me rather than one. They're just neatly packaged together."

"I'm afraid so."

Kirby rubbed her arms. "What about Rachel?"

Camille frowned. "What about her?"

"Well, a *manarei* wasn't sent after her, was it? So why not?"

Camille hesitated, then half shrugged. "It is possible she's more violent with those she holds responsible for her death. Helen and you were the ones who formed the circle, and it was Trina's power that killed Felicity."

Awareness flowed through her. Doyle had entered the other room. She turned and watched him approach.

His gaze met hers, and relief flicked through his thoughts. He'd been worried about leaving her, she realized then, even if she was with his friends. The thought made her heart do an odd little dance.

"Who's neatly packaged together?" he asked, stopping in the doorway.

Camille rose with a grunt. "Kirby can fill you in. Grab some names and addresses off Russell and keep looking for this Marline or Mariel Thomas. But I want you somewhere safe before sunset, understood?"

He nodded and motioned toward Trina. "What about her?"

"Russell's best suited to look after her. At least he can keep her controlled and quiet. I want you to keep in regular contact, understand?"

"Understood."

Camille's sharp gaze momentarily pinned Kirby. "I'll go get those herbs. Just make yourself a tea before you go to bed. It should take care of any lingering aftereffects."

Doyle moved to one side as Camille pushed past. "You feeling any better?" he asked.

Kirby shrugged. "I honestly don't think that's going to be possible until this whole mess is finished. Why does Camille want us tucked away before sunset?"

"A dark witch's powers tend to be greater after sunset."

She frowned, confused. "But she attacked you yesterday and Trina today. Both times were during the day."

"Yeah, and it's a sign of her strength, because she'll definitely get stronger at night." He walked around the table and held out a hand. "Come on, let's get moving."

She hesitated, not trusting the sudden hint of mischievousness in his expression. He wiggled his fingers impatiently. Knowing he was up to something, but not entirely sure what, she placed her hand in his. He pulled her to her feet, then pulled her close, amusement and desire darkening his eyes.

"Won't dare to steal kisses with my friends around, huh?" he murmured, his breath washing across her cheeks and setting her whole body alive. "Never tempt a thief with a statement like that."

His mouth captured hers. She meant to protest, meant to push him away, but the moment his lips touched hers all resistance seemed to melt away. All she could think about, all she wanted, was him. She wrapped her arms around his neck and pulled him closer still. Her breasts were pressed hard against his chest, and she could feel his strengthening desire. He deepened the kiss and, for one moment, it felt as if he were delving deep into the very heart of her. Her pulse raced and her whole body was on fire, every nerve ending gloriously alive and aching with the need for his touch. For him.

Then he pulled away, his breathing harsh, eyes filled with such heat she felt it clear through to her toes. "It hasn't faded, Kirby," he said softly.

"No." Quite the opposite, in fact.

"Nor will it, you know."

"I know."

He squeezed her fingers. "Shall we go?"

She raised an eyebrow. "Got the fast deflation model, have we?"

He grinned and brushed the hair from her eyes, his fingers trailing heat across her skin. "No. But I *have* got a coat. Wonderful inventions, coats. They hide many secrets."

"No doubt half of them stolen," she said dryly.

He grinned and didn't deny it. "I might even let you investigate one day, if you play your cards right."

"I wait with breathless anticipation."

His gaze found hers as he led her from the room. "So do I," he murmured. "So do I."

Heat crept through her cheeks. She pulled her gaze from his and knew, with absolute certainty, that if she survived the night without making love to him, it would be nothing short of a miracle.

FIFTEEN

THEY SPENT THE REST OF THE DAY CHECKING OUT THE
addresses of the various Marline and Mariel Thom-
ases, only to come up empty every time. They were all
either too young or too old. No one matched the image
of the child in her mind.

Not that *that* meant anything, Kirby thought sourly.
She closed her eyes, leaning back in the car seat. Trina
had looked nothing like her memories, either, so why
Kirby was so certain she would recognize the witch
was a puzzle.

Doyle climbed into the car and shoved several plastic bags onto the backseat.

"You've got enough food in those bags to feed an
army," she said with amusement. "You planning to
settle in for the long haul?"

"No, because it wouldn't be safe. I am, however,
starved."

"Does that mean you're planning to cook?"

He raised an eyebrow. "Can you?"

"Sort of." Helen was the expert in that field. Kirby
had only ever dabbled, and most of the time with disas-
trous effects. Which was why she'd been relegated to
cooking only two nights out of seven.

" 'Sort of' will ruin my soufflé."

"You're kidding . . . aren't you?"

He grinned and started the engine. "I certainly am. I can't stand soufflé."

She rolled her eyes. "So what *are* we having?"

"You'll just have to wait and see."

"You can be very irritating, you know that?"

He flashed her another grin that sent her heart into cartwheels. "Thank you. It's a skill I work hard at."

He pulled out into the traffic. She studied his profile, her artist instincts stirred by the sheer perfection of it. She'd paint him one day, though no doubt from memory. Pain twinged through her. She bit her lip and wondered again why he seemed so attracted to her. Was it just the danger pulling them close, or was there something more? He had the looks, and no doubt the money, to pick and choose as he pleased. Surely an unwanted brown mouse from Nowhereville, Australia, didn't have a hope of holding his interest for long.

And that was what was holding her back, she realized. As much as she wanted to make love to him, she was afraid that once she did, she'd want more. Want the whole nine yards. And she just couldn't believe he'd ever be content to stay with someone like her. Damaged goods, Helen had once called them both. Thieves didn't take damaged goods—they only went after the very best.

"I *am* going after the very best," he murmured.

She briefly closed her eyes. *If only I could believe you*.

But that was the trouble. She couldn't believe him. Couldn't trust that he meant anything he said. She'd learned the hard way that the world was filled with thieves—some, like Doyle, stole artifacts, jewelry and no doubt the occasional heart. Others, like the caretaker, stole innocence.

"Don't you dare put me in the same category as *that* animal," he said, voice cold and flat. "We're nothing alike."

"I know, and that's not what I meant." She hesitated, not really certain just where those thoughts had been headed, other than the fact that if Doyle stole her heart and then walked away, she'd never recover. Not without Helen around to pick up the pieces.

Tears stung her eyes. She blinked them away and risked a quick glance at him. His face was as stony as his thoughts. She'd annoyed him.

Hurt him.

And that was something she had never meant to do. "I'm sorry," she said softly. "It's just . . . I just need time." *Time to know you. Time to know me.* In two brief days, her life had irrevocably changed, and even the memories of her past had proven to be false. How could she possibly believe her feelings in such a situation? How could *he*? "You can't just walk into my life and expect me to be swept away on a tide of emotion. It's not that easy."

"It is that easy—if you trust me."

But that's the whole problem. I can't trust. She'd picked up most of the pieces and had continued on with her life, but her ability to trust people—and especially men—had never fully recovered. Somewhere deep inside her there was still a scared little girl hiding under the covers and listening to the sounds of trust being shattered.

She rubbed her forehead. Her headache was beginning to come back. "I really don't want to discuss all this right now."

He glanced at her, frustration evident in the blue of his eyes. "We have to discuss it sometime."

"Yes. But not now." Not until she knew whether she actually had a future to discuss.

They drove on in silence. The night shadows were creeping across the sky by the time they returned to the farmhouse.

Doyle ushered her through the back door. "Go have a nice, long bath. I'll prepare dinner."

"You don't want me to help?"

He raised a dark eyebrow and dumped the bags on the bench. "Did Helen?"

She grinned. "No, but that doesn't mean I can't help *you*."

"I think I'll take it as a sign." He tossed her one of the plastic bags. "Don't turn on the light. Use the candle I bought instead."

She looked inside the bag. There wasn't only a candle and lighter, but bath oil, herbal shampoo, conditioner and soap. "Why did you buy me these? I did bring my own toiletries, you know."

"You have a ceremony to perform at midnight, remember? There are rituals to follow if you don't want to attract the wrong sort of attention. One of them is cleansing."

Unease slithered through her. She'd all but forgotten about the ceremony. "So using these will help keep the bad things away?"

He nodded. "Partly. There are other things we have

to do, but we'll worry about them later. Go have your bath. Let me worry about that side of things."

When it came to magic, she had no choice but to trust him. She'd never really taken much notice of the ways of witchcraft, even though Helen had often warned her that she might regret it. Still, she hesitated. "What about the bandages I'm wearing?"

"Take them off. Camille's herbs should have worked their magic on the wounds by now anyway."

She nodded and walked into the bathroom. Turning on the taps, she poured in the oil, then sat on the edge of the tub as she waited for it to fill. Scents filled the air—an odd combination of basil, geranium and pine, mixed in with something else she couldn't define. It was relaxing and yet somehow invigorating.

She turned off the water, then stripped and climbed in. For a long time she lay there, enjoying the heat and the moment of peace. When the water finally began to cool, she reluctantly sat up and washed. Climbing out, she dragged some clothes out of her bag and dressed. Then she blew out the candle and walked barefoot to the kitchen.

Only to stop in surprise at the doorway. Doyle hadn't just cooked, he'd created magic. A pristine white cloth covered the table. Candles flickered in the center, flushing warmth across the length of the table but barely touching the darkness beyond that. Wineglasses and cutlery glimmered in the golden light, and the mismatched patterns on the side plates somehow added to the appeal.

He appeared out of the shadows and walked toward her, eyes as warm as the atmosphere he'd created. "Table for two? I think we can manage to squeeze you in. This way, my lady."

He offered her his arm. Smiling, she hooked her arm through his and let herself be led to the table.

"For your dining pleasure tonight," he continued, seating her, "we have a warm chicken salad, followed by a simple but appetizing dessert of strawberries soaked in Cointreau accompanied with freshly whipped cream."

He picked up a paper napkin, fluffed it out and placed it on her lap. His fingers brushed her legs, and warmth shivered through her. She wondered again how she was going to survive the night without giving in to desire.

Wondered if she even really wanted to survive.

He opened the wine and poured them both a glass. Then he disappeared into the shadows, coming back moments later with the two entrées. He placed them, then sat opposite her and picked up his wine.

"To the bravest woman I have ever met," he said softly.

Heat flushed through her cheeks. She wasn't brave. If she were, she wouldn't be sitting here dithering about her feelings for this man. She'd take what fate offered and let the future worry about itself.

She picked up her glass and met his gaze. No matter what her personal fears might be, right now he deserved some sort of honesty from her. "To the only man I have ever been tempted to trust. To the sexiest thief I have ever met."

His smile shimmered right through her, settling warmly in her heart. He touched his glass lightly to hers, then motioned to her salad. "Eat, before the chicken gets cold."

She ate. The meal was perfect, soothing her hunger without sitting like a weight in her stomach. She sighed with contentment when she finished and picked up her wine.

"Thank you," she said. "That was delicious."

He smiled and leaned back in the chair, his face half in the shadows, blue eyes gleaming cobalt in the flickering light. "Thank my mother. She was the one who insisted her sons know how to cook."

She raised an eyebrow. "Sons?"

He nodded. "I have three brothers, all younger, and two sisters, both older."

She couldn't help feeling a twinge of envy. It must have been wonderful growing up with so many siblings. Noisy, but wonderful. Especially at Christmas. Or birthdays. She blinked. Today was *her* birthday. And would have been Helen's, too.

She took a sip of wine, then said, "Do you see much of them?"

"No. They all live in Oregon, in a small town up near the Crater Lake National Park. My work—past and present—has always conspired to keep me away. But I'm in the process of buying a house up there and hope to correct that."

His words sliced through her. She lowered her gaze, concentrating instead on her wine. So, the truth was there for them both to see. No matter what happened between them, he wouldn't stay here in Australia.

"Kirby—"

She raised a hand. "Don't." *Don't tell me you care*

for me. Don't tell me you might love me, because in the end, it doesn't really matter. Nothing did, beyond the fact that he would go back to America.

Take heed, my foolish heart. Because knowing he would leave didn't alter the fact that she wanted him as she'd never wanted a man before.

"I'm not—"

She met his gaze. "Are you going to tell me you're not going back?"

"No, but—"

"Then I don't want to hear it."

"And you have the gall to call *me* irritating." He sighed and thrust a hand through his dark hair. "Whatever am I going to do with you?"

Take me with you, she thought, and she knew that just wasn't an option. His work was too important—to him and to the other people he was destined to save. He didn't need someone permanently in his life, particularly when that someone was as flawed as she was.

Besides, Helen was here, even if only in spirit.

She raised her wineglass. "How about pouring me some more wine?"

He did as she requested, then collected the plates and rose. "Do you feel like dessert now, or would you rather wait a little?"

"I think I'll let dinner settle a bit more, thanks," she said.

He disappeared into the darkness. Flame flickered briefly, then a tiny patch of warmth appeared. "I can't see how a flame that size is going to do you much good," she said, amused. "Why not borrow one of the candles on the table?"

"Because this candle suits my purpose just fine." He appeared out of the shadows, the tiny flame becoming a birthday candle sitting on the top of a cupcake.

"Happy birthday," he said, placing the cake in front of her. "Don't forget to make a wish."

Her smile felt tremulous. She blew out the candle, then closed her eyes and made her wish. Time was all she asked for. Time with Doyle.

She opened her eyes and he held out a small, carefully wrapped present. She didn't take it. Could barely see it through the tears stinging her eyes.

"You shouldn't have." Her throat felt so constricted, her voice came out as little more than a hoarse whisper.

"Birthdays are important." His smile was warm and sexy, and was reflected deep in his eyes. "And you should never let one go by uncelebrated. Go on, open your present. It doesn't bite and it doesn't hold any magic. I promise."

She smiled, and with trembling fingers began unwrapping the dark-red tissue paper. As the layers fell away, a long, plush velvet box was revealed. Her stomach churned. It looked expensive. Felt expensive. *I don't deserve something like this . . .*

She bit her lip and carefully opened the box. Her breath caught. Inside, attached to a flat silver chain, was a delicate, black stone panther. She picked up the necklace, and the panther's eyes sparkled in the golden candlelight. Diamonds, she knew without doubt.

"It's beautiful," she said. "But I can't—"

"You can and will," he said. "Here, let me."

He took the chain from her and placed it around her

neck. His fingers caressed her skin, chasing warmth down to her toes. She closed her eyes, enjoying the sensation.

"I couldn't resist buying this when I saw it," he said, his words brushing heat past her ear. "Especially given your reaction when you discovered I shapeshift."

"A constant reminder of what you are, huh?" She could barely get the words out, her throat was so tight. She quickly drank some wine, but all it did was make her head spin. Or was that merely a side effect of his closeness?

"Or maybe a reminder of what I am not."

She tilted her head back and met his gaze. "Will you show me?"

He frowned and brushed his fingers down her cheek and neck. A tremor ran through her, and deep down a familiar ache began.

"Are you sure you're ready to see it?"

"No." But she was sure she *had* to see it before their relationship could progress any further. To trust him, she had to know him—both versions of him.

He nodded, as if agreeing with her thoughts. "Then watch," he said and stepped away from her.

For an instant, nothing happened. Then motes of light began to appear around him, fairy dust that glimmered silver and gold. It snaked up his body, blurring the night and his outline as it did so, until there was nothing left of him except for that glitter. Then it was gone, and in his place stood a huge black panther with dark blue eyes.

She gasped softly, but not from fear. Far from it. His shifting shape had been nothing like she'd expected.

It was both awe-inspiring and beautiful—two words she'd never thought could be connected to such an act.

The shimmer appeared again, sweeping up from the big cat's tail and encompassing its body. Once again, Doyle stood before her.

"You didn't run screaming from the room, so I take that as a good sign." Despite his easy grin, there was a hint of worry in his eyes and in his thoughts.

She nodded and somehow found her voice. "That was amazing." She hesitated, a thousand questions tumbling through her mind. "But where the hell do your clothes go?"

He laughed—a rich sound that was edged with relief. "I don't know. It's just part of the magic, I suppose. I never really questioned it."

"Is there anything that doesn't change with you?"

He nodded. "Anything that's pure silver. That chain wouldn't, for instance."

She touched the panther. It felt warm against her skin, almost as if it were a living thing rather than being made of stone. "Why?"

He shrugged. "Pure silver is immune to the force of magic."

"Are your whole family shapeshifters?"

He nodded and sat down in the chair nearest hers. "Except for my mother and one of my sisters."

"And your children, when you have them?"

He regarded her for a minute, a slight smile tugging his lips. "My children, when we have them, will have a seventy-five percent chance of being shifters."

His use of *we* made her smile. He really *was* convinced they were meant to be; she just wished she were brave enough to feel the same. "Why seventy-five percent? If your mom is a normal human, why wasn't the distribution of shifter genes fifty-fifty?"

He shrugged. "Obviously the shifter gene is stronger. I'm not a scientist, Kirby. I'm a retired thief turned private investigator. Don't expect me to explain the technicalities. It just *is,* as far as I'm concerned."

"Well, a fat lot of good *that* does my curiosity." She hesitated and sipped her wine. "What about control? Is there ever a time you come close to losing it?"

"It hasn't happened yet." Amusement crinkled the corners of his eyes. "I can see the question burning through your mind, and the answer is no—not even in the heat of passion."

Heat flushed through her cheeks. "Well, I guess that's something of a relief for everyone involved."

He raised an eyebrow. "Everyone? Don't know about you, but I generally only go to bed with one woman at a time."

"And I," she said, in the haughtiest tone she could manage, "don't go to bed with any."

He grinned and saluted her with his glass. Then he froze. Her stomach fell through to her toes. "What?" she said, voice edgy and harsh.

"A car coming up the driveway." He quickly blew out the candles. Lights swept across the curtained windows, and the sound of a car engine seemed as loud as thunder in the silence.

Alarm raced through her. He touched her hand, squeezing her fingers lightly. "Don't panic."

"But what if they come into the house? What are we going to do?"

"Nothing yet. Stay here."

He left the chair and disappeared into the darkness. A moment later she saw the curtain move slightly to one side. In the stillness, two doors slammed. Jaunty whistling moved away from the house, and a water pump kicked into gear.

He's watering the stock.

What if he wants to feed them? Our car is in the shed.

He's making no move toward the shed just yet. If he does, I'll deal with it. He hesitated. *Someone else is moving toward us. Grab the glasses and wrap everything else in the tablecloth.*

She quickly gathered everything, her hands shaking so badly she could barely hold the glasses. He was beside her in an instant, one hand full of plastic bags and wet dishcloths. He took her free hand and led her quickly down the hall. *Did you leave much mess in the bathroom?*

Other than a damp towel, my bag and those oils you gave me, no.

Wait here. He let her go and disappeared again. She heard him moving about, then the sound of vigorous wiping. *What are you doing?*

Wiping the moisture off the bathtub.

Behind them, in the living room, came the sound of a key scraping in the lock. She shifted from one foot to the other, battling the urge to run. *Hurry.*

Hurrying will get us caught. Caution is the key—believe me.

Tension drew her muscles so tight they were beginning to ache. In the living room, the door opened and lights were swept on. *If you don't move right now, it'll be caution that gets us caught.*

He appeared out of the bathroom and ushered her into the nearest bedroom. *Quick, under the bed.*

She pushed aside the comforter and slithered under the old fashioned, high-off-the-floor wooden bed. Dust stirred, tickling her nose. She held back a sneeze and pulled in the bags, towels and tablecloth that he shoved in, trying to leave him some room.

He'd barely pulled the comforter back into place when the hall lights came on. Footsteps approached, loud and heavy despite the carpet. Fear squeezed her throat so tightly she could barely breathe, and for an instant, it felt as though her heart were going to leap out of her chest. She closed her eyes, battling the terror pounding through her.

It's okay. We're okay. He wrapped an arm around her shoulder, but his attention was on the hall outside. They were hardly out of the woods yet.

The footsteps moved past their bedroom hideaway, and another light burned brightly. After a few seconds came the sound of soft tinkling.

Despite her fear, laughter bubbled through her. The intruder was using the toilet?

Minutes ticked by. Finally, the toilet flushed, lights went out and the footsteps moved back down the hall. But they didn't entirely retreat. From the kitchen came the sound of running water.

She's filling something. He shifted around until he was facing her.

Oh God, don't tell me they're settling in to have a cup of coffee?

Could be. There's nothing much we can do but wait them out.

He pulled her close. Then he slipped his hand down to her rear and pulled her closer still, so that every inch of their bodies seemed to be touching. Her breath caught and her heart raced, but not from fear this time. Far from it. Her whole body felt as if it were on fire, and part of that came from the deliciously erotic sensation of lying here in the darkness with him, while the chance of discovery loomed only a few footsteps away.

We shouldn't . . . this is dangerous. Lord, even her mind-voice sounded breathless.

We're only lying here. What can be so dangerous in that? But even as the words whispered into her mind, he slowly began undoing her shirt buttons.

You need to concentrate on our intruders, not on trying to seduce me. She tried to add a touch of sarcasm to her thoughts, but failed miserably. They still sounded as breathy as she was feeling.

In reality, we're the intruders here. And if they move this way, I'll hear them, believe me.

She did believe him. He'd made a successful living from being a thief and had no doubt been caught in tougher situations than this.

His amusement washed through her. *But never before have I had such a lovely way to pass the time.*

The last of her buttons came undone. He brushed the shirt back over her shoulders, then teasingly ran his fingers across her bra and up her neck, until his hand cupped her cheek.

His lips grazed hers, feather light and tender. *I'll stop if you want me to.*

She closed her eyes. For an instant, she considered telling him to do just that. To back away and leave her alone. But only for half a second. He was going back to America once the murderer was caught, no matter what happened between them. Did she really want to lose him without at least knowing his touch, without feeling his caress, inside and out?

No, she thought. Definitely not. Damn it, she'd spent most of life erring on the side of caution, and what had it achieved for her? Very little. And certainly not happiness. If she lost her heart in the process of making love to him, what of it? At least she would have finally taken a chance, stepped beyond the shackles of memories and mistakes and done something simply for the hell of it.

Happiness doesn't happen all that often, Helen had been fond of saying. *So seize it by the scruff of its neck and enjoy it while it lasts. Let the future worry about itself.*

And just this once, she was going to do precisely that.

Don't stop. She turned her face and kissed his palm. He shifted his hand, running a thumb lightly across her lips. She caught it in her mouth, sucking on it gently.

His breath seemed to catch, and heat flowed through the link, setting her body alight. She let his thumb go and leaned forward, kissing his lips, exploring the warmth of his mouth with her tongue, greedy to taste him more fully.

He skimmed a hand across her shoulders and down her back, catching her bra and deftly undoing it.

She pulled back a little, her heart pounding and her breathing harsh. Lord, they'd barely even kissed and already she was aching with need. In some ways, it was scary just how attuned she was to him.

If we do have to run, this is going to be get awfully embarrassing, she thought, as he pushed the bra to one side.

That it will. He didn't seem unduly worried by the prospect. He ran a finger around the outline of her nipples, teasing them to aching life without actually touching them.

You're not playing fair. She tugged his T-shirt free from the waistband of his jeans, pushing it upward. He caught her hand, taking the T-shirt and deftly pulling it off.

You did that a little too easily. Are you sure you don't make a habit of trying to seduce women in confined spaces?

His amusement shimmered through her, spreading like a wave through her body, tingling even her toes. *I have to admit, this is not a place I've ever been tempted to try before.*

Oh yeah? So where have you been tempted to try? She touched his chest, running her fingers down the plane of his stomach, cupped her hand around the hard length of him, gently rubbing through his jeans. Desire burned through the link between them, ready to explode.

My favorite would be under the stars. He ran his hand down her stomach and began undoing the button on her jeans.

Her breath caught, the anticipation of his touch becoming a pulse deep inside.

There is something very erotic about two people making love under the light of a moon on a warm summer night, he continued, undoing her zipper.

There was something very erotic about making love under a dusty old bed with the chance of discovery only a quick gasp away, too. He pushed past her panties and touched her, slipping his finger down her wetness and thrusting inside. She shuddered, pushing against his hand and barely restraining her moan.

His lips caught hers. She kissed him hard and wrapped her arms around his neck, pulling him against her until her breasts were deliciously squashed against his chest and all she could feel was him caressing, thrusting, deep inside her.

Outside, in the hall, footsteps sounded.

Deep inside the ache was growing. *Oh God, stop . . . stop,* her mind begged, even though it was the last thing she wanted.

He stopped. She leaned her forehead against his chest, her breath ragged. The thunder of his heart rang through her ears but failed to drown out the thump of footsteps moving past. The bathroom light came on again.

What is it with these people? Haven't they got a toilet at home?

His smile shone through her. He brushed a kiss across the top of her head. *It's our male visitor this time.*

She looked up. *How can you tell?*

Lifted the toilet seat.

She smiled and began planting tiny kisses across his chin. He raised a hand, cupping her cheek, catching her mouth and deepening the kiss again. The toilet flushed and the footsteps moved away. A few seconds later, the back door slammed.

Alone again. Shall we continue this in a more comfortable position? He hesitated. *Or would you rather stop altogether?*

You stop now, and I think I will explode with frustration.

You wouldn't be the only one. He smiled and kissed her briefly, tenderly. Their minds merged, and just for an instant, his desire scorched through her. But right behind it, following like a tidal wave, came his feelings. She closed her eyes, shaken to the core. She didn't deserve the depth of those emotions. Didn't know if her own feelings could ever truly match his.

"I don't expect them to. Not yet." He brushed the hair from her eyes, his touch shivering heat through her heart, her soul. "You asked for time before, and that's all I want myself. Time together, so that you can more fully understand both my feelings and yours. Because those feelings *are* there, and so strong that I can almost taste them."

Her gaze searched his, and she wondered whether he was right or was merely hoping it to be the truth. The touch of wistfulness in his tone suggested it might be the latter, and it crystalized the fear that he would leave and not come back. But right then, she didn't really care. They had this moment to enjoy, and for once in her life, fear of the unknown was going to take a backseat.

"Kirby, you have to trust me—and trust the fact that while I may have to go back to the U.S., I *will* come back for you."

Maybe. Maybe not. "If they've left, can we please take this discussion elsewhere? The dust is starting to get up my nose."

He laughed softly and rolled out from under the bed. She followed, and he wrapped a hand around her forearm, helping her up, then pulling her close.

"Now, where were we?" He began sliding her shirt off her shoulders.

Excitement thrummed through her. She cleared her throat and raised an eyebrow. "Here? I thought we were moving to someplace more comfortable. You can hardly call a single bed comfortable."

"Depends who's in it with you." His grin was roguish and made her heart do somersaults. Her bra quickly joined her shirt on the floor. "Now, let's do something about those jeans, huh?"

He knelt, his tongue trailing heat down her stomach. She shivered in delight, anticipation growing. He slid her jeans and panties down her legs, allowing her to step out. Then he delved into her moistness, the caress of his tongue whisper soft and oh so arousing. She gasped, excitement pulsing through her, until every nerve ending screamed for release. He rose, claiming her mouth again and kissing her hard. He slipped his hand between her legs and stroked her, gently at first, then faster when the tremors began. She moaned, clinging to him, thrusting against his touch, climaxing hard and fast. She wished he were inside, climaxing with her, and yet not wanting it to end so soon.

"Nor shall it," he murmured. "That, my love, was merely an appetizer." He kissed her neck, her shoulders, then captured her nipple in his mouth, sucking lightly.

She gasped, and the embers she thought well sated sprang back to life. She pulled away from his touch. "Then by all means, let's share."

He arched an eyebrow and raised his hands, a teasing smile on his lips. "My body is yours to play with."

"And a beautiful toy it is, too," she murmured as she knelt.

She slowly undid his jeans and eased them down, taking his shorts with them. Allowed him to step out, then slowly ran her tongue up his leg and teasingly caressed the hard length of him until heat filled the link and threatened to burn them both.

She rose and wrapped her arms around his neck, pulling him against her, until the heat of his body seemed to invade every pore. She kissed him urgently, felt his hands cup her bottom and draw her closer, until his erection pressed deep into her stomach.

He kissed her neck, her breasts, trailing fire through her body. She groaned and pushed him back onto the bed, straddling him and pressing him against her moistness. Slowly, teasingly, she rocked back and forth. God, she wanted him inside so much she ached. But not yet. Not just yet.

He made a needy sound deep in his throat and reached for her, pulling her down against his chest and kissing her hard. She continued to rock, teasing them both, until the flames of desire burned through their minds and threatened to consume them.

Deep within her the trembling was growing, becoming a tide almost overloading her senses. She rubbed harder and heard his response—a quick, sharp gasp. Could feel him quivering and knew he was battling for control.

He released her lips, then ducked his head and caught her nipple, sucking hard. She gasped, and the tide became a wave of pleasure she could no longer hold at bay. Needing him inside, she shifted and captured him fully. He groaned, thrusting urgently, pushing her over the brink into ecstasy. She moaned and rode him hard, until their tremors had finally eased and they both were spent.

She collapsed against his chest, and he wrapped his arms around her, holding her as if he never meant to let her go. She closed her eyes and wished that were the case. And the doubts rose once more, teasing her insecurities to life.

"Tell me," she said into the silence. "Have you got a girlfriend back home in America? A wife, even?"

For several heartbeats he didn't answer, then he sighed softly. "Thieving was a job, not a philosophy."

She looked up at him. "What has that got to do with the question at hand?"

"Everything." He grabbed her waist and somehow reversed their positions. For several seconds, his gaze searched hers, then he smiled a warm, loving smile that sang through her soul.

"If I make a commitment to someone, I honor that commitment." He cupped her cheek, caressing her lips with his thumb. She didn't move—couldn't move, pinned by the emotion in his eyes as much as the weight of his body. "I've had girlfriends, yes, but the emphasis should be placed on 'friends.' I have never felt the need to take it any further. But after so many years of disbelief and denial, I have discovered I am my father's son after all."

His words confused and, in some sense, frightened her. She frowned. "What do you mean?"

"You need to know where I stand, and I guess I understand that." He hesitated, and the sudden seriousness in his eyes made her breath catch in her throat.

Don't say any more, she wanted to say. *I'm just not ready to hear any more.* But the words refused to come out, and all she could do was stare at him, an odd mix of yearning and trepidation filling her.

"I have never said this to anyone else. Before now, before I met you, I thought I never would." He hesitated again, and she felt her mouth go dry.

"Marry me," he added softly.

SIXTEEN

FOR SEVERAL SECONDS KIRBY SIMPLY STARED AT HIM. Part of her ached to say yes—to grab hold of him while she could and never let him go. But the other half, the part so afraid to trust, stepped back, unable to believe that any emotional commitment made in the midst of danger could be real and lasting. They didn't *know* each other, damn it! How could he possibly ask such a question after being with her for little more than forty-eight hours?

"Remember my father and grandfather," he said, a smile touching his full lips. "Forty-eight hours is a lifetime compared to them."

"I can't—" Her voice came out as little more than a harsh whisper. She hesitated, swallowing to ease the ache in her throat. "I can't give you an answer. Not now. Not until I'm sure." Sure that she had a future to consider. Sure that what she was feeling was real, and not just a side effect of the situation she found herself in.

"I know. And I don't really expect one. Not now. Not even in the next few weeks or months."

He brushed a kiss across her lips, and warmth shivered through her soul. If this wasn't love, then what the hell was it? She closed her eyes, battling tears. He continued softly, "But you needed to know what I planned, and now you do. I may have to go back home when all this is finished, but it won't be for long. I intend to come back, and I intend to make you part of my life, no matter how long that takes."

"But what about your work? Surely that's more important."

"Work can wait. I don't care."

"But—"

"Hush." He kissed her again, deeper and longer than before.

Longing surged through her, mingling with need.

When he finally pulled away from the kiss, he said, "Worry about the details later. For now, just concentrate on the only question that matters—do you love me? Once you answer that, everything else will fall into place."

"Nothing is that simple," she murmured, wishing that it were.

"I'll make it that simple." He caressed her cheek, gently thumbing away a tear. "Just tell me yes or no."

She closed her eyes. "What if I say no?"

He went still, but pain surged between them, so deep and stark that tears stung her eyes. He obviously feared this might be her answer, despite everything.

"If you say no, then I'll accept that and walk away."

The thought tore at her. While she wasn't sure of her feelings, she *was* sure of one thing. She couldn't let him walk away. Not yet. Maybe not ever. "I just need time," she repeated softly, more to calm her own fears than his.

She wrapped her arms around his neck and stared into his beautiful eyes. The sheer depth of love and understanding she saw there chased a shiver through her soul. She still wasn't sure if she was even capable of understanding such depths, let alone of returning them. Right now, she didn't even want to think about it. After all, the witch was still out there, and tonight might be all the time they had left together. "So, while I decide whether I'm a coward or not, what are we going to do?"

He raised an eyebrow and glanced at his watch. "We have two hours before we have to prepare for the ceremony. We could go eat those strawberries I prepared." He hesitated, shifting slightly, his eyes sparkling mischievously. "Or we could lie here and talk a bit more."

He slid inside her, hot and hard. She raised an eyebrow, amazed that he could be ready again so soon— and amazed that she could be. "Talking suits me just fine," she murmured, wrapping her legs around his so that he couldn't escape.

His smile shimmered through her heart. He kissed her, his mouth gently demanding. From that moment on, there wasn't a lot of conversation to be had, and she didn't give a damn.

DOYLE CROSSED HIS ARMS, WATCHING KIRBY CAREfully unwrap the present Helen had left her. Once the ribbon and paper had been removed, she peeled off the tape holding the lid down, letting it fly away on the wind as she opened the box. She didn't say anything for several seconds, but a frown marred her features.

"What's wrong?" he asked immediately.

"Nothing." She plucked a folded piece of paper

from the box. "I guess I was just expecting something more than a note."

If Helen had gifted Kirby with her powers, then she certainly *had* left more than just a note. "Open it."

She hesitated, then bit her lip and did so. Her voice was little more than a whisper when she finally spoke. "It's a spell. She's left me—"

"All that she was," he finished for her.

She nodded, blinking back tears as she met his gaze. "Why do that? Why the *hell* didn't she just keep her powers and save herself?"

"Maybe she couldn't. Maybe she knew there was no escaping her fate, and this was her way of stopping the witch from getting her powers." He glanced at the time. They would have to get moving if they were going to be ready by midnight.

"She could have run from her fate. It wouldn't be the first time we'd done it."

"Her name was given to the *manarei,*" he reminded her gently. "Not yours. She couldn't have outrun her fate, not without endangering your life as well."

She didn't reply, but he could feel her pain and her anger so fiercely it might as well have been his own. And while he ached to comfort her, they simply didn't have the time. "Kirby," he added, "we need to get ready."

She took a deep, somewhat shuddery breath, then nodded. "Tell me what to do."

He handed her a small dagger, then took the note from her. "Cut a circle around those items we have on the ground and make it large enough for you to sit comfortably in."

As she did so, he read the note. As he'd feared, Helen's instructions were quite specific on one point—no one could be in the protective circle with her when she invoked the spell.

It worried him. He had no doubt this spell was dangerous, which was why he was taking as many precautions as he could. But the best way of protecting her was to be with her, helping with the spell, sharing his energy with her and watching for dangers. With that option gone, he was left with little more to do than prowl around the outside of the circle and hope like hell nothing went wrong.

She finished the dirt circle and glanced up. "What now?"

"Pour the water along the line you've just drawn, but make sure you don't step out of the circle." Once she'd finished that, he added, "And do the same with the salt."

She nodded and walked around again. The wind caught at her nightdress, twisting it around her bare legs. Even though the moon was lost to the clouds and provided very little light, the outline of her body was visible through the sheer material. He scrubbed a hand across his jaw. While he understood the need for her to be wearing something special, something clean and new, for the spell, he wished it had been anything else but the nightie. She looked too vulnerable. Too desirable. It could attract the wrong sort of attention just as easily as the right.

Overhead, thunder rumbled, an ominous sound in the night's silence. He glanced at his watch. Helen's note said to be ready by midnight. It was three minutes to.

"Done."

He met her gaze, saw the fear lurking in the depths

of her eyes. Wished again that he could hold her. Comfort her. "Good. Now sit in the middle and take several deep, calming breaths."

She did, crossing her legs, her arms resting on her knees, palms up, as if meditating.

"Now, I want you to raise your body energy by tightening your muscles. Start at your toes, and work your way up. Imagine the energy as a purple mist . . . Squeeze it up through your body until it reaches your hands."

He hesitated, waiting. Saw her slowly tense, felt the thrum of magic beginning to pulse through the air. Midnight was a minute away. They didn't have much time. "Now, without moving, send that energy out through your fingers and in a clockwise circle around you. Imagine yourself encased in an orb of purple fire. Feel the power of it pulsing through you and out into the night."

The air shimmered, crackling with energy. Overhead, thunder ripped. Lightning forked across the skies, briefly turning night into day and electrifying the air around them.

"Now, repeat the spell exactly as Helen wrote it."

She began murmuring. Light flared across the night again, faster, closer than before. He frowned, looking skyward. He didn't like the feel of this.

Lightning split the night and crashed to the ground. Energy rippled through the earth, tingling through his boots and up his legs. Not energy from the fast-approaching storm, but from Kirby, from the spell she was murmuring. He clenched his fists and prowled around the circle, needing to move, to do something to ease the fear sitting like a weight in his gut.

Thunder rumbled again, a deep, dangerous sound. The wind became sharper, stronger, tugging at his coat, thrusting like ice against his skin. Kirby sat in a sea of calm, the circle untouched by the rising wind. But the sense of power was building, flaring across the night, reaching for the storm-held skies.

He thrust his hand into his pocket, wrapping his fingers around the silver knife hidden there. If all hell broke loose, it might be his only hope of protecting her. Silver was immune to magic—and it was the one weapon that could slice through the circle's protection.

Light leapt upward, following the trail of energy. The skies answered its call. Rain lashed downward, needle sharp and drenching. Water plastered his hair and ran like a river down his back. He ignored it, watching her, waiting.

Thunder rumbled again, long and hard. Lightning clapped, and the air shook at its fury. Energy streaked across the night and splintered into two—one jagged finger leaping back up into the fury of the clouds, the other arcing downward, toward the ground. Toward her. *No!* He stepped forward, but before he could do anything more, the fork of lighting crashed into the circle, through Kirby, and exploded into the earth.

The force of the blast lifted him off his feet and thrust him back. He hit the ground with a grunt of pain, for an instant seeing nothing but a shroud of darkness. He coughed, barely able to breathe, fear clenching his gut tight. What if he'd been wrong? What if this spell hadn't come from Helen, but from the witch who was trying to kill her?

I can't lose her now. He thrust to his feet, then

stopped, stunned. She wasn't even hurt. She was still sitting in the circle, but her arms were spread wide, as if greeting the electricity that played around her—through her. Another bolt arced down from the skies, splitting as it neared her outstretched hands, running across her fingers, her skin, until her whole body seemed to glow with the storm's heat.

The air screamed around him. Rain lashed him, lashed her, shredding her nightdress and pounding against her pale skin. Red welts rose, then just as quickly faded, but she didn't seem to notice—didn't even flinch. Her gaze was still skyward, as if entranced by the fiery light that danced through her. He tried to touch her mind, wanting to be sure she was okay. The wall of power that met him pushed him off his feet and nearly blew his senses.

He struggled up again. The thunder rumbled—a muted sound that quickly faded. A heartbeat later, the rain and wind also died, and the sudden silence felt almost eerie. Kirby was still sitting cross-legged in the circle, but she was slumped forward, as if all her energy had been sapped by the force of the storm.

He walked toward her. Energy tingled across his skin, a warning that the protection of the circle was still in place. He stopped at the perimeter, not wanting to enter unless it was absolutely necessary. He could hurt her if he did.

"Kirby?"

She stirred and rubbed her arms, groaned softly, then looked up. Her eyes were no longer entirely green, but ringed by a smoky silver band, as if the lightning had branded her. "God, everything is aching."

He wasn't surprised. After being hit by so much lightning, it was a wonder she was even alive. He clenched his fingers, wanting to touch her, hold her, make sure she was really okay. She *looked* okay—beyond her eyes, she looked amazingly untouched. But he still had to be sure.

"You have to close the circle. Imagine that orb again. Feel it, then draw its power back through your fingertips and down into your body. Relax with it."

She took a deep breath and resumed her meditation position. After a few minutes, the tingling sensation of power died. She opened her eyes. "Now the broom?"

He nodded. She grabbed the broom lying on the ground behind her, then pushed upright, her movements unsteady. He flexed his fingers, watching impatiently as she slowly brushed at the salt that defined the confines of the circle. It was a symbolic gesture more than a necessary one, a way of grounding her spirit back to the Earth after the spell's force. When the last of the salt had been swept away, he entered the circle, taking off his coat and quickly wrapping it around her. She huddled into it, body trembling and lips blue with cold.

"Let's get you back inside." He picked her up, holding her close as he raced back into the house. "I think you'd better take a shower and warm up."

"No." She touched his cheek, her fingers like ice against his skin. "Just lie with me, hold me."

Her voice was distant, frail. Worry snaked through him. He took her upstairs, peeling away the remains of the nightdress before tucking her under the blankets. He stripped off his own clothes and climbed in beside her, wrapping his arms around her and pulling her close.

"So cold," she murmured, nestling against him.

"I know." It felt like he was hugging ice rather than a flesh-and-blood woman. He pulled the thick comforter over them both, then ran his hands up and down her arms, trying to get some heat into her. "How are you feeling?"

"Sore. Cold." A tremor ran through her, through the link between them. But her thoughts, like her voice, were still distant, still weak. "My hair hurts."

No surprise there. Given the force of the energy that had flowed through her, it was a wonder she hadn't been burned to a crisp. "Would you like some coffee? Something to warm you up?"

"No. Just hold me."

He did, long into the night. It was close to dawn by the time the ice melted from her skin, and she began to retain some heat and regain her color. He didn't relax, just held her close, listening to her breathe and fighting the growing need to close his eyes and catch some sleep himself.

Dawn came and went. Light crept past the curtains, slithering heat and warmth into the room. Birds chirped noisily, cows mooed and, somewhere in the distance, a tractor spluttered and chugged. Finally, she stirred, though it was more a soft sigh of pleasure than any real sense of movement. The quick thrust of heat through the link told him she was not only awake, but aroused.

He ran his hand up the warm length of her body and gently teased a nipple to life. Amusement ran through her thoughts, warm and lazy. But she didn't stir and didn't open her eyes. Making him do all the work, he thought with a smile.

He kissed her shoulder, her neck, her ear, all the while continuing to stroke her breasts. Her breathing became sharper, and the link between them grew hazy with need—his as well as hers. He pressed himself against her, thrusting gently against the round perfection of her bottom. She sighed again and reached back, touching him. Her caress ran heat through his body and almost shattered his control. He groaned and ran his fingers down her stomach to the mound of her hair. She shifted slightly, opening her legs to his touch. Lord, she felt wonderful—warm and wet and oh so ready for him. He stroked her gently, teasingly, bringing her close to the edge of a climax before pulling away.

"Tease," she murmured, her breathing hot and hard.

He smiled and continued his gentle exploration of her body. Got lost in the wonder and warmth of it, until the ache in him was a fire that burned through the link, wrapping them in passion and love.

Love that was returned, even if she wouldn't admit it.

He ran his hand down to her hip and cupped her again, caressing her, gently at first, then more urgently as her breathing grew sharp and wildfire ran through the link, threatening to explode. As the shudders began to overtake her, he shifted, thrusting himself inside her. She groaned, a soft sound of pleasure he echoed. Her heat encased him, her muscles contracting against him as her climax grew. She touched his hip, holding him close, her movements as urgent as his. He thrust hard and fast, wanting, needing to come with her. Then the wildfire exploded, and her climax sent him spiraling beyond control and into bliss.

For several minutes he could do nothing more than simply lie there, wrapped in the warmth of her body, too contented, too spent, to move. *A man could get used to this*, he thought, and fervently hoped she'd give him the chance to do just that. While he had no doubts about his feelings—or hers—he still wasn't sure whether she'd step past her fears and look toward the future.

"How are you feeling?" he asked, after a while.

"Wonderful," she said, and turned to face him.

Her eyes were still ringed by the ethereal silver-gray of a storm witch.

"What?" she asked, the warmth fleeing her expression and replaced by fear.

"Nothing," he said, as calmly as he could. "It's just your eyes. They've changed color."

She scrambled out of the bed and ran to the mirror. For several seconds she simply stood and stared, her fists clenched and every muscle taut. Then she reached out, touching her reflection, as if not quite believing it was she. "How is that possible?" she whispered. "How could my eyes change like that?"

"I would say it has something to do with the spell and the powers involved." He hesitated. "Other than your eyes, do you feel any different?"

She shook her head, and outlined her reflection's eyes with her fingers. "I look like Helen."

"I've seen photos of the two of you, and you've always looked like her." The silver edge in her eyes only made it more noticeable.

"But . . . it's not me. I look in the mirror, and I see Helen. I don't see me anymore."

He rose and wrapped his arms around her, holding her close. She was trembling, but whether it was from fear or cold he wasn't sure. "What I see is what I have always seen—a beautiful, courageous woman with amazing eyes. Whether those eyes are green or gray or a bit of both doesn't really matter. It's only a surface alteration. It doesn't alter who you are inside."

"But I don't *know* who I am anymore." There was more than a hint of despair in her voice. "Everything's been twisted around. The past I remember has turned out to be nothing more than a lie, and it's killing people. It killed Helen . . ."

She broke off, a sob catching in her throat. He turned her around, and she buried her face against his chest. Tears tracked silently down his skin, their touch warm. He brushed a kiss over the top of her head and just held her. Nothing he said would make any difference right now. Too much had happened in too brief a period, and she just needed time to sort it all out.

Though time was the one commodity they didn't have a lot of.

As if to confirm the thought, his phone rang. Kirby jumped, her fingers clenching against his side. He brushed another kiss across her head, then released her and walked across to the pile of their clothes. He picked up his still damp coat, dug into a pocket and dragged out his phone.

"We got problems," Camille said immediately.

He rubbed a hand across his eyes. More problems was the last thing they needed. "What?"

"Russell's been attacked. They grabbed Trina and left him for dead."

But obviously not *dead dead*, he thought with relief, or Camille's tone would not be so calm. "How badly is he hurt?"

Camille snorted. "That fool witch obviously doesn't know much about vampires. Even Hollywood knows a stake through the heart is one of the better ways to incapacitate—"

"Camille—"

She sighed. "She shot him through the heart. Didn't even use a silver bullet. Then she roped him in front of the window. Maybe she just intended to let him fry."

"From what I've seen, that's more her style. She seems to like her victims to suffer." And thanks to that desire, Russell was still alive. It would have been a different story had she aimed for his head. "Where is he now?"

"Still at the motel. The manager heard the ruckus and called the cops, and by the time Russ had it sorted out, it was daylight."

Kirby stood beside him. He wrapped an arm around her shoulder and shifted the phone so that she could hear. "So, what's the plan?"

"I've done a reading from some hair I snipped off Trina. She's being held at some warehouse down near the docks."

Surprise rippled through him. "She's not dead yet?" Why? Particularly when every other time the witch had killed, she'd done so as quickly—and painfully— as possible.

"No, she's not dead yet, but I've got a feeling we'll have to move fast or she will be. I'll head over and pick up Russell, and we'll meet you around the back of the warehouse. You got a pen?"

He grabbed one and quickly wrote down the address. "What about Kirby?" he added, glancing down at her.

"She can't come with you. It's too dangerous. We'll just have to chance leaving her there."

"No, we can't—"

"We have no choice, Doyle. We must catch the witch, and this is our best shot. But if something goes wrong, we can't risk Kirby being close."

But dare they risk leaving her alone? He certainly couldn't.

She placed a hand on his stomach, her touch so warm against the ice suddenly encasing his gut.

"I'll be okay," she said, voice soft. "I can protect myself, and I still have Camille's beads. If the very worst happens and the witch turns up, I can use them to shield my appearance while I make a run for it."

"No. I'm not leaving you alone." Especially now that Russell had been attacked. If the witch could find him so easily, she might know where they were, as well.

"I heard what she said, shifter, and she's making perfectly good sense," Camille said.

Only if you didn't love the person in question. But he did, and there was no way on this Earth he was going to leave her here alone. "I don't care. I'm not leaving her unprotected."

"But I'm not unprotected." She raised up on her toes and brushed a kiss across his cheek. "I have both my abilities and Helen's."

"*If* the spell worked. We don't know that it did."

"I trust Helen, and we have no reason to believe that it didn't work."

"Kirby—"

"No. We both know this might be your only shot to stop this woman, and you can't risk that by worrying over my safety. I'll be okay. I promise."

He sighed. She was making perfectly good sense,

and he knew it. The only way she was ever going to be totally safe was by them finding and killing the witch. He just wished there were a way they could do that without leaving her unguarded.

"Okay, okay, I give in." He glanced at his watch, then asked her, "How long will it take me to get to the docks from here?"

She shrugged. "Maybe an hour, maybe more, depending on the traffic."

"Let's just hope our witch hangs around that long," Camille muttered. "See you there in an hour, Doyle."

He hung up, then brushed his fingers across Kirby's cheek, tucking her hair back behind her ears. "I don't want to do this."

Her smile was tremulous. "And you think I want to be left alone? Knowing that witch might be out there, just waiting to send her beasties after me the minute you leave?"

"Then why—"

"Because it may be the only chance we get, and you have to take it."

She reached up and kissed him. He wrapped his arms around her and deepened the kiss, all the while wishing he had the time to do more. Lord, she'd barely even touched him, yet he was aching with the need to make love to her again.

"Just make sure you come back to me," she murmured, her breath warm against his lips.

"Always." He pulled back a little, staring into her smoke-colored eyes—something he hoped to be doing for the rest of his life. "Just promise me you won't go anywhere unless that witch turns up."

"I promise."

He kissed her again, briefly, urgently, then grabbed his clothes and quickly dressed. "Call me if anything happens," he said, and scrawled down his phone number.

She nodded and accepted the scrap of paper with a look of trepidation on her face. "I'll see you when you get back, then."

"Count on it." He kissed her a final time, then before he could change his mind and give in to the desire to stay with her, he grabbed the car keys and headed out the door.

Kirby crossed her arms and watched him leave, an uneasy chill running down her spine. It wasn't so much that she feared being left alone, but more that she feared something *would* go wrong. That this was the opportunity the witch had been waiting for. Goose bumps chased their way across her arms. She shivered and quickly dressed before heading down the stairs to make coffee.

The silence seemed to close in on her, and the natural creaking of the old house made every nerve ending jump. She wandered around aimlessly, looking for something to do. In one of the bedrooms she found a stack of romance novels, and after sorting through them, she settled down to read.

The hours ticked slowly by. Outside, the wind called. She frowned, put aside her book and walked to the window. Beyond the curtains, the light was bright, almost harsh, but the day itself looked warm. The breeze stirred the trees, rustling through leaves and tugging at the brightly colored daisies in the garden beds below. She frowned and closed her eyes. Beneath the whispered song of the wind came the soft but clear call of her name.

She bit her lip and wondered if she was imagining things—wondered if all the events of the last few days had tipped her over the edge and into insanity. The call came again, more urgently this time. Definitely *not* imagination. She dropped the curtains back into place and headed outside.

The afternoon sun was as hot as it was bright, but it failed to chase the chill from her skin. She walked down the slight slope of grass and sat under the gums. The leaves stirred, stronger than before, and through their murmuring she heard her name. The voice was soft, warm, and oh so familiar. Vanilla drifted on the breeze, entwined with the slightest hint of lime. Helen's favorite scents.

Pain welled. Kirby closed her eyes and somehow found her voice. "What did your spell do to me?"

The leaves stirred and answered. "Nothing more than return what was rightfully yours."

"What do you mean?" She stared up into the gum tree's dark canopy, wondering if Helen's spirit danced with the wind among the leaves.

"There is a reason we always felt drawn to one another. We were not just friends, dear one, but sisters. Twins."

"Twins." It came out harshly, her throat too constricted by sudden tears. "But how do you know this? How can you be sure?"

"The wind told me, long ago."

"So why didn't you tell *me*? Damn it, I had the right—"

"But you never showed *any* desire to uncover the past

and the reason we were abandoned as babes," Helen interrupted. "And how many times have you said you have no desire to meet the people who could abandon you to such misery?"

"Yes, but parents are far different from a *sister*—from a twin."

"We found each other in the end, and that is all that matters. And deep down, you knew. You felt our connection as keenly as I did."

Yes, she had. From the moment she and Helen had met in that facility, it had felt as though she'd found the other part of herself. Which she had, because they were twins. She took a deep, quivering breath. "Did you ever find out anything about our parents?"

"No. Not even the wind could tell me that. But it was my search for answers that brought us to this point, Kirby."

"I have my own powers, Helen. I never wanted yours."

"Perhaps not, but they are now where they should have been from the very start."

Kirby frowned. "What do you mean?"

"I mean that we are not just twins, but the much rarer semi-identical twins," Helen said. "One egg, two sperm. It means the abilities that should have been yours were split between us. You were and are the binder, but you should have been a whole lot more."

Kirby's frown deepened. "Meaning I should also have been a storm witch?"

"And air elemental. But those two came to me, in a somewhat diluted form. I was never a very powerful witch, nor could I control air as I should have. That is because some remnants remained in you."

"But I never—"

"Because you never wanted to. You had your one weapon—a weapon that was born from all the elements that once resided in you—and you had no desire to learn or use anything else. But you must use them now, Kirby. You must stop that woman's murderous ways."

Alone? How the hell was she supposed to stop a woman who was now half demon? "Doyle's gone after her."

"No. The witch has set a trap. It is your task, your fate, to stop her."

Fear ripped through her, and she scrambled upright. "Doyle? Is he—?"

"You have no time to worry about him now, sister. The witch has the fourth point. You must save her."

"But—" She hesitated, battling the tide of fear. "I can't fight her alone. I need help."

"You need nothing more than courage. Remember, you are the one that combines and controls. She cannot hurt you with what is yours to command."

What in hell was that supposed to mean? If the whispering leaves knew, they didn't say. "I don't want to do this."

"You must. We started this, albeit unknowingly, so long ago, and we have run from our responsibilities for too long. But revenge has overtaken us, and now you must see this finished. For the sake of us all."

She closed her eyes. She didn't want this responsibility. Didn't know if she had the courage to face this woman alone.

"You must, sister. Or the cat will die."

It felt like someone had grabbed her heart and squeezed

it tight. For a minute, she couldn't even breathe. "What do you mean?" she somehow ground out.

"In protecting you, he will draw the witch's ire and die. I have heard it whispered on the wind."

The wind didn't whisper unchangeable truths, only possibilities. How often had Helen told her that? Yet it was a possibility she dare not risk. She drew in a deep breath. In one sense, Helen was right. If they hadn't sidetracked fate so long ago, then none of these murders would have happened. They certainly couldn't change that now, but they could stop a madwoman's quest for power and send a demon back to hell.

Maybe. She shivered and rubbed her arms. "Where do I go?"

"To an abandoned building in Port Melbourne. She will perform the ceremony tonight, when she has more strength. You have to stop her."

Kirby closed her eyes. *Have to* and *would* stop her were two very different things. "The address?"

It was the wind itself that answered, burning the address into her thoughts. Another tremor ran through her. The spell had worked after all.

"Call the storms, and they, too, will answer." Helen's words were barely audible. The dance of the leaves was dying, as was the wind. "Take care, sister . . ."

"Goodbye," she whispered, and felt the quick kiss of wind on her cheeks before the day went still.

Swallowing heavily, she climbed to her feet. The chill seemed to have settled deep in her bones. She rubbed her arms, knowing it came more from fear than the wind—and from the knowledge that she might not survive this encounter with the witch. Despite Helen's words, she was under no illusions. The witch was far stronger than she ever would be.

But she had no choice. If she contacted Doyle and told him what she was about to do, he'd either tell her to stay put or accompany her. And if the wind's whispers were right, he'd die. Or maybe his friends would. Either way, she couldn't take that risk. If anyone else had to die, then let it be her. This was her fault, after all. Helen was right. It was time to stop running from the past and start making things right, no matter what the consequences.

Sighing softly, she headed back to the house to collect her things and call a taxi. And while she was waiting, she'd write a note of apology to the man she feared she'd never see again.

The man she might just love.

DOYLE DUCKED PAST THE FILTH-RIDDEN WINDOW AND moved to the back door. It was padlocked, but the screws holding the latch in place were loose and rusty. Nothing a good kick couldn't dislodge. He leaned back against the wall and glanced at his watch. Ten seconds to go.

There was no movement inside the warehouse, no smell of life. But the feel of magic lay heavy in the air—as did the smell of death. Zombies, and God knew what else, waited inside.

He glanced at his watch again. *Time,* he thought. From the front of the warehouse came the sound of squealing tires, then a loud bang and the sound of metal grinding. Camille, reversing the van right through the warehouse's main doors.

He stepped away from the wall and kicked the door. It flew open, the lock flying sideways and clattering noisily to the floor. He rolled into the gloom, coming to his feet fast, silver knife in one hand and gun in the other.

Nothing but dust stirred. He rose and cautiously edged forward. Light filtered in through the filthy windows, washing hazily across the semi-dark hallway. Doors lined the walls to his left and right—and from the one at the end of the corridor, he heard the rattle of a dead man breathing.

He put his weapons away, then took a deep breath and opened the door. The zombie lunged toward him, hands clawing for his neck. The smell of decay hung heavy in the air. This one had been dead for quite a while before it had been called from its grave. He ducked under the creature's blows and thrust his fingers deep into its neck, shattering its windpipe. It gurgled, hands grasping wildly at its throat, as if desperate for air it didn't need to survive. He stepped behind it, grabbing its neck and twisting hard. Bone snapped, and the zombie fell dead at his feet.

Unease ran through him. One zombie, and not a very strong one at that. As traps and this witch went, it just didn't mesh. Something felt wrong. Very wrong.

He got out his weapons, then stepped over the mildewed body of the zombie and continued on down the corridor. At the end, he found a set of stairs leading downward. He took them cautiously, pausing after each step. The silence felt so intense it almost seemed to be buzzing. Where the hell were Camille and Russell?

He reached the last step and stopped again. The room that stretched before him was long and narrow and wrapped in a blanket of gloom. Dust stirred, but little else. There were doors to his left, and another set at the end of the room. He hoped they led into the main section of the warehouse. Though he could hear no sound, he had a horrible feeling Camille and Russell needed help.

He moved left and tested the handle. Magic tingled across his fingers, sharp enough to burn. He jerked his hand away, then carefully brushed his fingers across the door itself. The whole thing was spelled.

If this door was trapped, then no doubt the other one would be, too. He stepped back and studied the wall. No windows, no vents—nothing he could use to gain access to the next room.

Frowning, he moved right, running his hands across the wall. Plasterboard. Maybe he could kick it in and gain access that way. He walked to the middle of the wall, far enough away from both doors to ensure he didn't trigger either spell, then began kicking. White dust flew and the plaster gave way, revealing the struts and wall beyond. He kept kicking until there was a hole large enough for a cat to fit through, then shifted shape. But he didn't enter, not immediately.

The silence in the room beyond felt tense, electrified. Magic stirred, breezing across his senses, but its touch had the feel of distance. He padded a little closer, listening to the undertones of the silence. He could hear breathing, sharp and rapid. Could almost taste the sting of sweat, the acrid smell of fear. Human smells and sounds, not animal. Not zombie or any other nightmare creature.

There was no one close. He pushed through the hole,

then shifted shape and reached back for the knife. The gloom in this part of the warehouse was not as intense, the sunlight filtering in from skylights dotted across the ceiling. In the middle of the large room stood a crate. On it was an odd-looking parcel. His gut clenched. He had a horrible feeling he knew what that parcel was. This time, the witch wasn't taking any chances with magic alone. This time, it looked as if she'd set a bomb to ensure their destruction.

He looked quickly to the right, wondering where the hell his friends were. The van was half in and half out of the main entrance, the roller door still wrapped around it. Camille had jumped out and was standing next to the door, reaching back into the van. Russell had thrust open the van's side door and had one foot on the ground, but he was more in the van than out. Neither of them appeared able to move any farther.

Frozen by magic, he thought, and he smelled again the sting of fear, the sense of urgency. He ran toward them, looking at the parcel as he passed it but not daring to go any closer. He had no experience in dealing with bombs and no desire to go near it and risk blowing them all up. All he needed to know was the time they had left, and the clock showed that all too clearly—less than two minutes.

Magic thrummed against his skin. He skidded to a stop, his gaze sweeping the floor. He saw the wide semicircle drawn onto the concrete and the wards spaced at regular intervals along that line. They'd had no hope. The minute they'd breached the warehouse's entrance, the spell had been activated. It had snared them the moment they touched the concrete. No doubt a similar spell had been set on the doors. No wonder

Trina was still alive. It would have taken a tremendous amount of personal energy to set these spells, and it would take the witch more than a few hours to recover.

He squatted, eyes narrowed, watching the slight ripple of energy cutting the air. Urgency beat at him, through him. Though he couldn't see the timer, he knew the seconds were slipping away too quickly. But if he hurried, if he touched this spell the wrong way, it would snare him too and they'd all be blown up.

He studied the curve of energy to his right. It pulsed rich and strong, cutting the air as cleanly as a knife. But to his left, down near the entrance, the shield rippled. One of the wards had been knocked slightly off-line by the van's impact as it came through the door. All he had to do was knock it out of line completely, and the circle would be broken.

He rose, putting away his gun and switching the knife to his right hand. He glanced at the clock and saw they had less than a minute. Sweat trickled down his back. He quickly followed the arc of energy and stopped near the ward. The knife wasn't long enough to break through the shield and reach it. He cursed vehemently. He certainly couldn't touch the circle. The minute he did, he'd be caught. And the energy would repel anything except silver. He glanced at the clock again. Forty seconds. No time, and no choice. He'd have to throw the knife and hope like hell the impact was enough to knock the ward off-line.

Otherwise, they were all dead.

He ran back until he was at the right angle and took aim. He threw the knife as hard and as fast as he could. It pierced the shield cleanly, light flaring like lightning down the blade as it arrowed toward the ward. It hit dead center, sliding the ward several inches sideways. Not far, but enough to break the circle. Energy exploded, a wave of heat and power that knocked him off his feet.

Hands grabbed him, hauling him upright. "Ten seconds!" Russell yelled. "Move, Camille."

Doyle pulled away from Russell's grip. "I'm okay. Go!"

He thrust Russell forward, then grabbed his knife and followed him. Behind them, the timer beeped. For several heartbeats, nothing happened. Relief swept through him. Maybe the witch wasn't as clever as she liked to think . . .

The bomb blew. A fiery wave of destruction picked him up, thrusting him sideways. A second later, the heat hit, searing him. Pain surged, and a scream tore up his throat. Then the darkness encased him and he knew no more.

SEVENTEEN

KIRBY STEPPED INTO THE SHADOW OF AN OLD ELM and studied the building halfway down the street. It was nothing spectacular—a square, five-story brick affair, surrounded by a high chain-link fence that almost looked solid, thanks to the weeds and rubbish that clogged it. If the smashed state of the windows and the amount of graffiti scrawled across the walls were anything to go by, the building had obviously been abandoned for some time.

Why here? It seemed a strange sort of place for a witch to be conducting a spell. Though admittedly, she didn't know an awful lot about witches or spell casting, despite the fact that Helen had been involved in both. But it was too late now to regret her reticence when it came to learning anything about the subject.

She glanced down at the bag clutched tightly in her hand. She had no idea why she'd bothered to bring it. It wasn't as if she were going to need it, particularly if she didn't beat the witch. She thought of the note she'd left behind, of the things she hadn't said, and wished she could go back to yesterday, to the moment in time when she lay wrapped in the warmth of Doyle's body and he'd asked her to marry him. Wished she'd had the courage to take the chance rather than giving in to fear yet again.

At least then she would have had a moment of happiness to remember now, when death was so close she could smell it.

Terror stole through her heart, squeezing it tight. She took several deep breaths, trying to calm her nerves, then resolutely headed toward the building. She couldn't delay any longer. Dusk was beginning to creep across the sky. If she waited until night, Mariel would be at full strength, and she wouldn't have a chance.

The gate was locked, but the wire in the nearby fence had been cut and pushed back, leaving a small gap. She threw her bag through, then squeezed in after it. The sharp ends of the wire brushed her back, snagging through her T-shirt and tearing into her skin. She cursed and pulled away, leaving a jagged scrap of material hooked on the wire.

Great, just great, she thought, twisting around in an attempt to see the cut. Though she couldn't see it, there was warmth trickling down her back. It didn't feel like much, so with any luck, the cut wasn't all that bad. The last thing she needed right now was to be leaving a trail of blood. Who knew what sort of attention *that* might attract?

Goose bumps fled across her body. Trying to ignore the growing sense of danger, she picked up her bag and headed down the driveway. Several stacks of crates lay to her left and she hesitated. She had to stow her bag somewhere, and they looked just as safe as anywhere else. She doubted there would be any kids around. Surely the witch would have made sure there was no one near to disturb her spell casting.

In the distance, thunder rumbled. She glanced up. The skies were blue and clear, yet electricity thrummed through the air—through her. Sparks danced across her fingers, but it wasn't that energy she felt. It came from the sky itself, from the distant hum of a waiting storm. Hers to call, thanks to Helen's sacrifice.

An all-too-familiar ache washed through her. *I have to win this. For Helen, and for the other girls in the circle.*

She tucked her bag under a couple of nearby crates, then turned, her gaze sweeping the front of the building. Where would a witch go to perform a ceremony?

She bit her lip, remembering the vision she'd had— the concrete walls slung with slime, and the feel of empty desolation. *The parking garage,* she thought, gaze sweeping to the side of the building. There, near the end of the building, she saw the entrance.

A tremor ran through her, and the energy playing across her fingers became fierce enough to stand on end the hairs along her arms. She continued on down the driveway.

The garage loomed, dark and cavernous. No sunlight filtered in past the entrance; it was almost as if a curtain of night had been drawn across it.

Might as well be entering hell itself, she thought, and had a horrible feeling that might be the case.

Thunder rumbled, closer than before. She looked up one more time at the blue skies and hoped she lived to see them again.

Then, taking a deep breath, she stepped past the curtain and entered the parking garage.

* * *

THERE WAS SOMETHING ON DOYLE'S BACK, PRESSING down hard, squashing him. Every breath hurt—the air burned, scorching his throat and his lungs. Heat licked at his feet, his legs. He groaned and tried to move. Fire twisted down his side, a living thing that threatened to consume his consciousness.

He groaned again and tried to open his eyes. Couldn't. Something seemed to be gluing them shut. He sniffed the air and regretted it almost instantly. It was pungent and gaseous, and seemed to burn through his entire body. He coughed so hard it felt as if he were tearing apart.

"Doyle!" Russell's shout seemed to be coming from a great distance.

"Here." The word came out harsh but little more than a whisper.

The weight pressed deeper. He fought to breathe, to stay conscious. The heat of the flames danced across his feet, and the smell of burning leather joined the junket of toxic odors surrounding him.

"Doyle! Answer me, damn it."

Here, he wanted to say, *here!* But the words lodged somewhere in his throat and refused to budge. Sounds reached through to his prison—the scrape of metal against concrete, a grunt of effort, the sharp sound of swearing. He smiled. Camille had never been much of a lady.

Dirt showered him. The weight on his back shifted, and pain shot through his leg, reflecting across his entire body. A scream tore at his throat, but it came out as little more than a hiss. Swearing filled the air, as colorful as the smoke surrounding him. He coughed again, harsher and longer, until spasms shook his body and it felt like he was going to throw up. Then the weight lifted from his back and leg, and suddenly he could breathe again. Only the fresh air sent him into another spasm of coughing and made him wish for the bliss of unconsciousness.

Hands grabbed him, hauling him upright. The world blurred, and then he was out in bright light, with the warmth of the late afternoon sun glaring down on him. That was quickly replaced by cool darkness. The van, he thought vaguely, looking around. But hadn't that been blown up?

Moisture dribbled across his lips. He licked at it quickly, desperate to ease the burning in his throat.

"Easy with that," Camille said from his right. "Not too much or he'll throw up."

"I know, I know." Russell's voice sounded impatient and worried.

I'm okay, he wanted to say, but his vocal cords still refused to work. Something cool and moist touched his face, wiping the stickiness from his eyes. He blinked and opened them. A man knelt in front of him, his head and hands swathed in bandages that were covered in soot and dirt. He blinked, but the vision refused to go away.

"Russell?" His question came out as little more than a harsh croak.

The bandaged face nodded. Doyle looked to his left and saw the bright sunshine peeping past the black plastic covering the van's back windows. He realized then that Russell was wearing the bandages for protection. It was the only way he possibly could have ventured out into the sunlight without burning up.

"Keep still a while," Russell said. "Camille's fixing your leg."

Russell lifted the cup, dribbling more moisture into his mouth. He swished it around, then swallowed. The fire in his throat began to ease. He looked down, but couldn't see anything beyond Camille's back. Couldn't feel anything beyond an odd sort of numbness in his right leg.

Fear stirred his gut. "What's wrong with my leg?"

"A large chunk of metal has speared your thigh. It missed the bone, but that's about all it missed," Russell said. "Camille's plastered the area with a numbing salve and has cut off what she could, but basically, that's all we can do beyond getting you to a hospital. If we try to take it out here, you'll bleed to death."

At least that explained the numbness in his leg. He drank a few more drops of water and rolled his neck, trying to ease the ache. It felt as if someone had played baseball with his entire body.

"Not if I shapeshift. It'll heal enough to stop me from bleeding out."

Camille's expression showed serious doubt. "I'm not sure—"

"But I am. Do it, then bandage it tight. It'll hold, Camille." He sure as hell wasn't going to any damn hospital. Not when that mad bitch was still running around out there.

Camille took a deep breath, then nodded. "You ready?"

"Go for it." He released his grip on the knife and tensed, even though he knew it was completely the wrong thing to do. He felt the momentary pressure on his leg as Camille gripped the rod; then, without warning, she ripped it free. A scream tore up his throat, and for a moment, everything went black. He could feel the warmth gushing down his leg, and he knew that if he didn't do something quick, he'd die.

"Fuck, Doyle, change—now!"

He called to the magic and felt it rip his body, reshaping flesh and bone, the process as much about healing as shifting. He remained in panther form for several minutes, his breathing rapid and head light, then shifted back to human form.

And promptly blacked out. He must not have been out for long, though, because Camille was still bandaging his leg when he woke. "Why in hell did you detour for that damn knife? It almost cost you your life." Anger edged Russell's words.

Doyle shrugged. "It's silver, and the only one I have with me."

"So? Steal another. It wasn't worth almost losing your life over."

"Russ, silver is the one thing immune to magic. We may yet need it." Especially if the witch went after Kirby. He went still, and in that moment knew beyond a doubt that she was in trouble and needed help.

"Kirby," he said urgently, struggling to rise. "We have to get back to her!"

Camille swore at him, and Russell held him down. "Don't move, damn it!"

"You don't understand—"

"No, *you* don't understand," Russell said vehemently. "We need to get that leg tightly bandaged, otherwise you'll break the wound open again and bleed to death. How is that going to help Kirby?"

He relaxed a little and closed his eyes. Tension rode him, as sharp as the fear stirring his gut. "Okay. But once my leg is bandaged, we go get her."

Russell glanced at Camille. "I don't think—"

"I don't care what you think, my friend. She's in danger, and it's far more important that we save her than get me to a hospital."

"As much as I hate to say it," Camille said into the tense silence, "he's right. We can't let the witch get her hands on her."

Camille shifted slightly, revealing the massive blob of bandages on his leg. What was left of his jeans below the wound was soaked in blood. No wonder he felt light-headed. "How come the van survived the explosion?"

"Because I jumped in and drove it off," Camille said. "It runs a might faster than these old bones, let me tell you that. Besides, it was Russell's only hope. The sunshine would have killed him." She rose and lurched toward the driver's seat. "Now, where's this farm you two were staying at?"

He gave them the address, then added, "It's out along the Calder Freeway."

"Wherever that is. Russell, type it into the sat-nav while I get us moving."

The van started. Doyle closed his eyes, letting the movements of the old van lull him into a semi-sleep. Pain drifted through him, but at a distance. No doubt Camille had put something in the water to diminish it.

The noise of city traffic gave way to the hum of free-way travel. *Not far now,* he thought wearily, and hoped Kirby was okay. Hoped he was worrying over nothing.

Awareness tingled across his senses, and a wave of tension and fear rushed through his mind. Not his—Kirby's. He sat up abruptly. She was somewhere close. He scooted down to the back windows and tore away the plastic.

"What's wrong?" Russell said, voice sharp with concern.

"She's here." They were still on the freeway. There were no cars immediately behind them, but across the other side, a yellow cab sped by. "Turn the van around," he added, urgently.

Camille didn't argue. Tires squealed, then they were bouncing through the dividing strip of grass. "What car?" she asked, once they were on the other side.

"The cab. Hurry!" He leaned back against the side of the van and closed his eyes, wondering if she was a prisoner to evil or merely breaking another promise.

The traffic closed in around them again. Camille swore, and the blast of the van's horn was almost lost in the squeal of tires. "Idiot!" she yelled out the window.

Doyle edged forward and peered out the wind-shield. Not a cab in sight.

"It turned left two streets down," Russell said, glancing at him. "But from there, it's anyone's guess. How good is this connection between you and Kirby?"

"Good enough to find her, I think." *I hope.*

Camille turned left, then slowed. The street stretched before them, devoid of traffic of any kind. "Where to now?"

He frowned, reaching for the link. Though her thoughts were still distant, her fear surrounded him, so sharp it became his own. He flexed his fingers, trying to control the growing knot of anxiety in his gut. "Take the next right."

Camille swung into the street. Down at the far end, a yellow cab cruised out of a side street and drove toward them. Kirby wasn't in it. He knew that without looking.

"You want me to stop in front of that sucker and ask where he dropped her?"

He hesitated. Could they afford to waste the time? Could they afford not to? "Do it," he said.

The van slewed sideways, blocking the road. The cab stopped and the driver rolled down the window as Camille hustled over. Three minutes later she was back. "Rodger Street," she said. "Outside some sort of packing factory. He didn't have a specific number."

"Was she alone?" Some part of him hoped she wasn't. Hoped that she was being forced into this action. He just didn't want to believe she was breaking another promise.

Camille nodded. "Whatever she's doing, she's apparently doing it willingly."

"Damn." Why? What could have gone so wrong in the few hours he'd left her alone that she was now willing to risk her life going up against the witch?

Camille patted his hand, then reversed out of the cab's way before continuing up the street. They quickly found Rodger Street and slowed to a crawl.

"There's the packing factory," Camille said, pointing to the right.

He knew without looking that she wasn't there. "Keep going."

They continued to cruise down the street. "Heartbeats, coming from that abandoned building up ahead," Russell said. "There are at least three that I can hear."

"Human or otherwise?" Doyle asked. Not that it really mattered beyond knowing what he was up against.

Russell hesitated. "Hard to say."

Camille pulled into the driveway and stopped. "The gates are padlocked," she said. "If I drive through them, they're going to know we're here."

"She didn't enter via the gates." He spotted the brief flutter of material on the fence several feet away from the gate and thrust open the van's side doors, clambering out.

"Damn it, shifter, get back in here. Let us deal with this. You can't go wandering around with that leg of yours."

He ignored her and hobbled over to the fence. Pain rose—a promise of the agony he would no doubt be in once the painkillers wore off. He plucked the thin scrap from the wire and sniffed it quickly. Basil, geranium and pine—the oils she'd soaked in last night. He clenched his fingers around the material, his gaze searching the structure. She wasn't in the building itself, but underneath—in the parking garage.

"Damn it, Doyle—"

The rest of Camille's words were lost to the buzz of magic as he shifted shape. Even in panther form, his leg was useless. It didn't matter. As a cat, he had three other legs and could move faster than any human. He slipped past the wire and ran for the parking garage.

KIRBY STOPPED AT THE END OF THE RAMP. ELECTRIC-ity danced across her fingers, shooting slivers of light through the veil-heavy darkness. Somewhere in the distance water dripped, a steady sound like fingers tapping impatiently. She shivered and thrust her imagination back into its box. The last thing she needed was to be imagining the worst. No doubt the witch would be doing *that* soon enough.

She edged forward, her steps becoming surer as her eyes grew used to the darkness. Columns loomed before her, some hung with slime, others scrawled with graffiti. Beer bottles decorated the far corners, scattered about like abandoned toys. The air smelled stale and was perfumed with the rich scent of rubbish and urine. Her vision, come to life.

A chill crept icy fingers down her spine. She shivered again, wondering why the parking garage was so cold when the air outside was so hot. Surely this close to the entrance, some of the day's heat should have crept in. Or maybe the unnatural curtain of darkness that seemed to hang over the entrance somehow blocked the heat as well.

She continued to follow the ramp down, reaching the next level. Mariel would be on the last one, though why she was so sure of this, she couldn't say. Oddly enough, the air here seemed warmer. The dripping water had faded, to be replaced by a hum that seemed to reverberate up through her feet. She hesitated, listening. And heard, underneath the hum, the soft chanting.

A spell of summoning, she thought. And wondered how the hell she knew.

And what the hell Mariel was summoning.

The closer she moved to the last level of the parking structure, the louder and stronger the humming became. Wisps of red and purple light flickered across the walls, and the air seemed to vibrate with urgency and power. Then it was gone, and a dead sort of silence prevailed.

Goose bumps crawled down her spine. There was something in the darkness with her. Something not human. She froze. A footstep scraped against the silence. Breathing, harsh and heavy, approached. She didn't move, pinned by fear, her hands clenched against the energy burning across her fingertips.

A man lumbered into view. Only it wasn't a man, but a decayed replica, its clothes little more than tatters of material that barely covered the skeletal remains of its body. It reeked of death and rotten meat. Her stomach stirred, threatening to revolt. She bit her lip, watching the creature plod by. Why was Mariel summoning things like that into being? Surely, if she was going to summon the dead to help her, she could get something a little more . . . lively? Like the zombie that had attacked Doyle . . .

Pain rose, and she closed her eyes. God, he was going to be so angry at her for doing this! But what other choice did she have? She couldn't be responsible for his death. She couldn't live with that on top of everything else.

She continued on. Ahead in the darkness, light beckoned. Someone was humming—a happy tune that set her teeth on edge.

She rounded a corner and stopped. A fire burned within a circle of stone, but its flames were an unnatural purple and green and cast sick shadows across the darkness. A tripod had been set up over it, and from this hung a steaming kettle. To the right of this was a black stone table. On it lay Trina. Even from where she stood, she could see the rise and fall of the other woman's chest. Relief swept through her. At least she wasn't too late to stop this madness.

A woman swept in from the darkness. She had sharp features, short brown hair, and a lanky, almost boyish body. Mariel. She hadn't changed all that much since Kirby had last seen her. She'd gained some height, but other than that, she could still have been the child that had chased them with dead bugs. Kirby flexed her fingers, needing to move, to hide. But the minute she did either, the witch would spot her. All she could do was remain still and hope fate was on her side for a change.

It wasn't.

Mariel bent over the fire, grasping the kettle with a gloved hand. Then she hesitated and looked up. Kirby met her gaze and saw only madness.

"Well, well, this is a nice surprise," Mariel murmured. Her voice, unlike her gaze, was warm and pleasant, her tone that of a friend rather than a foe. "Please, do come down. I've just made a cup of coffee, if you'd like to share it."

"Thanks, but I'm comfortable right where I am." Kirby flexed her fingers, trying to ease the tension knotting her muscles. The energy that danced across her fingers shot fiery sparks across the darkness.

If Mariel noticed, she gave no indication. "Maybe

so, but I prefer you to come closer— and you will do so, or the tramp on the table shall suffer the consequences."

She raised a hand and a knife appeared from nowhere, hovering above Trina's stomach. Kirby drew a deep breath. If she didn't do what Mariel wanted, if she tried to retreat or attack, it would be Trina who suffered, not her. She stepped into the circle of light provided by the fire and stopped.

"One wrong move and that knife will taste blood," Mariel said, then bent and poured some water in her mug. "You sure you don't want a cup?"

Kirby nodded, fingers clenched by her sides. Thunder rumbled, closer and sharper than before. But would it be able to help her this far underground? Or didn't that matter, given that Helen hadn't been just a storm witch, but the air elemental?

"Must be a storm brewing," Mariel commented, holding the mug in two hands, as if warming them. "But you wouldn't know anything about that, would you?"

Kirby shook her head, watching her cautiously. It felt as if she'd stepped into the Twilight Zone. The last thing she'd expected to be doing right now was standing here having a semi-normal conversation with the fiend who'd murdered her friend—*her sister.*

Mariel considered her for a second. The firelight cast shadows of green and purple across her features, making her face look gaunt, almost skeletal. She seemed in no great hurry to do anything more than talk, and that in itself was worrying.

"How did you find me?" Mariel asked, eventually.

"Does it matter?" Kirby glanced across at the black stone table. The knife still hovered above Trina's midriff, rotating rapidly, as if it were a drill barely held in check. Attack Mariel, and the knife would drop. Attack the knife, and Mariel would use the moment to attack *her*. She shifted her weight from one foot to the other, wanting—*needing*—to move, to do something to end this impasse. Every second she delayed bought them a second closer to night and to the witch gaining full strength. Yet right now, she had no other option than to play this Mariel's way.

"I guess it doesn't." Mariel sipped her coffee, watching her steadily, her blue eyes filled with a mix of hate and madness.

It was the hate Kirby couldn't understand. What had they ever done to Mariel to deserve such depth of feeling? Yes, they'd killed her best friend, but that had been an accident, and Mariel herself had been the fire elemental . . . Her thoughts stuttered to a stop. If Camille was right, it wasn't just Mariel who stood before her now, but Felicity—or at least, Felicity's spirit. A spirit that may well have been dragged from the depths of hell. "Tell me, when did you raise Felicity's spirit? And why?"

Mariel raised an eyebrow. "You are well informed, aren't you?"

She shrugged. "Sometimes it pays to know what you're up against."

Mariel nodded serenely. "Yes, I guess it does." She sipped her coffee again, then tilted her head, her gaze narrowing a little.

The sense of danger leapt tenfold, squeezing her throat

so tightly that Kirby could barely breathe. Yet Mariel hadn't moved, hadn't done anything beyond change her expression. *I'm out of my league,* Kirby thought, and flexed her hands, her fingers aching with the energy that burned across them. The sparks danced in jagged lines across the darkness, clashing with the dirty light of the fire. Mariel glanced down briefly, a slight smile touching her lips.

"The power of air," she said. "I'm keen to see how well it stands up to fire and water."

Kirby wasn't. The only thing she was keen to do was get the hell out of here. But that wasn't an option—not yet, and not without Trina. Then she blinked. Mariel had said *she* was air—did that mean she wasn't aware that *she'd* been the binder, not Helen? "You didn't answer my question."

"Didn't I? How remiss of me."

Her smile was cold, cruel. It whispered of death, of a darkness so deep Kirby felt the chill of it clear through to her soul.

"Do you know how hard it is to find information about raising the dead? It took me five years to find anything decent on the subject. Five years is a long time in hell, you know."

Her hands clenched around the cup, shattering it. Shards of china clattered over the concrete, a brittle sound that sawed at Kirby's nerves. "Then you were sixteen when you raised her. So why wait until now to go after us?"

"You really don't know anything about magic, do you?" Mariel snorted and shook her hand. Blood splayed across the concrete and into the flames. They hissed and recoiled. "It takes time to learn the craft, time to gain strength and knowledge. And time to find what the government had scattered."

So, it was true. In trying to track down their origins, Helen and the other girls had led a killer to their door. Kirby rubbed her arms, showering herself with sparks that did little to ease the chill from her bones.

"Why? Answer me that. It can't be all about revenge." Surely no one, no matter how mad, would go through all this for something as simple as revenge.

"I thought you would know the answer to that." Mariel hesitated, then shook her head, as if in disbelief. "You felt the power we all raised. How could you not want to feel all that again?"

Kirby stared at her. Was that what this was all about—the need to control? The need to be the most dominant force? Mariel had never been entirely sane. Anyone who raised dead bugs for the sheer fun of terrorizing other children could never be described as sane. But that night, when they'd joined hands and raised a force that had shaken the very foundations of the world around them, they'd obviously destroyed what little rationality she'd had. For one brief moment, Mariel had had a glimpse of the absolute power she'd craved—only it wasn't hers to control. It would never be hers to control.

Unless she destroyed the circle and sucked its powers into her own being.

"So you went after Helen?" Kirby said, keeping her voice low. Right now, the last thing she wanted was to antagonize the bitch and force her into action. But she needed time to think—to plan. And she needed to know what assumptions Mariel had made.

"At first, I thought Helen controlled the powers of air. But when I killed her and there were no powers there to steal, I knew I had been wrong. Then I knew that she was the binder, and you controlled the air." Mariel sniffed. "The two of you always were a bit interchangeable, so it's no wonder I got confused."

But Kirby could see the sudden flare of rage in her eyes, and knew this was the reason why Helen had been torn apart so brutally; Mariel never had liked being made to look the fool.

"And you didn't care about her powers of binding?" Kirby hazarded.

Mariel wrinkled her nose. "Why should I? What use are the powers of binding when I will have all four bound within *me*?" She gave a short, brutal laugh. "I already control two of the four elements. And now I have the final two here, awaiting my gift of darkness."

Tension ran through Kirby. Her fists were clenched so tight her nails were cutting into her palms. No wonder her name hadn't been on Camille's list; she had become a victim in Mariel's twisted mind only after Helen's murder.

But Kirby did suspect that Mariel's assumptions were wrong in one important way. She had bound together the power of four elementals on that one fateful night. She had felt how her powers changed and magnified what was already present. To gain the powers she wanted, Mariel *would* need the powers of binding— but if Mariel succeeded in killing Kirby, she'd not only get Helen's power, but become the binder as well. And all the Circle's worst nightmares would come true.

"I must say," Mariel continued serenely, and absently waved a hand, "that you've caught me by surprise. I was expecting to have to pry you away from the hands of that damn shifter." She hesitated, smiling again. It was a picture of maliciousness itself. "I set a trap for him, you know. Just how well do you think a shifter can survive a bomb?"

Kirby's stomach churned, her mind snared by the sudden image of Doyle being caught in flames and imprisoned under a mountain of concrete. Fear rose, threatening to engulf her. She took a deep breath and thrust the images away. Doyle wasn't dead. She'd know if he was.

She opened her mouth to reply, but the words froze in her throat. The wind stirred, caressing her cheeks. They were no longer alone. Something was creeping up behind her—something that smelled like death.

She spun and thrust out her hand. The pent-up energy surged from her fingers, lashing the darkness, thudding into the chest of the dead man behind her. Fingers of blue-white light webbed across his body, pinning him to the spot and burning him to a crisp in seconds flat. The smell of burnt flesh stung the air, and her stomach roiled.

He's dead, she reminded herself fiercely. *You can't feel responsible about killing a man who is already dead.*

The air behind her boiled with heat, reaching toward her with fiery fingers she felt rather than saw. She dropped, her hands and knees smacking painfully against the concrete. Heat seared across her back, burning her T-shirt but barely touching her skin. She rolled to smother the flames, then saw something glitter out of the corner of her eye, and kept on rolling. Ice exploded against the floor, showering her with shards that tore at her skin and hair.

She flung out her hand, imagined fingers of air wrapping around the knife and flinging it back, deep into the darkness. There was a whoosh, and the knife disappeared. Without pausing, she shifted, this time aiming her net at Mariel. Energy cut through the darkness, momentarily highlighting the surprise on the witch's face before she dove out of the way. The lightning exploded against the edge of the fire and scattered the ring of stones. With an odd sort of sucking sound, the purple flames died and darkness swept in—a black curtain she could almost touch.

"Now, that's just plain nasty," Mariel commented from the darkness to Kirby's left. "Do you know how difficult it is to raise one of those fires?"

Trying to get around me, Kirby thought. She slid off her shoes and edged barefoot toward the table. If she could just get Trina down . . .

Flames shot across the darkness and she cursed and dove away, hitting the concrete again and skinning her chin in the process. She wiped away the blood dribbling down her neck, then yelped as fiery fingers of heat licked toward the soles of her feet. But the flames never touched her, recoiling millimeters away from her feet before dying. She frowned and remembered Helen's words—*she cannot hurt you with what is yours to command.* Did that mean the powers of fire could not be used against her? She fervently hoped so, if only because it gave her some sort of chance.

She pushed upright. Thunder rumbled again. The

storm was close, so close. She could feel the power of it beginning to thrum through her body, her soul.

Then the wind stirred again, whispering its secrets. Kirby spun, but far too late. Something hit the side of her head, and darkness closed in.

A RING OF DEAD MEN SURROUNDED HIM. DOYLE HESitated in the parking garage's entrance, studying the zombies for several heartbeats. There were six of the stinking things. At any other time, it wouldn't have much mattered. These six didn't possess the size or the brute strength of the zombie that had attacked him at Rachel Grant's and, even though he was wounded, generally wouldn't have caused him much of a problem.

But right now he couldn't afford any kind of delay. Kirby's fear was like a blanket, threatening to smother him. She was with the witch and in trouble. Any delay might have deadly consequences for them both.

The zombies lunged toward him. He sprang over their backs and shifted shape, then wrapped an arm around one of the creatures' necks and twisted hard. Bone snapped, and the zombie went limp. He thrust it into the path of another one, then backpedaled as fast as his injured leg would allow as a third zombie lurched at him. He twisted away from its grasping fingers, and pain shot up his leg. He cursed and limped away, aware of the warmth dribbling down his thigh. The wound had obviously opened a little, but it was nowhere near as bad as before. The creatures formed a pack and ran at him as one. He shifted shape and leapt away, but the grasping fingers of a zombie on the outskirts of the pack caught him, bringing him down before it jumped on top of him. He slashed at the creature's face with his paws, cutting deep, then shifted back to human shape and smashed his fist into the face of the creature pinning him. Bone shattered, but the blow itself had little effect. Fingers grasped at his neck, seeking to choke him, while others grabbed his legs and feet and pulled, as if intent on ripping him apart. Agony burned through his body, and the rush of warmth from the wound became stronger.

Behind the pack of zombies, the darkness shifted and became Russell's bandaged form. He picked up the creatures by the scruff of the neck, tossing them back into the shadows as if they were nothing more than unwanted garbage.

Then he held out a bandaged hand and hauled Doyle to his feet. "You keep going. I'll take care of these maggots."

For an instant, the darkness swam around him, and pinpricks of heat danced before his eyes. Sweat broke out across his brow, and he knew it was only Russell's grip on his arm that was keeping him upright.

"You look like shit," Russell continued, the concern in his voice deeper.

"That's because I feel like shit." The scuff of a foot against concrete told him the zombies were on the move again. "Where's Camille?"

"Turns out the gate was spelled. She's disconnecting it so she can bring the van in." He hesitated, then shoved something into Doyle's hand. "You may need this."

He glanced down. It was the silver knife. He squeezed Russell's shoulder. "Thanks. And be careful."

The vampire snorted. "I'm not the one in danger of bleeding to death here. Now, go and rescue your lady before you fall down dead."

Doyle limped away. One of the zombies tried to follow, but Russell grabbed its arm and tossed it back at its brethren. The sounds of the ensuing scuffle followed Doyle into the darkness.

Light began to dance across the wall, but its color was the sick hue of dark magic. He was so close now that it burned across his skin—a foul sensation that churned his gut. Kirby's fear sharpened abruptly, then both the light and her thoughts cut off, leaving an odd sort of emptiness in his mind. She wasn't dead, but he wasn't certain of anything more than that. Apprehension became a blade digging deep into his gut. He shifted shape, then picked up the knife between his teeth and hurried on, his breathing sharp and with a bitter taste in his mouth.

In panther form, he could hear the sound of movement more clearly. Could hear someone grunting in effort, then the slap of flesh against stone. He heard the sharp click of heels moving away through the darkness.

He reached the parking garage's bottom level and stopped in the shadow of a concrete pillar. The witch squatted near a ring of stones, rearranging them and muttering something under her breath. Kirby and Trina were both lying on a sacrificial table. Neither of them moved, but they both breathed, and relief washed through him.

Yet even from where he stood, he could smell the blood that had leeched into the stone over time. Death had tasted the life of its victims many times on that table. If he weren't very careful, it would savor the taste of two more.

He padded forward. The witch stood, and her muttering grew more intense. She produced a knife and slashed her wrists, dripping the blood into the ring of stone. Magic stirred, caressing his skin with evil. Light woke in the ring of stone, flickering sick shadows across the darkness.

He didn't have much time left. He shifted shape near the table and rose, quickly slashing the ropes binding Kirby and Trina's limbs.

Behind him, the chanting grew, becoming feverpitched. Magic seared the air, and the night shifted as flames began to dance and burn within the ring of stones.

No time left. Nor was there any chance of him getting Kirby out of here without being seen. The only option left was attacking the witch.

He hefted the knife and turned to throw—only to find himself eyeballing a gun.

THE SOUND OF A GUNSHOT JERKED KIRBY AWAKE. Fear filled her mind—fear and pain—a wave of red heat that almost suffocated her.

Doyle was with her here in the darkness, but he was hurt. Seriously hurt. Just as Helen had warned.

Biting her lip and fighting the need to get up and look for him, help him, Kirby opened her eyes. Cold stone pressed against her back, and darkness loomed above her. Trina was lying beside her, as cold and still as death itself. Terror rose, grasping her by the throat, threatening to strangle her.

Sound scuffed to her right, then the sharp click of heels approached. She closed her eyes, feigning unconsciousness, knowing that until she knew where Doyle was, it was better not to move. Better if the witch thought her still unconscious.

Mariel stopped beside her. She ran her hand almost lovingly down Kirby's arm, and it took every ounce of willpower to remain still and not shudder away from the sting of her touch.

Then she turned away and addressed the shadows. "Come into light where I can see you, shifter, or the next shot will remove your charge's toes."

A chill ran through Kirby. She had no doubt Mariel meant what she said. Obviously, neither did Doyle.

He moved into the circle of dusky firelight, and her breath caught. Blood glistened wetly on his arm and darkened his jeans almost black. He was barely even standing—most of his weight seemed to be resting on his left leg. Sweat beaded his forehead, and his eyes were little more than deep blue slits. He was a bloodied warrior ready to die to protect her, and she knew she could do no less for him. She shifted her hand carefully, reaching for Trina. Found her fingers and clasped them tightly.

Overhead, thunder rumbled—a violent sound that seemed to shudder through the very air around them. Energy burned into her body, her soul. Though her eyes were still closed, she could see the swiftly running clouds far above them, could feel the lick of their power, as if they were her own.

Mariel glanced at her—a brief but heated touch she felt rather than saw.

"Drop the knife, shifter," the witch said after a moment, her voice filled with sudden anxiety.

The knife clattered to the concrete. Doyle's concern ran around her, through her. *Are you okay?*

Tears stung her closed eyes at the sheer depth of concern—and love—in that one question. *I'm certainly better than you.* She hesitated, wishing she could say more but not daring to tempt fate just yet. *I'm about to test Helen's spell and call the storms down, so be ready for it.*

Be careful, he said. *She still has the gun.*

Not for long she doesn't. She clenched her fist, fighting back the bitter taste of fear and any form of doubt. This would work. It had to work, or they would all die.

Within her mind, she reached for the clouds high above. Power surged, sharp and clean, running through every muscle, every vein, until her whole body ached with the force of it.

Mariel's snort raked the silence. "Sometimes men are simply too predictable." As she raised the gun, Kirby called to the wind. It swept in, fierce and cold, swirling around Mariel, thrusting her sideways and wrenching the gun from her hands. And with the wind came the rain, a torrent that soaked the three of them near the table and yet left Doyle untouched.

He shifted shape and leapt toward the witch. Fire burned through the night, and he twisted. The flames singed his coat, and the smell of burning hair and flesh stung the air and churned Kirby's stomach. He hit the ground and became human again but remained on all fours, as if he didn't have the energy to move any farther. Agony surged through the link between them, and for several seconds she couldn't even breathe.

"Bitch!" Mariel spun and lashed out.

Kirby dodged, but not fast enough. Mariel's nails raked her face, as sharp as any panther's claws.

"For that, you will both pay." A knife appeared in midair. Mariel waved a hand, and the blade arrowed toward Doyle. He didn't move. He wasn't even looking.

Kirby called the air, directing its power at the blade, then lurched up and grabbed Mariel's hand while tightening her grip on Trina's.

The witch's eyes widened, and for the first time, fear flickered in the depths of her madness. But she could no more fight Kirby's hold on her than she could the energy that now rushed between them.

Once again, the circle of five had become one.

Power surged, crackling sharply across the silence— a rich, throaty roar that made the storms pale in comparison. The earth shuddered in response, and the sharp sound of shattering concrete filled the air.

Kirby!

Doyle's shout seemed a million miles away. Energy burned, became a song only she could see and control. Her whole being danced to its tune, aching for its caress.

Kirby! Listen to me.

She frowned, but the music of the energy beckoned and his voice seemed to fade. She smiled, in her mind's eye seeing the witches' stones tumble and leap like frogs in the pond that the garage had become.

You must control it, or you'll kill us all.

The desperation in his voice reached past her euphoria. Memories shuddered through her. She couldn't kill—not again.

Not innocent bystanders, anyway.

She took a deep breath, then focused the force in on Mariel herself.

Pain exploded—pain so deep it tore through every fiber of her being. She screamed—a sound echoed by both Mariel and Trina. Then the whole world seemed to tear itself apart and she knew no more.

EIGHTEEN

"ARE YOU SURE YOU WON'T COME BACK WITH US?"

Doyle shook his head. "I have to find her, Russ. I can't leave until I at least talk to her."

Five days had passed since that fateful fight in the parking garage that had killed the witch and damn near killed him as well. Five days in which he'd been stuck in the hospital, recovering from the wounds the witch had inflicted. He might be a shapeshifter, and capable of fast healing, but even *he* needed medical help sometimes.

And in those five days, he hadn't seen or heard from Kirby.

She'd checked out of the hospital the day after they'd both been admitted and had simply disappeared. Worry and fear had been his constant companions from that moment on. What if she was still lost in the dance of energy she'd raised? What if the energy that had blown apart the witch had somehow backwashed and taken her spirit and her mind, as well?

What if she was running from *him,* from the emotions she feared to face?

The wind stirred, running heated fingers through his hair. He squinted up at the clear blue skies. Though dawn had barely passed, the promise of another hot day was already evident. A good day for hunting, if nothing else.

"You'd better get inside," he said, returning his gaze to Russell's bandaged face. "Before the sun hits full strength and you start burning."

Russell nodded and held out a bandaged hand. "Good luck, my friend."

"Thanks. I think I'm going to need it." He glanced past the vampire as Camille appeared in the doorway of the Circle's private jet. She looked around quickly, then clattered down the steps and bustled toward them. "Looks like you're about to get in trouble," he added.

Russell groaned. "It's going to be a long trip home if the old witch is going to start nagging now."

"If you don't watch that smart mouth of yours, vampire, you'll well and truly hear me nag." Camille stopped and glared up at Russell. "Now, get that bandaged butt of yours into the plane. We've got to get going."

"My butt isn't bandaged. Only my face and hands."

"Seems to be no difference from where I'm standing," she muttered. "Now, move it."

Doyle choked back his laugh as Camille turned the full force of her glare at him. "As for you, shifter, be careful. There's no telling what her state of mind is going to be."

"I know." But he couldn't leave without trying to find her. Without knowing, one way or another, whether she wanted to be a part of his life.

Camille pulled a brush and a scrap of paper from her pocket and slapped both into his hands. "My finding spell finally pinned her down for you. The address where you'll find her is written on that paper."

He clenched his fingers around both. "Thanks."

Camille studied him for a moment, her expression troubled. "What are you going to do if she says no?"

He shrugged. It was a question that had preyed upon his thoughts more than a few times. And the truth was that he simply didn't know. He loved her, and he would always love her, no matter what. And while he was certain she returned his feelings, he wasn't sure she had the strength to follow her heart and trust what she felt.

"I'll see you in a week," Camille said. "One way or another, this will all be sorted out by then."

Hopefully for the better, he thought bleakly. He kissed Camille's leathery cheek and watched her power back toward the stairs. She waved from the top, then ducked inside. Doyle thrust his hands in his pockets and turned away. Time to go find a cab and search out the woman who could still shatter his heart.

KIRBY PLUCKED THE DEAD FLOWER HEADS FROM THE small rosebush, then sat back on her heels. The silvery-purple blush on the remaining flowers seemed to glow in the bright morning light, as if lit by an inner fire.

Helen's body had been released to the funeral parlor five days ago—the same day she'd checked herself out of the hospital—and while the police investigations were still ongoing, she knew they'd never get their answers. Mariel was dead—blown apart by the very forces she'd tried to control.

They were forces that would not—at least in Kirby's lifetime—be joined again. She'd felt both the earth and fire powers slip from her grasp as she'd fallen unconscious. She had no idea where they went or what would happen to them. Perhaps they waited in the ether. Perhaps sometime in the future, two children would be born with the ability to raise fire or shake the earth. She hoped those children would not be forced to kill, as she and Helen and the other girls in the circle had.

Kirby closed her eyes. She'd killed once again, but this time she didn't really regret it. Mariel had deserved her fate.

At least Helen had been cremated, as she'd wished. This rose and the small nameplate underneath it were all the indication that anyone of any importance lay buried here under the turf. It didn't seem right, somehow. Surely Helen deserved more.

The wind stirred, briefly kissing her cheeks. She closed her eyes, reaching for that faint caress.

"Remember, sister, all that lies under the rose are the ashes of my body." Helen's voice was distant, as gentle as the breeze itself. "I am one with the wind now and forever within your reach."

Tears stung her eyes. Because of Helen's sacrifice, she would never be alone, no matter what happened between her and Doyle. And yet, given the option, she'd rather have a flesh-and-blood sister standing beside her any day.

"I'm finally happy, Kirby, and I'm not alone. Other storm witches glide the breezes with me." Fingers of wind playfully tugged at her hair. "Don't be compelled to stay where my ashes lie. They don't matter in the scheme of things. It is time you looked after yourself."

As Helen's words swirled around her, Kirby felt the last vestiges of guilt vanish. She'd done all she could— not just for Helen, but for Trina. Helen's insurance money would pay for the care Trina needed, and the doctors were hopeful that, with time, she'd return to normal. Or as normal as any of them could ever be, given what they'd been through.

Helen was right. There was nothing to be gained by staying here, mourning someone whose spirit had not died. It was time for her to move on, to put the half-forgotten memories of the past behind her forever and start looking toward the future.

A future that depended greatly on the reaction of the thief who'd snuck past her defenses and stolen her heart.

She rose and turned—only to freeze in surprise. Doyle stood twenty feet away, his arms crossed and stance casual.

Joy surged within her, fierce and hard, and for an instant, all she wanted to do was run into his arms and shower him with kisses. But the eyes she loved so much were wary, and the link that had allowed them to read each other's thoughts and emotions was still, as devoid of life as his expression. Fear stirred in her stomach. What if, sometime in the last five days, he'd changed his mind?

She licked her lips. "How are you feeling?" It was an inane thing to say, but the words she wanted to say lay lodged somewhere in her throat, frozen by the caution in his eyes.

"Better now, knowing that you are whole and sane."

She winced at the soft rebuke in his voice, but knew it was well deserved.

"I'm sorry. It's just that with the police and Trina, and . . ." Her voice faded. It sounded like she was putting him behind everyone else on her list of priorities, and that was far from the truth. He'd been in her thoughts every hour of every day, even if she'd made no effort to contact him. But then, she hadn't really needed to. She'd known he was okay, just as surely as he'd known she was.

But it wasn't their physical well-being that hung in the balance right now—it was their emotional one. *Had* he changed his mind? She couldn't tell, and it scared her more than anything ever had.

There was only one way she was going to find out. She took a deep breath and gathered her courage.

"Do you remember that question you asked? The one I wouldn't answer?"

He didn't move, didn't react in any way. "I'm not likely to forget such a question."

Her stomach tightened. She stared at him for a moment longer, then said softly, "The answer is yes."

He didn't react for what seemed like an eternity. Then a sexy grin split his lips, and the link opened between them, flooding her entire being with warmth, love and happiness. She ran toward him and he laughed, lifting her off her feet and twirling her around until her head spun. Then he kissed her, his lips hot and urgent, devouring hers until it felt like her heart was spinning as fast as her head.

Breathless and giddy, she broke away, staring into

his beautiful blue eyes. "I gather the answer is something of a relief?"

"You could say that." His thumb traced the line of her cheek, his touch gentle yet making her whole body tremble. "Do you have anything else here that you need to do?"

She glanced down at Helen's grave, then wrapped her arms around his neck and shook her head. "Why?"

"How long would it take you to pack?"

"Five minutes." Everything she wanted to keep was already in storage. Everything else had been given away. "Why?"

"I'm asking the questions here, missy." Mischief and love danced in his eyes. "What about a passport?"

She smiled. "I ordered one four days ago and paid extra for priority service. It arrived this morning."

"Then how do you feel about a Las Vegas wedding?"

Her heart danced at the thought. She raised her eyebrows, barely checking her grin. "Making sure you get me to the altar before I change my mind, huh?"

"Exactly." His mouth claimed hers again, but this time it was more a lingering promise of the night yet to come.

She sighed against his lips. "Las Vegas seems so far away."

"More than twenty hours," he agreed. He slid his hand down her back, cupping her rear and pulling her so close that their bodies almost seemed fused together. "Of course, I have several suggestions that'll while away the flight time."

"In front of a plane full of people? I thought you weren't an exhibitionist." She raised her eyebrows again, even though her pulse quickened at the thought.

"I'm not. I own a jet, and it comes complete with discreet staff and a bed big enough to get lost in."

"My, we *were* a successful thief, weren't we?"

"Yes. But my greatest acquisition is the one I'm now holding in my arms." His smile shimmered through her. "I do love you, you know."

"And I you," she said, then added dryly, "Mind you, if all you're intending to do is merely hold me and talk, I may have to reconsider my answer."

He laughed—a warm, happy sound that sang through her entire being.

"Las Vegas, here we come," he said, grabbing her hand and racing her toward the waiting taxi.

If you loved *Circle of Fire,*
be sure not to miss the exciting final novel
in the Damask Circle series

CIRCLE OF DESIRE

by

Keri Arthur

And stay tuned for the start of the riveting
Spook Squad trilogy with *Memory Zero,*
coming in Fall 2014.

Here's a special preview:

AIR HISSED THROUGH THE SILENCE. TENDRILS OF smoke began to curl past the window frames, its color luminous yet sickly. Katherine Tanner tugged one of the two white ash stakes strapped to her jeans free and clenched it tightly. On the opposite side of the room, a little girl slept on, oblivious to the smoky slivers of evil beginning to slip past the window. Kat hoped she remained unaware, but how likely was that, given her kidnapper seemed to be targeting children born into shifter families? While not all shifters were sensitive to magic, many were. It was a part of their soul, after all, even if a child this young would not be able to shift form. Not until puberty, anyway.

Kat was keeping her fingers crossed that this kid *did* get the chance to hit puberty.

Because if Gwen's premonition was right—and her grandmother's premonitions usually were—this child would be the next to go missing. They'd done everything they could to prevent that. They'd nailed the windows shut, they had cops patrolling close by, and warding stones had been placed around the child's bed to prevent any magic from coming close.

But these wards weren't designed to stop evil itself—and that's what was seeping into this room tonight. Kat's stomach began to churn. Though she'd spent the last ten years hunting the rogue elements of the supernatural community that preyed on humans, she'd never come across anything that went after kids the way this thing did. She had never met anything that did to them what this thing did.

She closed her eyes, fighting tears, trying not to relive the moment two nights before when they'd stepped into that old factory and found the body of the second missing four-year-old. Daniel had been unmarked except for two small puncture wounds on his neck. Though he'd been drained of blood, this was not what had caused his death. Only those gifted with psychic sight would ever see *that*.

Something had stolen his soul—had ripped it from his body between the beats of his heart. He'd died quickly, but in pain. Terrible, terrible pain.

She didn't want to face the thing that could do something like that. No one in their right mind would. But she had no choice, simply because the Damask Circle's resources were stretched to the limits right now, and there was no one else free to make the trip to Oregon.

She gripped the stake tighter and watched the

smoke draw together and find shape, becoming a scantily clad, extremely beautiful woman.

Evil came in all shapes and sizes, but for some reason Kat hadn't expected it to take the form of such Oriental perfection. And maybe it was just her own maternal instincts coming to the fore, but she just couldn't understand how *any* woman could harm a child—particularly one so young.

But this *was* the thing snatching the kids. It had the same sense of deeply entrenched corruption that she'd felt in the other bedrooms.

The woman stepped toward the child. Kat tensed but fought the urge to move, sensing the show wasn't over yet. Her fingers ached with the force of her grip on the stake. She had no idea whether it would actually kill the soul-sucker or not, but at the very least it would do some serious damage and give her time to yell for reinforcements.

A cold smile touched the woman's bloodless lips, then she turned and tried to open the window. It didn't budge, held steady by the nails placed there earlier. The woman stepped back and energy surged, crawling like fire across Kat's skin. The nails slithered from the wood and dropped softly to the floor. The woman lifted the window and leaned out.

A gaunt, dark-haired figure appeared, and the sensation of evil increased tenfold. The vampire's dead gaze scanned the room, stopping when it reached the shadows in which Kat stood. Though

she was certain he couldn't see past her grandmother's wards, he really didn't need to. Not with
the frantic beat of her heart.

He snarled softly, revealing stained canines. The
soul-sucker spun, the malevolence in her dark eyes
overwhelming any lingering impression of beauty.
With an inhuman growl, she leapt for the sleeping
child. Kat raised her hand, thrusting a lance of kinetic energy at the soul-sucker, flinging her away
from the bed. The woman hit the wall with enough
force to dent the plaster and shatter the nearby
window. As glass fell to the floor, the child woke,
her shriek almost ear-piercing. Hurried footsteps
began to echo down the hallway, but it was doubtful the cops would get here fast enough to even see
this thing, let alone catch it.

As the child's screams continued, the woman's
gaze met Kat's. In the dark depths of the creature's
eyes, she saw the promise of retribution. A chill
chased through her soul and she shivered.

Then the woman's form disintegrated, becoming
little more than mist that eddied out the open window. Kat cursed and ran across the room. The
woman had regained shape near the back fence,
and though the vampire was nowhere in sight, the
scent of his evil stung the night.

The bedroom door burst open and police poured
in. They called to her to stop, but their voices were
almost lost beneath the child's continuing screams.
So Kat ignored them and climbed out the window,

simply because she had no other choice. By the time she stopped to explain what had happened, the soul-sucker and the vamp would have disappeared. Besides, she doubted the cops would believe her anyway. The only person who *would* understand would probably be scrying right now, staring into her crystal ball in an effort to track the creatures and perhaps discover their daytime hideaway.

Smoke swirled up the wooden fence and disappeared over the top. Kat scrambled after it and sprinted down the alley, her footsteps a lone echo in the night. Ahead, streetlights shimmered and traffic rolled, but it all felt a world away. The creature she chased wanted seclusion and darkness—at least for the moment.

It turned left into another small alley. She followed, leaping over the rubbish and battered trash cans strewn across her path. She was tempted to shift shape and hit the night sky in her raven form, but she didn't dare risk it with the stakes she carried. And she wasn't about to leave them behind—not when the vampire still lurked. Her quarry ran past one of the gates leading into an old factory. Metal creaked, as if stirred by a wind that didn't exist, and another chill ran down her spine. The vampire was out there, pacing her. Watching her.

If he was the soul-sucker's partner, why didn't he attack?

The smudge of vapor continued on, moving toward

a squat-looking building at the end of the alley. Kat slowed and half wished she'd brought a flashlight. The moon above was almost full, yet its light struggled to touch the shadows lining the small alley. Though her night sight was generally better than a human's, even she would struggle to see through the pitch blackness inside that warehouse.

The soul-sucker wrapped itself around a window and disappeared. Kat stopped and scanned the outside of the building. It was a two-story brick structure, though the color of the bricks had long since been lost to thick layers of dirt and graffiti. Most of the windows on the lower floor had been boarded up, and the upper ones were all smashed. There was a small door to her right. The thick chains that had locked it were shattered.

An invitation, if ever she saw one. But an invitation to what? Was she walking into a trap, or had she merely found the most recent hiding place of these creatures?

The pounding of boots against concrete echoed against the night—probably the cops coming after her. She couldn't let them find her. The vampire could take out a dozen men in the blink of an eye. Even her powers gave her no certainty against him, despite her experience and psychic senses. Especially with that other thing wandering around.

She flipped the stake in her hand, then walked across to the entrance. Raising her fingers, she sent a sliver of kinetic energy at the door and pushed it open. It didn't creak. It didn't make any sound at all, not even from the chains that swung gently back and forth.

Her unease stirred anew. She stepped to one side and studied the darkness. Though the moon caressed the outer wall with light, no brightness shone through the doorway. It was as if a blanket of night hung over the entrance, sucking in all light.

She stepped inside. Nothing stirred the blackness except the wild beat of her heart. Yet she wasn't alone. The vampire and the soul-sucker were both here—along with someone new. Another shapeshifter.

Taking on two was tempting fate; three was inviting a trip to the nearest morgue. But she couldn't retreat. Not when the image of little Daniel Baker rose in her mind.

She edged forward. The farther she moved into the warehouse, the heavier the air became. The scents of age and rotting rubbish mingled with the ripe aroma of evil, turning her stomach and making it difficult to breathe. Breathing through her mouth didn't help, either. The air tasted as bad as it smelled.

Her foot hit something solid, and metal rattled across the concrete floor, the noise deafening in the silence. She cursed under her breath, but the night seemed to amplify her words and echo them across emptiness. Laughter answered, deep but feminine.

She hesitated, her gaze sweeping the night. The

soul-sucker wasn't running anymore. It was out there, watching Kat struggle through the dark. Waiting for her slightest mistake . . .

Despite the chill in the air, sweat trickled down her back. A white ash stake suddenly seemed woefully inadequate against the creatures that waited ahead.

Her fingertips touched a wall. It was wet and slimy, even though there didn't appear to be any water running down its surface. She skated her hand across it, using it as a guide as she moved deeper into the darkness. Concrete eventually gave way to metal—a staircase, leading down into a deeper gloom.

Down to where they waited.

God, she *so* didn't want to go down there. She didn't want to confront these things. In ten years of fighting evil, she'd never been this scared, and she'd faced some pretty foul beings during that time. But none of them had the power to suck the essence from her body and destroy all that she was, all that she could be—both now and in future reincarnations.

Once again the image of Daniel rose, and she took a shuddering breath. He would have been just as scared. And he'd certainly deserved more than four years of life. While she and Gran had been placed on the trail too late to save him and the other two kids, they were here in Springfield, Oregon, now. They had a chance to stop this.

All she had to do was go down into that darkness.

She took another deep breath, then felt for the edge of the step with her toes. She kept hold of the banister for guidance and repeated the process, moving slowly down.

The chill in the air grew until it felt like she was breathing ice. Her fingers were so cold they ached, and despite the fact that she'd put on extra-thick socks, her toes felt numb.

Or maybe it was just fear, paralyzing her from the extremities up.

She reached the bottom and stopped. Nothing moved. Her breathing rattled across the silence, and the wild beat of her heart echoed in time with it. The vampire and the soul-sucker stood to her left. The shapeshifter was more distant and to her right. There was no sense of evil coming from his direction, just wave after wave of anger and hostility. It didn't seem to be aimed at her, or even at the duo she chased. It seemed to be aimed at the world in general.

And it was odd that she was getting such a strong impression of a man she hadn't even met.

Evil stirred, splitting up as it moved forward. She backed away until she hit a wall, her grip on the stake so fierce her knuckles ached.

Air rushed at her from the left. She slashed the stake across the night and felt the slight resistance as the sharp point tore into flesh. The vampire howled but didn't stop. She dove out of his way, hit the concrete with a grunt, and rolled back to her feet. Tendrils of softly glowing smoke reached for her. She hit it with kinetic energy, momentarily fragmenting it.

The darkness stirred, then lashed out, connecting hard with her chin. The force of the blow sent her sprawling backward. Her back hit the floor, and her breath left in a whoosh of air. For a moment, stars danced in her vision.

Then, the weight of another hit her, pinning her in place. Though gasping for breath and fighting the blackness invading her mind, she still heard the vampire's snarl. She looked up in time to see the shadows unravel around him. His dead brown eyes were inches from hers and his teeth were extending, dripping blood in expectation of a feed. Tendrils of smoke gathered above him, pulsing red. *Excitement,* she thought. *Need.*

With as much force as she could muster, she smacked the heel of her palm into the vamp's nose. At the same time, she sent a surge of kinetic energy at the vapor, again tearing it apart.

"Bitch!" The vampire's voice was hoarse, his breath full of dead things.

"Bite me," she said—and yelped when the bastard did. She stabbed the stake into his side, using kinetic energy to force it deep.

Blue fire flickered, and the smell of burning flesh rent the night. The vampire howled and slashed at her, not with his teeth but with fingernails as sharp as claws. They tore across her face, and she cursed him fluently. Kinetic energy surged, but before she could release her weapon, the vampire was torn from her.

"You all right?"

The voice was rich, husky, and called forth fantasies of long nights and silk sheets. She blinked, wondering where the hell her mind was. "Yeah."

A hand appeared in front of her eyes. "Then get the hell up, because that thing is coming back."

The shifter's fingers were a furnace compared to hers, and he pulled her up with an ease that spoke of strength. He was a warm, solid presence she could feel but not see. A man whose emotions she could taste as easily as she tasted the evil of the other two.

And she had no idea why. Empathy with the living was not one of her talents.

"Thanks." She pulled her hand from his, and the emotive swirl died a little. But his hostility lingered, mixed with some deeper emotion she couldn't quite define. Yet it stirred her senses. Made her pulse race.

"Get out of here," he said. "This place is too dangerous for a woman. I'll keep the creature occupied."

"It's not alone," she retorted. "And this place is just as dangerous for a man who has no idea he has two opponents rather than one."

"Listen, lady—"

"No."

Tendrils of smoke formed behind the shifter's solid presence, ready to caress and kill. Kat hit the soul-sucker kinetically, dissipating it yet again, then was flung sideways by the shifter.

She flailed her arms, battling to keep her balance, then heard a grunt as the shifter was hit by the vampire. Blue fire flickered across the darkness— evidence that the stake was still buried deep in the vampire's flesh. So why didn't he damn well die, like all bad little vampires should?

She dragged the second stake free and clenched it tightly. The two men were slugging it out, the shifter apparently giving as good as he got. But he obviously knew he was up against a vampire, so why didn't he just grab the stake and thrust it into the bastard's heart? Surely he *had* to know it was the best way to stop a bloodsucker? Going toe to toe with one generally never ended well—for the attacker, not the vampire. Hell, the only reason he could even *hit* the vampire was the stake holding it in human form.

She shifted her weight from one foot to the other and fought the need to move. She didn't dare attack until the shifter was clear. The stake she held was just as deadly to him as the vampire, and the slightest mistake could prove costly.

The mist began forming again. She swore and slashed it with the stake. The air howled—an inhuman sound that sent a chill down her spine. The vapor disappeared, and the sense of old evil retreated, flowing up the stairs and out the door.

If she didn't follow it, she'd lose it. But she couldn't leave the shifter here alone, either. Not when instinct suggested he would not come out of this warehouse alive if she did.

"Back off, shifter, and let me at it," she said.

"Like . . . hell." His words were punctured with the smack of flesh against flesh.

"Hitting it is not going to damage it." Exasperation edged her voice. If she lost the soul-sucker's trail because of this man's stubbornness . . .

"He's injured. Bleeding."

"And already dead," the vampire snarled. "As you and the bitch will be by the time I'm finished with you both."

"As I said to the lady, like hell."

His words were emphasized by a grunt of effort and another smack of flesh. The vampire made an odd sound deep in his throat and staggered backward. It was the break she'd been waiting for. She reached deep, drawing on all her remaining kinetic strength, and flung the shapeshifter back—far back, across the warehouse. Surprise whisked around her a moment before he smacked against the wall, then all emotion died. *He hit his head*. At least she didn't have to worry about him getting in the way.

She raised the stake and ran at the vampire. He snarled and tried to dodge, but his movements were slowing, and he was nowhere near fast enough. She drove the stake through his chest into his black heart, then leaped sideways as he lashed at her with clawed hands. His fingers slithered down her leg, tearing through her jeans and into flesh. She cursed and kicked him, shoving him backward.

He hit the ground with a splat and didn't do anything more than writhe. Blue fire encased his torso, and the smell of burning meat churned her stomach. She climbed to her feet, brushed the dirt from her hands, and watched the vampire incinerate. She felt no elation at her victory. She couldn't. Not when there was one more horror still running free.

When there was nothing left but ash, she turned and ran for the stairs. The shifter was safe enough now that the vampire was dead, and with any luck, Gran and she would be well gone by the time he awoke. Because if the hostility he'd projected was anything to go by, it wouldn't be pleasant to be within a ten-mile radius of the man when he eventually stirred. Especially after she'd knocked him cold.

The moonlight seemed abnormally bright after the shuttered darkness within the warehouse. She blinked and hesitated, searching for some sign of the soul-sucker. Evil was a distant echo, moving away fast.

She shifted shape and flew down the alley, skimming past the cops who raced toward the warehouse. This time, the creature headed for the main street. Perhaps it hoped the noise and motion might loosen any psychic hold she had on it—which was a definite possibility after all she'd been through tonight.

The soul-sucker hit the street, its ethereal form getting lost in the warm glow of lights. It whisked away to the right, and the psychic leash she had on it snapped with a suddenness that had her plummeting to the ground.

She hit with a grunt, then shifted shape and rolled onto her back, staring up at the moon.

She'd lost it.